FIRST
CONTACT

FIRST CONTACT

David Hiers

By David Hiers

FIRST CONTACT

FIRST CONTACT - RETURN

FIRST CONTACT - CUBE

For more information on this
or other books by David Hiers,
or to place orders,
Go to: **www.dhiers.com**

ISBN: 0692206825
ISBN-13: 9780692206829

Acknowledgements

I would like to thank Deborah and Catherine Deborah for their assistance, encouragement and patience throughout the creation of this book. Without their kind words, I would never have succeeded.

PROLOGUE

Pulsing red light bounced off cylindrical walls. Running footsteps echoed loudly on the metal floor. An airlock spiraled open and two jumpsuit-clad figures jumped through and scanned the corridor; large, oblong eyes dilating under the prominent bony ridge crests across their foreheads. They sprinted down the corridor toward a distant airlock. Scraping noises echoed from a side corridor between them and the airlock, the sound of claws against metal, moving fast and getting louder. Sliding to a stop, they brought up their weapons. A blur of fur rounded the corner. One fired and dove to the ground. The other fired, but missed, as the creature leaped to the side, bounding off the wall straight at him. Searing pain laced into his forehead as the creature's front claws grabbed him. His head jerked back, knocking him off balance. Then came the rear claws...

Mark awoke with a start, heart racing, covered in sweat. Claws dug into his throat and he screamed, jumping up in bed. A blur of fur leaped off his chest to the floor with an angry hiss. White light filled the room.

"What's going on?"

Mark stared at his wife lying next to him, her hand on the nightstand lamp. He turned and saw the cat on the floor, staring at him accusingly, before it turned and stalked away.

"What's going on?" his wife repeated. "Did you have a nightmare?"

Nightmare? Mark couldn't remember dreaming. His forehead hurt and he absently rubbed his throat. "We need to stop letting the cat sleep inside," he said as he lay back down, his heart still pounding in his chest.

CHAPTER 1

Fireball detection

IR sensors aboard US DOT satellites detected the impact of a bolide over the southeastern US on 29 August 2011 at 05:22:15 UTC. The object was traveling roughly east to west. The object was first detected at an altitude of approximately 68 km at 30.43 North latitude, 87.19 W. longitude and tracked down to an altitude of approximately 27 km at 41.3 N., 77.3 west. The impact was simultaneously detected by space-based visible wavelength sensors operated by the US Department of Energy. The total radiated energy was approximately 1.31×10^{12} joules.

Deep within Cheyenne Mountain, the most secure facility in the world, Second Lieutenant Dennis Morris read the fireball detection log for the hundredth time. He practically knew it by heart, he had read it so many times. He glanced up at the four monitors in front of him. Who would have believed that working at NORAD, the North American Aerospace Defense Command, could be so boring? And to think how hard he had worked to get here, even landing a coveted position in the Aerospace

Warning Center. AWC had been exciting when he had started. The sheer novelty of controlling spy satellites and to be able to monitor virtually anything down to the size of a paint fleck. And the security made him feel so important. But before long the monotony of the job started to take its toll. The computers did all the work and nothing ever happened. He hadn't even seen a meteor, or bolide to use the professional terms now. At least that would break up the monotony.

He glanced back at last week's fireball detection entry, mentally calculating its trajectory. Entry would have been around Jacksonville, Florida, heading west past Tallahassee towards the Gulf Coast. Should have been visible from the ground if anyone was looking up at midnight.

His mind wandered. The cavernous room was quiet. Monitors flickered, the occasional click on a keyboard. But there was nothing to report. Years of schooling, training, and never-ending testing, and where did it get him? Monitoring thousands of pieces of drifting space junk. Sitting deep within the most high-tech mountain in the world, where he could virtually spy on anyone anywhere on the globe with the most sophisticated satellites at his command, and he was stuck monitoring space junk. 'Oh no,' he thought sarcastically, 'the space shuttle screw is spinning out of control! Or, the lost glove is nearing the missing wrench!' How did one lose a glove in space? And why did he have to watch it?

His phone beeped. "NORAD, AWC, Lieutenant Morris, this is an unsecure line," he answered.

"This is John Davis. I'm a graduate student at Space Watch Project. They told me I should give you a call."

Lieutenant Morris couldn't decide whether to welcome the interruption or be irritated with the inefficiency of dealing with civilians, particularly Space Watch, a civilian organization created to catalogue the heavens, or at least the near Earth heavens.

"Who told you to call me?" Lieutenant Morris asked.

"Oh, Dr. Brendenmeyer. We found a bolide which appears to have a trajectory towards us, I mean the Earth. It's coming in pretty fast. Initial calculations place it around 84 km/second. Dr. Brendenmeyer believes entry will be somewhere in the Pacific, perhaps between Guam and Indonesia. Hold on, I'll give you the coordinates."

Lieutenant Morris typed in the coordinates. "What's its mass?" he asked, his stomach tightening as he wondered if this might be the "big one" the scientists all worried about. Space Watch found a lot of asteroids, but their detection range was only down to about one kilometer. They couldn't even see most of the stuff he routinely tracked.

"We don't know. We don't have a radar image on it. We picked it up when it blocked the light from an asteroid we were tracking. It doesn't appear to be very big. Might burn up in the atmosphere if it fragments. But Dr. Brendenmeyer said you would probably like to watch. Between you and me," John Davis lowered his voice and added conspiratorially, "I think he really just wants to show off that we saw it before you did. After all, our equipment is not designed to spot things this small, it appears to be about forty meters."

"Thank you for the report," Lieutenant Morris responded. Forty meters gave it a shot of hitting Earth if it did not break up, but it was not the 'big one' Space Watch was dedicated to finding. Damn egotistical professors trying to show up NORAD. "Now where is it?" he wondered aloud as his fingers flew across his keyboard.

Radar negative. Infrared negative. Radiation negative. That left visual light only. And black against black, he would only be able to spot it when it blocked light from another object. He wondered briefly if this was a test, or perhaps a joke. He glanced around the large room, but no one seemed to be paying any attention to him. He plotted a probable trajectory from the last known point to the general impact area. This still left a rather large search window. And not much time to search. Nothing. He glanced at his watch. Quick calculations told him that impact would be in less than 30 seconds. He frantically searched the heavens, but to no avail. Ten seconds, nine, eight, seven. He still couldn't spot it. He would be the laughing stock of NORAD. Three, two, one.

Dejectedly, he checked the IR monitor for atmospheric impact. Nothing. Was this a joke? He started getting mad, but continued to scan. And then he spotted it. Much higher than he had calculated. He zeroed in with a visual image satellite, the only one that was currently registering. The bolide was much higher and slower than reported. Slower did not make any sense as it had not yet entered the Earth's atmosphere and should, if anything, be picking up speed as the gravitational pull increased. Two satellites were able to lock onto the object, giving him more data. It was actually about three minutes from impact with Earth's outer atmosphere. He would turn the tables now. Space Watch's calculations were completely wrong. Forget to carry the two, boys? He was already planning his retort. New data streamed in. Thirty meters long, somewhat oblong, still hard to tell at this distance. And it was decelerating. Impossible. He checked and rechecked the readings. It was definitely decelerating: sixty kilometers per second, fifty, thirty.

"Marcus, check this out!" He blurted out to the Lieutenant next to him. "What do you make of this? It's a bolide, thirty meters long, but it's decelerating."

Marcus studied the screens. "Did you set this up, or is it real?" he asked seriously.

"No, I didn't. It's real. The guys at Space Watch found it and called it in a couple minutes ago."

Marcus studied the screens a moment longer and then turned to his phone and punched one of the preset direct dial buttons. "This is Lieutenant Hodgkins in AWC, we have an unidentified incoming at..." he paused before reading off the latest coordinates. "Object is decelerating, repeat, decelerating. Impact with upper atmosphere currently estimated at," he paused again, "two minutes, thirty-two seconds." The announcement set off a flurry of activity throughout NORAD as various departments responded.

"No launches identified."

"No known craft in vicinity."

Lieutenant Morris had to laugh at that one. The only craft in vicinity would have to be a spacecraft. Which meant either the space station or one of the satellites he monitored. Satellites! He quickly checked to make sure that the current trajectory did not bring it close to any of his assets. That would have been really embarrassing.

In another section of NORAD, Major Young picked up his phone and punched the preset for COMPACFLT and requested a direct patch to the *USS Ronald Reagan's* carrier task force, which he was watching on his satellite display as it traveled through the area of estimated impact.

Ensign Nichols, the duty officer aboard the *USS Ronald Reagan*, was enjoying his watch as he "commanded" the Nimitz class carrier as it headed to the South China Sea. He was imagining leading a heroic response to a Chinese provocation when a voice interrupted him.

"Sir, urgent voice traffic for the commander," the communication specialist reported.

Ensign Nichols picked up the secure phone: "*USS Ronald Reagan*, CVN 76, Ensign Nichols duty officer, this line is secure."

"Major Young, NORAD," was the terse reply. "You have an unidentified incoming object entering the atmosphere near your location, probably a bolide. However, it is acting peculiarly and we want you to put eyes on it. Coordinates and probable trajectory following in flash traffic. You should be getting a visual within the next five minutes. Deceleration is extremely erratic which prevents me from giving you a better estimate. Target is radar negative."   As this was said the specialist was handing a flash traffic sheet to the Ensign. "Report on visual ASAP."

"Yes, Sir, I have the coordinates. Will report back ASAP." Replacing the receiver he called across the CIC: "Commander Jones, flash traffic from NORAD; incoming bolide. Requesting visual confirmation. Impact in less than one minute. Coordinates are," he glanced at the flash traffic sheet and called out the latest coordinates and trajectory information.

Cmdr. Jones took the flash traffic sheet and studied the situation board. Turning to the air wing Air Traffic Controller he ordered, "ATC, have Red 1 leader take his flight to this area and give us a visual. He is authorized supersonic." He studied the coordinates and the situation board again. "Jones, tell CTV 30 to get out of there. He's in the impact area." He paused. "Put all ships on air defense alert!"

A klaxon blared, followed by the intercom: "Man all air defense stations. Repeat, Man all air defense stations. This is not a drill."

As ships' personnel ran to their stations, Lieutenant John Thompson, otherwise known as Red One leader, was swinging his F-18 Hornet to his new heading. He was doing what he loved best, soaring through the sky. He had always wanted to be a pilot and had realized his dream eight years ago after what seemed like ages of training. Now he was on his last sea tour before joining the Blue Angels in Pensacola. He had received his wings in Pensacola and was looking forward to going back, particularly to the beaches. And flying with the Blues would be a plum assignment. But meanwhile, he could still fly free, and here was another chance to really soar. "Ready, Red Two?" he called out to his wingman.

"Roger, Red leader."

"Let's light it up," Lt Thompson replied as he pushed his throttles forward. A double sonic boom traveled across the ocean as the two Hornets streaked into the upper atmosphere.

"Keep your eyes open," Red leader radioed, rather unnecessarily.

"I have visual," Red 2 transmitted about thirty seconds later. "Bright dot at 1:30 high."

A pause, then, "Roger, I have it. Nose camera on." They turned to follow the meteor that was now quickly passing their altitude, leaving a fiery trail in its wake. Still supersonic they shot down after the meteor, trying to keep it in the camera's field.

"Red One, ATC."

"ATC."

"Red One, we have good visual. Bright object, leaving fire trail. Heading almost straight down, slight bearing of two-forty degrees. We are approximately twenty kilometers from it and losing. Negative on all radar systems. Visual and IR only." He didn't bother adding his speed or heading, as he knew the ATC would be plotting it already. It was a clear, almost cloudless day, so he had no difficulty following the meteor as it burned its way toward the blue sea. At this speed he would have to pull up in a few seconds or he would impact also. Just a few more seconds for the camera, he thought. "Object is not breaking up," he reported, "looks like it will impact... Oh s…!"

On the *Ronald Reagan* the ATC watched Red flight on the radar screen. Suddenly, both aircraft pulled out as if taking evasive action and then pulled tight turns while dropping speed dramatically. The ATC resisted the urge to ask for a status, he knew a report would come as soon as the pilots were able.

"Red One," the report finally came. "Object has stopped, repeat, object has stopped in mid-air. We overran it."

'Probably almost hit it,' the ATC thought to himself.

"Object is back in our sight, still glowing hot, now dropping fast. Object just hit the deck. Large splash. Huge cloud of steam. Passing it now. Red Two, what do you have?"

"Red Two; I'm back two klicks. Approaching. Large cloud of steam, no sign of object or debris. Passing now. Banking for another pass."

"Send a search and rescue helicopter out there," ordered Captain Peters, who had entered CIC just a minute before. "Upload the nose camera's feed from Red flight. NORAD is going to want to see that."

"I would like to hear NORAD explain how a meteor can stop in mid-air," a whispered voice broke the ensuing silence in CIC.

"So would I," said Captain Peters quietly. "So would I."

CHAPTER 2

"I love these quaint old houses, 1920's you said, didn't you?" Mrs. Frances Oglethorpe, a spry 83-year-old widow, gazed appreciably at the gleaming hardwood floor of her attorney's office.

"1928," answered Mark Williams patiently as he stood to escort her out. Mrs. Oglethorpe's monthly visits rarely required any legal work; they were more social affairs for an elderly lady intent on staying active. "I really like this old building," Mark continued as he led her to the door. "Heart pine floors and walls. Much better than the cubicle I started in."

"They just don't make buildings the way they used to," Mrs. Oglethorpe complained. "Hardwood floors, expansive windows, high ceilings and ceiling fans. This is what the South is supposed to look like. I tell you, it's a good thing the lawyers and accountants are using these old houses as offices, otherwise we would lose the charm of our town to those horrid steel and glass monstrosities going up everywhere else. You know my accountant has one of these charming houses down on Alcaniz Street. She has fixed it up very nicely."

"I've seen it," Mark agreed, as he led her through the reception area to the front porch. Ms. Oglethorpe paused to admire the front porch swing. "Would you like to sit a while?" Mark asked.

Ms. Oglethorpe shook her head reluctantly. "I do like to sit on the front porch. I sit outside when I can't sleep at night. I let the frogs serenade me. They are quite wonderful, you know."

"They are nice," Mark said. "You can sit here as long as you want. But I can't promise tree frogs, only traffic."

"I was sitting out last week about midnight and saw a meteor. It was quite low, very bright. Did you see it?"

"No. I didn't hear anything about a meteor."

"That's because no one spends time outside anymore. It was very special. It seemed like it slowed down when it got to Pensacola. Probably so I could get a good look at it," she chuckled.

"Probably."

"But I see you have more clients," she said, clearly referring to the man they had passed in the reception room. "And he doesn't look like someone who likes to be kept waiting," she added.

"No, he doesn't," the lawyer said before adding in a conspiratorial whisper, "He looks like a government man. They are always so businesslike, no sense of humor."

She laughed. "How right you are. Fortunately, we know how to enjoy life."

"Yes, we do. Now you have a good weekend. And call me if you have any further questions."

"I will, and say hello to your wife for me."

Mark waited on the porch as Mrs. Oglethorpe walked to her car. As he waved goodbye, he noted two, non-descript, dark colored sedans parked on the street behind Mrs. Oglethorpe. Their similarity and plainness cried out "unmarked cars." The first car had the cheap "cop" hubcaps and short antennae on the back window. Glancing at the second car, Mark noted a military license plate on the front. Two men were sitting in it watching him intently. Mark shook his head as he turned to go back into his office. His joke to Mrs. Oglethorpe about the "government man" was running wild with his imagination. However, he did not have another appointment scheduled that morning. Puzzled, he stepped back into his office.

"Mr. Williams, I need to speak to you," the government-looking man said.

"Sure, what can I do for you?" Mark asked as he evaluated his unannounced visitor. He didn't need his overactive imagination to start typecasting. He had dealt with law enforcement long enough to recognize the unofficial uniform: gray slacks, white button-down shirt, and navy blazer. Probably a fed, Mark concluded. He made no move to take the man back to his office, as he did not intend on prolonging this meeting, not with all the work waiting for him on his desk.

The man looked uncomfortably at the receptionist. "Could we talk privately?"

Mark paused for a moment. "Come on in," he reluctantly agreed. "But I don't have long," he added, hoping this intrusion would not interfere too much with his schedule. As it turned out, it was a futile wish.

Mark escorted the man back to his office and motioned for him to sit down in a chair in front of his desk. "What can I do for you?" Mark asked as he sat behind his desk. Still standing, the man hesitated before sitting in the offered chair. His posture was aggressive; he sat straight up, more on the front of the seat and leaning slightly forward, blazer open. Mark caught a glimpse of dull metal under the man's left arm and was slightly relieved when the man identified himself.

"My name is John Parker. I'm a field agent with the FBI, Pensacola division. Washington called and asked that I escort you to NAS."

"NAS?"

"Yes, Naval Air Station, Pensacola," the agent responded.

"I know what it is," Mark said. "I just wondered why NAS?" Oddly, Mark felt a bit apprehensive. Why did the FBI want to escort him to NAS? Despite living in a navy town, Mark had few dealings with the base. And why the FBI? There had to be some mix-up, maybe identity theft?

"You are to come with me. Now," the agent's command interrupted Mark's thoughts.

"You are arresting me?" Mark asked, his voice incredulous.

"No. I'm here to escort you to NAS. There is something they need your assistance on, something they want you to see," he replied authoritatively. "So they asked me to assist."

"Okay," Mark replied, relaxing a bit and now very curious. "What is it they want me to see?"

"I don't know. They wouldn't tell me." The agent answered, slightly embarrassed. "So if you'll come with me..." he finished, authoritative again as he stood up.

Mark leaned back in his chair. "Let me understand this. I'm not under arrest. But you want me to drop everything and come and look at something at NAS?"

"Yes, that's exactly correct," the agent replied expectantly. "Shall we go?"

Mark looked at the agent and then at his day planner, which was covered with projects of varying importance. His curiosity was piqued, but he was also put out by the agent's attitude. He had always hated the self-important and bossy attitude law enforcement often affected and it was this emotion that finally won out. "No, I don't think so," he said, enjoying the look of surprise on the agent's face. "I have a very busy calendar," Mark continued. "If you provide me with more information, I am sure I can make an appointment to see what ever it is you want me to see. Perhaps sometime next week."

The agent stepped to the edge of Mark's desk. "My orders are to escort you to NAS. This is a matter of national security and of utmost urgency. You will come with me."

The agent's aggressive manner irritated Mark, who took a calming breath before replying. "As important as I would like to think that I am, I fail to see how a small-town lawyer handling little old ladies' wills, traffic accidents and similar legal matters has any bearing on national security. So you will excuse me if I am less than impressed with your claim of national security."

"You are coming with me," the agent stated loudly.

"You have a warrant?" Mark asked, amazed at how quickly the situation was escalating.

"No. But I'm an FBI agent."

"And I'm a lawyer. And my partner is a lawyer. So if you take me out of here without a warrant, she will have a federal judge on the line in two minutes and this nonsense will be stopped before we get to Navy Boulevard." Mark paused and watched the agent consider his threat. Thinking it best to try to defuse the situation, Mark continued. "Now look, I have a lot of things to do. I would like to help you if I can. I just don't respond well to someone asking me to drop everything without an explanation. So if you can find somebody to explain this to me, I am sure that we can work something out." When the agent had still not responded, Mark added. "Or we can get the federal judge on the line, the choice is yours."

"You will comply if we explain it?" The agent asked.

"If the explanation is good enough, sure."

"Wait here, I'll get someone."

"Someone from that other car?" Mark guessed.

The agent looked back quickly and then went out the door, saying only, "Wait here, I'll be right back."

Mark watched out the window as the agent hurried out to the second car parked out front. To Mark's surprise, after a short conversation two uniformed Navy Officers got out and accompanied the FBI agent back to Mark's office. Leaving the window, Mark walked to the reception area to meet them. No sense in going through the formal buzzing from his receptionist. That would be too petty.

As Mark directed the group to his office, the Navy officers instructed the FBI agent to stay in the reception area. Once seated in Mark's office, the first officer started the conversation: "Mr. Williams, I am Commander Mike Matthew and this is Lieutenant Steve McKnight. We are with Navy Intelligence here at Corry Station. I understand that there was a... misunderstanding with Agent Parker. Perhaps we can answer your questions and avoid any," he paused again, "more confusion."

"Gentlemen, as I told Agent Parker, I would like to help you if I can, but he basically ordered me to drop everything and come with him and would not explain why. And quite frankly, I just don't respond well to intimidation techniques."

"Understandable," Commander Matthew responded. "The problem is that Agent Parker does not know why you're being requested. Actually, I don't understand why the FBI is involved at all. Someone in Washington thought the FBI needed to come with us. Obviously, that was a mistake."

"Okay, so what's the deal? What do you need me for?"

"Before we start, and without sounding melodramatic, I need to tell you that what we are dealing with right now has been classified top-secret. Therefore we have to ask you to agree not to tell anyone what we are about to tell you. We also need you to sign this Official Secrets Act agreement before we proceed." He handed a three page single spaced document to Mark as he said this.

Mark quickly scanned the document before handing it back unsigned. "Even when I had a secret clearance in the Army, I don't remember having to sign anything like this. I'm sorry, I do not know where this is going, but it does not look like something I want to get involved in."

The two Navy officers glanced at each other and then the Commander continued. "Okay, I'm going to go out on a limb. We need your assistance and I'm going to assume that after you have heard what we have to say, you will agree it needs to remain confidential."

"Okay, convince me."

"Let me warn you first, this is going to sound extremely strange," the Commander said. "Two days ago Space Watch, which is a civilian organization that monitors near-Earth asteroids, detected what they thought was an incoming meteor. They notified NORAD, which noticed that the object was decelerating before entering the Earth's atmosphere. It happened to be entering the atmosphere near the *U.S.S. Ronald Reagan*, one of our aircraft carriers sailing near Guam. NORAD notified the *Ronald Reagan* in just enough time to have two fighters attempt to intercept. The fighters managed to film the object as it streaked towards the sea. At this point they still thought it was a meteor. But, then it stopped. Actually, it slowed significantly before splashing into the ocean. Once in the ocean, we were able to track it with one of our submarines attached to the battle group. The object changed course a couple of times as it headed to the bottom."

"So what is it?" Mark asked, now quite interested.

"We don't know," the Commander responded. "Like I said, at first we thought it was a meteor. But meteors do not slow down before they enter the atmosphere and they certainly don't stop right before hitting the water. And the course changes that it made in the water are not explained by mere deflection. So it is clearly some type of craft that can control its course. There was no radar signature, so we only have visual readings and the ambient noises it made when entering the water."

"So you are saying this is really a UFO?"

The Commander hesitated before replying. "It is a UFO in the sense that it is an unidentified flying object. It was first spotted just prior to entering Earth's atmosphere, so we can't rule out the possibility that it is a man-made vehicle."

"Rule out?" Mark asked puzzled.

"The trajectory and flight characteristics are beyond our technical abilities."

"So why don't you go down and find out what it is?"

"Because when it changed course, it headed to the bottom of the Challenger Deep in the Mariana Trench, which as you may know is the deepest part of the ocean. There are not many vehicles that can go that deep."

There was a moment of silence as Mark digested what they told him. Finally, he asked, "So what does this have to do with me?"

"That's what we would like to know."

"Well I didn't fly it there and then come back to Pensacola to prepare a will," Mark said with a laugh. "Seriously, why are you telling me about this?"

"That is the strange part," the Commander said. Mark resisted the impulse to say that they were already way past the strange part. "One of our submarines has been trying to communicate with it by sending signals at various frequencies. This morning, our time, we received the first response: an image." The commander paused and reached into his briefcase and pulled out an 8 x 10 photograph and placed it on Mark's desk. "This image."

Mark looked at the photograph. It was a picture of a computer monitor, probably military, judging by the surroundings. But what got his attention was the image on the monitor; it was his office website, complete with his photograph. Mark stared at the photograph in disbelief. "Let me get this straight," Mark asked incredulously. "A UFO lands in the ocean and instead of saying 'take me to your leader,' it asks for a lawyer. More specifically, it asks for me? You've got to be kidding."

"That's what happened," the Commander responded.

"What is this, Candid Camera?" Mark asked. "Okay folks, I need to get back to work," Mark added as he got up from his desk.

"I wish we were kidding," the Commander stated. "But I can prove to you that I'm not. Will you give me five more minutes?"

"You're kidding," Mark repeated.

"Five more minutes, that's all I ask."

Mark paused. "Okay, five minutes, that's it," he relented as he sat back down.

The Commander motioned to the Lieutenant who pulled out a laptop and turned it on. "May I close the blinds while I show you this please?"

"Go ahead," Mark said resignedly.

When the computer booted up, the Lieutenant pulled up a file. "This is the gun camera feed from the fighter that followed the object. You can see the object here as it first entered the camera's field of view. Let me turn the audio up. You can hear the pilot talking to the ATC." Mark watched the computer screen. "Okay, here's where the object stops, or almost stops. The pilot was traveling at over Mach one and almost hit it. You can see him take evasive action right now. In a moment he'll come around. There. The object has dropped. All you can see now is dissipating steam from the impact. By the time Search and Rescue arrived, there wasn't a trace." The Lieutenant turned off the program.

"I'm sorry. I'm still having a little trouble understanding this. The video is cute, but my daughter could probably do something like that on her computer. I'm still not convinced this is not Candid Camera."

"So what can we do to convince you?" the commander asked.

Mark thought for a moment. "Let's start with your identification."

Mark studied the proffered ID badges. "They certainly appear to be authentic. But I guess it's still possible to get Navy officers to moonlight for Candid Camera. Let me ask you this, what is it that you want me to do?"

"We want you to fly to the *Ronald Reagan* and see what happens next. We do not know why we are receiving your website. The only thing that we can guess is that it wants us to bring you there."

Mark laughed out loud. "This is just too weird. This sounds like a Google ad: Even space aliens will find your website as number one! I'm sorry, I'm just not buying it. You did have me going there for a moment. Whichever one of my warped friends put you up to this, you can tell them they did a really good job. But now I really must get back to work."

"I understand why you would think this was a joke," the Commander stated. "In fact, I thought so too when I first saw it. But then I saw how it was routed through the military and realized it was serious. You, of course, only have our word. Let me assure you that this request comes from the very highest level."

"Right. Like the President?"

"Yes, the President."

"Then I suggest he should call me and ask," Mark said with a laugh.

The Commander paused, "I think we can do that. Give me a minute." With that he picked up his cell phone and made a call. Mark overheard him say, "We are having some difficulty convincing Mr. Williams this is not a joke. We need the President to make the call. Okay, I'll hold." A minute later the Commander turned to Mark and said, "Bear with me just a couple more minutes."

A short time later Mark's office phone rang. His receptionist answered and then buzzed his office; "A Mr. Nichols is on the phone for you. He says you are expecting his call. Would you like to take it?" she asked.

"Please take the call," Commander Matthew requested.

Mark picked up the phone. "This is Mark Williams."

"Hold for the President, please," was the reply, followed a moment later by a familiar sounding voice, "Mr. Williams, this is Barak Obama."

"Yes, Mr. President, and I'm Tinkerbelle," Mark responded with a laugh.

"Excuse me?"

"I'm sorry, you really don't expect me to believe this is the President of the United States, do you? I mean this joke is getting rather elaborate. Can't we all say that we had our fun and move on? I will admit that y'all had me going. But now let it go. I've got to get back to work."

"Mr. Williams, I can understand that this is hard to believe. I am still having trouble believing it as well. But let me assure you, what you have been told is true. We are trying to find out as quickly as possible what is going on and we ask that you help us."

"If you were the President," Mark replied, "I would say 'yes.' But since you're obviously one of my warped friends who is very good at imitating voices, let me suggest that we all go down to McGuire's Irish Pub instead. It's Friday afternoon and I'm obviously not going to get any more work done today."

There was a slight pause and then the voice on the other end of the line said, "How about if you call me. Will that convince you? I'll give you my number."

Mark had really expected everyone to start laughing over the joke by now and was getting irritated by the increasingly elaborate hoax. "Okay," he sighed. "I suppose you are at the White House?"

"Yes."

"Since you have gone to such trouble to set this up, I will make a fool out of myself just a little longer. I will call the White House number, the listed White House number, and ask for the President. If he answers, then I will fly to the *Ronald Reagan*. If he doesn't, then you buy the first two rounds at McGuires."

"Fair enough."

"See you at McGuires," Mark replied as he hung up the phone without waiting for a reply. He turned back to the Navy Officers, who were sitting there stunned.

"You need to make that call," the Commander said quietly.

"I think I have played along quite long enough," Mark replied.

"You really need to make that call," the Commander repeated.

"Hasn't this gone far enough?" Mark asked.

"Call the number," the Commander repeated earnestly. "Please."

Mark sighed. "Then you owe me some hor d'oerves, too. If I'm going to be a complete fool, then at least I'm going to be fed while you all laugh at me."

"Deal, you can order anything you want," the Commander agreed. "Now call the number."

Mark started to feel uneasy. He turned to his computer and typed in www.whitehouse.gov and pulled up the official website. From it he found the White House phone number and dialed.

"This is the White House," a cheerful female voice said. "How may I help you?"

"This is Mark Williams," Mark said a bit nervously. "You might be expecting my call," he added, suddenly fearing the answer.

"Oh, yes, Mr. Williams. Please hold while I connect you to the President."

CHAPTER 3

Strapped into the back seat of an F/A 18 Hornet, traveling almost twice the speed of sound at 40,000 feet, Mark wondered at how quickly his world had changed. One moment he had been finishing up a will for Mrs. Oglethorpe. Less than three hours later he was hurtling halfway around the world at the special request of the President of the United States in an attempt to make contact with a UFO. He couldn't believe that he had actually hung up on the President. But, he had thought this was all an elaborate hoax. Now that he was actually underway, the enormity of the situation started to overwhelm him and he wondered if he would not have been better off if it had been a joke.

Sitting in the back of the jet fighter, he replayed the events of the last couple hours. After talking with the President, he was informed that arrangements were being made to transport him to the Mariana Trench as fast as possible. He had left his office with the navy personnel, leaving a bewildered FBI agent behind, while telling his secretary that there was a court-martial on base he had to review. Having defended court-martials at NAS previously, this explanation was not unusual.

Complications occurred when they got in the car. "We have to stop by my wife's office first," Mark had said. "She's an accountant with Norton, Dunn & Blue. It's just a couple blocks down the road," Mark added when he realized the navy officers might not recognize the firm.

"That's not possible," the Commander said. "This mission is classified. And the President was emphatic that we get you to the *Ronald Reagan* as soon as possible."

"You expect me to leave without telling my wife?" Mark asked incredulously. "Are you serious?"

"This mission is classified," the Commander repeated.

"Well, you are just going to have to unclassify it as far as she is concerned," Mark said. "Besides, do you really think she will remain quiet if I just disappear for a week? How are you going to explain my absence?"

"You call your office and claim a family emergency and instruct your staff to cancel your appointments for the next week," the Commander explained.

"That won't work unless my wife is on board," Mark objected.

"We don't have time for any delays. We already have a jet warming up on the airfield."

"Then just swing by her office and we'll pick her up. We can explain it to her en route," Mark said. "Or, you can just drop me off here and explain to the President why I refused to go," Mark added when the Commander hesitated.

After a moment's consideration, the Commander acquiesced and instructed the Lieutenant to head for Mark's wife's office. "She will have to agree to keep this confidential," the Commander said.

"Trust me," Mark said. "She is not going to tell anyone that her husband is out chasing UFO's. We both have businesses to run and that is not good for business."

When they arrived, Mark ran in and got his wife, explaining that he needed her to meet a client right now. When she climbed into the car, Mark explained what he had learned at his office, while the Lieutenant drove toward NAS.

"You pull me out of my office to play some practical joke?" Beth asked hotly. "I have a lot of work to do today."

"I felt the same way," Mark protested, "until I talked with the President. Here, let them show you the video clip they have."

The Commander had been on his cell phone while Mark was talking to his wife. He paused long enough to boot up the laptop and pull up the video.

Beth was still not convinced fifteen minutes later when they went through the NAS gates and headed for the airfield. It wasn't until they were waived through the airfield gates and out onto the tarmac in front of a hanger where a two-seater fighter jet was warming up, did Beth start to believe him. "You are really serious, aren't you?" Beth said.

"I don't know what is going on," Mark said. "But something is going on that has the President's attention. There is no harm in checking it out."

Beth looked skeptical.

"You need to get going," the Commander interrupted. "They have some gear you have to put on," he added, motioning to three crewmen standing by the aircraft holding a flight suit and helmet.

"Wait just a minute," Mark said before turning back to Beth. "I did tell the President I would go."

Beth looked at the jet and then back at Mark. "You are looking forward to this," she said.

Mark looked sheepish. "It should be a fun ride."

"Men!" Beth said. "Let them play with some toys and they will agree to do anything."

Mark gave his wife a hug, promising he would be safe and would call as soon as he could. The three airmen approached and helped Mark put on a flight suit before they assisted him aboard the fighter. After a very cursory introduction and safety briefing, the canopy was closed, Mark gave a final wave to his wife, and then he was roaring down the runway and lifting off into the setting sun.

"You must be in a hurry," the pilot's voice came across Mark's headset, breaking him out of his reverie. "They don't usually allow us to go supersonic in the States as the citizens don't like the sonic boom. However, we'll be going supersonic the whole way. That's Mach 1.8. We'll be traveling 6,800 nautical miles; that's about 7,800 miles. Flight time is six and a half hours, plus four in-flight refueling stations. Sit back and make yourself comfortable. And don't touch anything."

The pilot did not ask Mark any questions throughout the trip. Occasionally he would point out a particular landmark or city they passed or explain what was going on when he slowed to rendezvous with a refueling tanker. Otherwise, the trip was relatively uneventful, which was fine for Mark as he was preoccupied by what would happen when he arrived at the *Ronald Reagan*. He could not imagine why a UFO was broadcasting his website. Who knows, he thought, maybe nothing will happen when I get there and it will all be rather anticlimactic. In the meantime, he may as well enjoy the flight as it sure beat flying commercial through Atlanta.

The last half of his trip was over the Pacific, which did not provide a lot to see. He looked up, but it was still too light to see the stars. He tried to imagine being in a spaceship instead of a fighter. What mysteries were out there? More importantly, if this really was a UFO, would these beings be friend or foe? Unbidden, all the science fiction movies and books he had seen or read flashed through his mind: from friendly aliens like *ET*, to *War of the Worlds*, or the most terrifying ever, *Alien*. Would this be like *Star Trek* or *Star Wars*? And how did he fit in? He never had any unexplained alien encounter and had certainly never been abducted by space aliens. He had scoffed at those who claimed they had seen the Gulf Breeze UFOs that made headlines several years back. Just another bunch of crackpots. But now he wondered. Could they have been real? He kept coming back to the same question, why him? But he never could come up with a plausible answer. He was just your everyday lawyer, working in a two-person office doing routine legal work. I don't even do immigration work, he thought with a chuckle.

He was still trying to figure it out when the pilot told him they would be descending as they approached the carrier. Straining to see past the pilot's seat, he finally spotted the carrier. It seemed impossibly small and he prayed that this would not be one of those landings when they missed the wire or something else went wrong. He wished now that he had not spent so much time on YouTube watching carrier-landing mishaps as those images filled his mind. Finally, he managed to control his imagination and convinced himself to sit back and enjoy the ride. That is, he thought wryly, if you could truly enjoy crashing onto a carrier deck at 150 miles an hour. He was, after all, someone who never went to the Fair and did not enjoy riding roller coasters or any spinning attractions.

The aircraft carrier came up surprisingly fast. He leaned back, bracing against the seat for the impact. Closer, closer, and then they slammed against the deck as the jet's engines roared. The end of the ship raced towards him and then stopped as the arresting cable held. That was certainly something he would not want to do again. He watched as yellow vested crewmen directed the aircraft to a spot near the tower. Once stopped a number of crewmen ran out and helped him out of the cockpit. They escorted him into the tower and helped Mark strip off the flight suit and helmet. "I've been ordered to take you to the Captain," one of the crewmen told Mark when he finally finished peeling off the flight suit.

"Not until you show me the head," Mark said. "It was a long flight." Although the crewman clearly wanted to get Mark to the Captain as soon as possible, the irrefutable logic of Mark's request could not be ignored. The crewman was standing impatiently in the hallway when Mark stepped out of the head. "Lead on," Mark said, much to the relief of the nervous crewman. "By the way, do you have anything to eat on this ship? I'm starving."

"Galley's open 23 hours a day. Best food in the fleet," he replied proudly. "But you need to see the Captain first," he added, perhaps to keep Mark from requesting yet another detour.

"He better not take too long," Mark said. "I've traveled halfway across the world on a bag of peanuts." Mark was amused to note the look of horror on the crewman's face when a civilian even implied walking out on the Captain. Mark remembered his days in the Army. Although he could not figure out the crewman's rank by his Navy insignia, he assumed he was talking to the equivalent of a private.

Mark was led through numerous narrow corridors and climbed several flights of steep metal stairs before finally arriving in a small briefing room, complete with a podium, flat screen TV monitor and about a dozen metal chairs. "Here you are, Sir," the crewman stated, evidently relieved he had finally completed his mission.

"That will be all," the sole occupant in the room said to the crewman.

"Aye, aye, Sir," the crewman replied and made a hasty exit.

An officer approached Mark with his hand outstretched. "I'm Bob Humphreys, the XO. Welcome to the *Ronald Reagan*." As Mark shook Humphreys' hand, the XO added, "How was your flight?"

"Pretty fast. Although a bit cramped and not many stewardesses."

The XO laughed. "Yes, I suppose it does lack some of the amenities. Speaking of which, if there is anything you need during your stay with us, please just let me know."

Mark was about to reply when the door opened and a fit looking man walked in. Mark guessed him to be late forty's, judging by the graying hair. His bearing placed him as an officer.

"Mr. Williams?" The newcomer asked rather unnecessarily. Who else would be standing in the briefing room wearing a rumpled business suit?

"Call me Mark."

"I'm Joseph Peters, Captain of the *Ronald Reagan*. We've been looking forward to your arrival."

"Well," Mark said a bit self-consciously. "I'm not sure what I can do to help. I'm sure they briefed you on my interview back in Pensacola." The Captain nodded his head affirmatively and Mark continued. "I don't know anything about your UFO other than what your people showed me. I'm not a UFO expert, or ever had any close encounter with one, at least not to my knowledge. I have absolutely no idea why you are receiving my website, of all things. In fact, I had to be convinced that this was not just some big, elaborate hoax."

"Is it true that you hung up on the President?" the Captain asked.

"I'm afraid it is."

The Captain laughed. "I would love to have seen that!"

"Yes, in hindsight it is rather funny. I guess it's fortunate that I'm a civilian."

"If you weren't," the Captain added, still chuckling. "You would be now."

"Anyway," Mark added. "I'm here to help if I can, but I have no idea what I can do."

"Fair enough," the Captain replied. "That's why we have a briefing scheduled. To make sure you have as much information as we do and to bring you up to date. Although nothing new has happened since you were contacted."

"Okay, when is the briefing?" Mark asked hesitantly.

"Right now," the Captain said.

"Oh. All right. Afterwards would you mind showing me where the galley is?" Mark asked. "As I was telling your XO, your flight lacked any in-flight meals and I think my body is at least four feedings behind right now."

"Can you wait thirty minutes?" the Captain asked.

"Sure, particularly since I don't know if it's time for breakfast or dinner."

"It's dinnertime," the Captain stated as he signaled to the XO, who opened the door, letting in about eight officers. Mark took the proffered seat next to the Captain and the briefing began. It was odd, Mark thought. He had attended a number of briefings back in the Army, but this one was directed solely to him. It started with the announcement, "This is a top-secret briefing." They repeated the NORAD report and followed with the video footage from the gun camera, which Mark had been shown back in his office. The rest of the briefing tracked what he had previously been told. The only new information was that provided by the submarine, which evidently was able to track the UFO into the Mariana Trench until it was lost in the Challenger Deep. Several hours later the submarine picked up a signal being transmitted from the depths, which it transmitted to the carrier. It was this signal which contained Mark's website. When the briefing concluded, the briefer looked at Mark expectantly. When Mark had nothing to add, the Captain motioned for the briefer to have a seat.

"I still don't know how I can help you," Mark said. "Although more detailed, this is still the same basic information I was told in Pensacola."

"We've discussed this while we were waiting for you," the Captain explained. "The consensus is that the ball is now in the UFO's court. We just have to wait to see what happens next. In the meantime, why don't I show you the galley?"

"That would be great," Mark replied. "And if it's on the way, I would like to see first hand the monitor that is receiving my website. I am still having trouble believing that a UFO is beaming my website to the United States Navy."

"You're not the only one confused about that," the Captain replied as he led the way out of the briefing room. "We'll swing by sonar first so you can check on your website and then we'll head to the galley."

"Captain on deck," a voice rang out as they entered the sonar room. The Captain led Mark to a station at the side of the room. "Still getting a live feed?" the Captain asked.

"Yes, Sir."

Mark stared at the monitor. There was his website with his photo staring back at him. After a moment he asked the operator, "Can you activate the links?"

"No, Sir. This is not on the internet, it's just a picture. Like a screen print." The seaman glanced up to see whom he was addressing. He glanced back down and did a double take, evidently recognizing Mark. "Nice website, Sir," he added.

"Thanks," Mark answered. "I knew Google advertising was good, but never thought it was this good." The joke fell flat. Well, most of his did, he thought.

The Captain led him out of the sonar room and through another maze of gray corridors and stairwells. Finally, they reached the galley where a long line and tantalizing smells greeted them. The Captain looked over at Mark. "I don't normally cut in line. But you have had a long trip and if you're absolutely starving..." he let the question hang.

Mark looked at the line and felt his stomach growl. "Just this time I wouldn't mind sneaking to the front," Mark replied. The Captain led him to the front of the line where he was greeted with the sight of shrimp, snow crab legs, steak and every vegetable imaginable. After filling their plates, Mark, the Captain and the XO found seats at a corner table complete with a tablecloth and silverware. "You certainly could teach the Army something about cooking," Mark said as they began their meal.

"We work our people hard," the XO explained. "Twelve hour shifts, seven days a week. But we feed them well. That's a morale builder."

Mark thought the XO's speech sounded like a training script. "Works for me," Mark agreed as he dug into his food. The Navy officers talked with Mark about Pensacola, sharing stories from past tours they had done there. When the conversation turned to the workings of the *Ronald Reagan,* Mark's attention drifted as he thought about his website staring at him from the Navy monitor and tried to figure out what it all meant. As they were finishing their meal Mark realized that the XO was speaking to him. "Sorry, what?"

"We are assigning a Marine escort to you while you're here," the XO repeated. "He'll be your tour guide. Get you where you need to go. Keep you from getting lost, which is very easy in a ship this size. If you need anything, ask him and he'll take care of it. Unless there's anything else you want right now, we'll have him escort you to a berth so you can get some rest."

"That would be great," Mark said as he realized how tired he was. "By the way, what day is this?"

It's Saturday evening.

"I've lost a day," Mark complained.

The Captain laughed. "It's easy to get disorientated when you are flying around the world. We are fifteen hours ahead of Pensacola. It is 18:25 here, that's 6:25 in the afternoon.

"That means it's about 3:25 in the morning for me," Mark calculated. "That explains the jet lag. I guess I won't call home right now to tell my wife I arrived. But later I will need to give her a call and let her know I made it. She hates flying and worries when I fly."

"We can arrange that," the Captain said. "But you will be limited in what you can tell her."

"She knows why I came out here," Mark objected.

"It's not that," the Captain replied. "She will be on an unsecure line. We have to be careful what we say on it. I'll have a communications officer brief you first, but basically we can't say anything that will compromise our mission or our position."

"Okay," Mark agreed. "But just out of curiosity, with satellites today, doesn't everyone know where we are anyway?"

"Not everyone," the Captain said. "But yes, with satellites it certainly is not like it used to be.

After a pause, Mark added, "If I could ask one other thing; perhaps a toothbrush and a change of clothes? I wasn't given time to pack anything and I rather not walk around your ship in this suit for the next couple days," Mark added.

"Bob will take care of that for you," the Captain answered. As they stood up a Marine approached and reported to the Captain. "Here's your escort," the Captain explained. I will see you in the morning."

Mark shook the Captain's hand. "Thank you for the hospitality."

"This way, Sir," the Marine said as the Captain and XO left. Mark glanced at the Marine. He was shorter than Mark, but had that solid look and crew cut that all Marines seemed to possess. Not someone to mess with, Mark thought. By the stripes on his uniform, Mark figured he was a Staff Sergeant, or whatever the Marine equivalent of an E-6 would be. Once again Mark was led through a maze of corridors and stairwells. Mark was quickly lost and saw why the Captain had assigned him an escort. Finally, they reached their destination. The Marine opened a narrow door and motioned Mark into a small room. Mark looked around the small gray berth. It contained a bunk, complete with a utilitarian looking pillow and wool blanket, a small gray table attached to the wall, a built in TV, and even a bathroom, with a narrow shower. The Marine showed him the amenities in the small room and stated that he would be waiting outside if needed. Mark took a cramped shower and climbed into the bunk. Despite the thin mattress and the strangeness of past events, he finally succumbed to sleep.

CHAPTER 4

Mark was awakened at 06:30 by the same Marine Sergeant. "These should fit you, Sir," the Marine informed him as he placed a pile of clothes on the small desk. They are basically one-size-fits-all. Well, you know that. They told me you are ex-Army. These are basically your modern-day BDU's. I also have some sneakers, size ten. Anything else you need we can get at the store after breakfast."

"You have a store on board?"

"Actually, two. But we do not have time for that now. Captain wants you to attend the morning briefing, which he has scheduled for zero-seven-hundred this morning, to allow you time to sleep. If you hurry, you have time for a quick shower and breakfast before the briefing. You did tell me last night to wake you up as late as possible."

Twenty-nine minutes later Mark was hustled into the briefing room by his Marine escort, while he swallowed the last piece of a bagel that he had snagged as they passed through the galley. Once again he was given the seat next to the Captain, who had not yet arrived. Precisely at 07:00 the Captain entered the room with the accompanying cry of: "Attention on Deck." Mark smiled to himself when he jumped to attention also. He had been out of the military for over 20 years and still some habits came right back. I guess it's the same as standing up for a judge, Mark surmised.

The briefing started, as all military briefings seemed to begin, with the weather - although on a ship it made much more sense, which is probably why they spent so much time discussing a low-pressure system off the western coast of Mexico. Being from Pensacola, Mark had great respect for low-pressure systems that could turn into hurricanes; no, typhoons, he corrected himself. This was the Pacific after all. The briefing summarized the politics of South East Asia, which is where the battle group had been heading, and then the myriad details of running a ship, a battle group, and the welfare of 5,000 seamen. All of this was accomplished in less than 30 minutes, at which point the last briefer announced, "My briefing is top secret; all unauthorized personnel please depart." There was a shuffling to the door as a number of individuals, including Mark's escort, left the briefing room. With that accomplished and the obligatory guard posted at the door, the briefer continued.

"As you know, Mark Williams arrived on station at 19:25 hours last night. Since that time there has been no change in Bogeyman. That's the codename we have given the UFO," the briefer added for Mark's benefit. "Once it stopped moving we have not been able to detect it on any of our instruments or by our underwater asset. That's our escorting submarine," he added again for Mark's benefit.

"Our detection ability at that depth is not optimal. And we have identified what appears to be a thermal vent in the area, which further complicates detection. We still are receiving the same broadcast without interruption and it appears to be originating from an area near Bogeyman's last known position. Whether Bogeyman is there or the signal is coming from some type of relay, we can't confirm. There is no new data from NORAD. Any questions?"

"What is the status of the submersible?" the XO asked.

"They estimate another seventy-four hours before they can clear port in California. Barring any unforeseen delays, the earliest they could be here is ten days."

An uncomfortable silence followed, as Mark believed all personnel were waiting for him to solve the problem. As the silence continued, he turned to the Captain and asked, "Does this bogeyman even know I'm here?" The question seemed to take everyone by surprise.

"Your arrival here was not hidden," the briefer replied. "We assume that it monitored your arrival."

Mark pondered this for a moment before replying. "You're assuming that it is conducting surveillance on us and that it could recognize me when I got out of that fighter, wearing a flight suit and helmet. That could be perfectly accurate or it might be a huge assumption. After all, we might all look alike to them." Mark had trouble not making a joke as the absurdity of what he was saying struck him. Here he was on an aircraft carrier seriously talking with the officers about aliens and whether they could recognize him.

"So what are you suggesting?" the Captain asked.

"Maybe we should tell it that I'm here," Mark continued, still feeling like he was playing in some huge joke and that any minute everyone would shout "April Fool" or point out the hidden camera.

"How?" a voice from behind Mark asked.

"I don't know?" Mark replied. "You are receiving a signal from it. Why don't you send a signal back?

"What kind of signal?" someone asked. "The sub already tried and this is all we get."

Mark thought for a moment. "It sent you a visual. Send one back. Maybe a picture of me standing on the flight deck? You could alternate between my website picture and the flight deck picture so there is no misunderstanding that it is the same person. You could add a caption saying that I am here, but then you are assuming that they read English and since they are only transmitting a picture, pictures are probably a safer bet. I guess it all depends on how long they have been sitting up there watching us," Mark added, still thinking this was the weirdest conversation he ever had.

After a moment of deliberation the Captain replied, "That makes sense. Jones, get some photographs of Mr. Williams on the flight deck and put together a short signal alternating it with the web site signal that they are sending to us. When it's ready, let me review it. We will have to clear it with CINCPAC before we start sending. That's Commander-in-Chief Pacific," the Captain added for

Mark's benefit. "I think that's a good idea." With that the meeting ended. As they left the Captain turned to Mark, "I see we have found something for you to wear. Get with Commander Jones about arranging the photos; then you're free to tour the ship. We can always find you through your escort."

"Thank you," Mark replied. "Is there someway I can call my wife? I need to let her know I made it safely." There was a pause while the Captain discussed Mark's request with the XO.

"Bob will clear it with the communications officer," the Captain agreed. "But remember, you won't be able to tell her where we are or about the mission. Her side of the transmission will not be secure," the Captain explained.

"Don't worry," Mark said with a laugh. "I don't even know where I am."

As they exited the briefing room, the Marine Sergeant walked up to Mark and asked, "Where to now, Sir?"

"I need to get with a Commander Jones about a photo op and then you need to show me a phone booth. After that you can give me a tour of this floating city of yours, including that store you were telling me about. Looks like I may be here for a while."

They shot photographs of Mark wearing his suit, as it seemed closer to the website photograph than his current look with the BDU's. When he had changed back to BDU's the Marine took him to a communication center, where they patched a call through to Mark's wife. The communication officer stayed to monitor the call.

"Hey Honey, it's me," Mark said when they finally got through.

"I was getting worried. You haven't called in almost twenty-four hours. Was the flight okay?"

"Sorry. Things were a bit hectic, and of course, there is a time zone difference."

"What time is it there?" she asked.

"I can't say," Mark answered when the Officer shook his head no. "They are concerned that this is an unsecure line."

"What can you say?" she asked, clearly a bit put out by his reply.

"Well, the flight was fine. Pretty uneventful, which are the way flights should be. It was interesting."

"I bet you loved every minute of it," she replied knowingly.

"Yes, it was fun," Mark conceded. "I could get used to riding up front."

"So, is it there? What you are looking for," she asked hesitantly.

Mark paused. "Nothing has changed from what they told us before. It is just like they said," he answered carefully.

"So what are you going to do now?" she asked.

"I really don't know. Just wait and see, I guess. It looks like I may be here for a little while. I'll call when I can," Mark continued. "But don't worry if you don't hear from me for a while. The time change here is a bit drastic." They talked a little more before he finally hung up, promising to be careful and call again when he could.

After that, Mark took a tour of the ship. At first he was fascinated. But before long the endless gray corridors and countless stairs became routine. During the tour Mark questioned the sergeant about his background. Staff Sergeant William Jeffreys was from a small farming town outside of Des Moines, Iowa. He had enlisted in the Marines after high school in order to pay for college, had enjoyed it, so he stayed. Now an E-6 at age 26, he was halfway through a four-year college program and currently assigned to the *Ronald Reagan* as part of a Marine security detachment. He planned to put in his 20 years, but did not have any plans after that. He was single and enjoying the opportunity of a lifetime; visiting foreign ports all over the world.

"I think I've had enough exercise for a lifetime," Mark complained after the five-millionth staircase. "Why don't you show me to the nearest galley so I can put back on some of the calories you burned off me."

"I thought you were an Army officer?" Sgt. Jeffreys asked with a laugh, relaxing as he got to know Mark.

"I was, twenty years ago. And a JAG officer at that," Mark explained. "And I was assigned to an armored division. That meant we rode, not walked everywhere we went. This aircraft carrier is like living in New York City, but without any subways or taxis. No wonder everyone is in such good shape! Everyone has to walk to work."

Laughing, Sgt. Jeffreys led Mark through several more corridors and staircases until they arrived at galley

number two. "This is more like it," Mark said as he
loaded his plate with stuffed shrimp, steamed asparagus
and potatoes au gratin. "Now if it weren't for all the
walking, I could get used to this."

As they sat down to eat, Sgt. Jeffreys' radio beeped
and he held a hushed conversation into it. When he
finished he jumped up and said, "We have to go. They
want you on the bridge ASAP."

"But I'm having lunch," Mark protested. "Just
kidding," he quickly added when he saw the look on Sgt.
Jeffreys' face. "Damn Marines," he muttered as he
scooped up two stuffed shrimp in his hand before
dumping the otherwise untouched plate of food. "No
sense of humor." He followed Sgt. Jeffreys through the
ship as he led him back to the bridge at a fast pace,
wondering if he would be able to keep up with the young
Marine. However macho pride, or as his wife always said,
"testosterone poisoning," would not allow him to slow
down. Five minutes later he was entering the bridge,
tired, winded and already regretting wolfing down the two
stuffed shrimp. He was escorted to the briefing room
where a number of officers were already assembled. He
sat down in his customary chair next to the Captain and
tried to catch his breath. "Sorry I'm late," he said. "I
think I was on the opposite end of the ship and forty
flights down when you called."

The briefing officer started with the usual preamble:
"This is a top-secret briefing." After that all normalcy
ended. "We have a response from Bogeyman." Mark sat
up in his chair. "We began transmitting the new signal

consisting of Mr. Williams' photograph on the flight deck and his website at 09:45 hours. At 13:21 hours Bogeyman's signal to us changed. Here is the new signal." The officer turned to a display screen behind him. "This is a real time feed from Bogeyman." Mark stared at the screen. On it he saw his website displayed for about 10 seconds, and then the scene shifted to a dark picture, which lasted for another 10 seconds before the sequence repeated. "We have enhanced this picture," the briefer continued. "If you look here," he stopped the sequencing and pointed to the top corner of the dark photo, which was now obviously lighter, "You can clearly see the outline of a submarine. This appears to be *SSN Louisville*," the officer continued. Turning to Mark he added, "That's the Los Angeles class submarine attached to this battle group. It's currently patrolling deep in the Mariana Trench in the area where we believe Bogeyman is located. This is not a file picture. We believe it is a recent picture taken by Bogeyman."

"I bet Commander Hastings was not happy when he learned he was being shadowed by Bogeyman," the XO remarked to the Captain.

"That's an understatement," Captain Peters agreed.

Silence filled the briefing room as the officers watched and absorbed this new information. "What do you make of this transmission?" the Captain asked, although it appeared that he already had an answer.

"Sir, I would say that Bogeyman wants Mr. Williams on the *Louisville*," the officer answered.

"Damn," Mark said in the ensuing silence and then glanced around guiltily when he realized that he had been heard.

The Captain turned to Mark. "Do you agree with that interpretation?" he asked.

"I'm afraid I do. As much as I would like to come up with a different interpretation, it certainly makes sense."

"Will you go?" The Captain asked.

Mark took a deep breath. "Yes."

"Okay." The Captain turned to another officer. "Tom, contact the *Louisville* and arrange for the transfer." Turning back to Mark the Captain continued, "We'll have a Seahawk helicopter take you out to the submarine. After that you will be Commander Hastings' guest."

Mark only nodded. This did not sound like it was going to be fun. The idea of being cooped up in a submarine hundreds or thousands of feet below the surface was not something he relished. He was not very claustrophobic, but he did not want to test it in this fashion, particularly when they were going down to investigate a UFO.

CHAPTER 5

Once again Mark found himself flying in a military aircraft, this time an HH-60 Seahawk helicopter. He was wearing a bright orange exposure suit, which they had explained was in case he missed the drop-off and landed in the ocean. It should keep him alive and on the surface long enough to be recovered. That thought was not comforting at all. Nor was the thought that he would be dangling out of a helicopter, trying to land on the bridge of a submarine, while both were underway in the middle of the ocean. A crewman provided Mark with a myriad of instructions, none of which he understood. Sgt. Jeffreys had helped, obviously jealous, and wishing he could rappel down to the submarine for, as he put it, "a joyride."

Mark would have gladly changed places with Sgt. Jeffreys. He had nothing against helicopters. He had enjoyed riding in them whenever he got a chance in the Army. But that was over dry land and he wasn't jumping out of them. He was also, he kept reminding himself, twenty years younger back then and "bulletproof." And he certainly did not want to think about crawling inside the submarine and diving down to whatever depth it could go. All he could think about were the old submarine movies where the subs went too deep and their hulls collapsed, killing all aboard as the compartments flooded.

Mark sat in the open door of the Seahawk helicopter, his Gumby suit keeping him warm against the blowing wind and a harness keeping him from exiting the aircraft before the proper time. He could hear the military chatter in his helmet headphones, most of which he ignored until he heard one of the pilots say, "There she is." Straining his head out the door he could just make out the submarine's conning tower in the sea below. The helicopter circled and approached from the stern, coming lower and lower as it approached the conning tower. At the pilot's signal, the crew chief checked Mark's harness, tightened a safety strap around Mark's arms so he couldn't flail around, and then disconnected the helmet audio plug. 'That would have been funny,' Mark thought wryly, being lowered from the helicopter only to have forgotten to disconnect the headphones. 'Oops.'

The helicopter hovered about 50 feet over the submarine's conning tower as the crew chief prepared to lower Mark. The first step is always the worst, Mark reminded himself as he thought back to the rappelling classes he had taken back in college. That's when you found out if the rope was connected properly. Mark didn't budge when the crew chief signaled him to step out into space. When he tried to turn to ask what he was to hold on to, the crew chief pushed him out and Mark spun on the cable, unable to even grab the cable as the safety strap pinned down his arms as he swung out helplessly over the submarine. The helicopter held station while the crew chief lowered Mark down to the pitching submarine. Waves crashed against the conning tower, sending cold spray across Mark's face. Dangling in the down thrust from the helicopter, while being sprayed from the waves below, Mark finally appreciated the cumbersome Gumby suit. Down, down, he went, slowly spinning on the cable. He barely noticed a seaman touch the cable with a pole to ground it out before waiting hands grabbed him and lowered him into a tiny space at the top of the conning tower. They quickly disconnected his harness and safety strap and waved the helicopter off.

"Welcome to *SSN Louisville*," one of the submariner's yelled above the departing helicopter's noise. "We need to get below so we can dive." Having no interest in being left alone on the conning tower, Mark quickly followed them down the narrow ladder into the submarine. The deck was pitching beneath his feet as he was led to a corner and instructed to stand there and hold on. He listened as commands were given and felt the deck pitch forward. It was almost like riding a trolley, except he leaned back, not forward. After what seemed like several minutes the submarine stopped pitching and the only sensation of movement was that the deck appeared to be sloped slightly downward. At that point one of the sailors walked over and introduced himself. "I'm Commander Hastings. Welcome to the *SSN Louisville*. They shook hands as Commander Hastings added, "Once you get out of that suit, we will go to my cabin and discuss your business here."

After a sailor helped him peel off the exposure suit, Commander Hastings led Mark down a narrow corridor to a small cabin containing a berth, desk and not much more. "Probably not as much space as you were used to back on the *Ronald Reagan*. But down here space is at a premium," Commander Hastings explained as he sat at the desk and motioned Mark to sit on the bed. "The flash traffic I get is rather cursory," the Commander continued. "I would appreciate it if you could fill me in on the details."

Mark had not been told to keep any secrets from Commander Hastings, nor was he inclined to anyway, so he explained what he had learned in the briefings and his confused involvement. He ended with, "So you see, I have no idea what is going on and certainly no idea why this UFO seems to like my webpage or wants me down here. The thought is not only confusing, but also a bit scary. However, here I am; for whatever it's worth."

The Commander thought for a moment before responding. "Your rendition tracks with what they have been telling me. I guess I was hoping that you had the answer."

"You and me both," Mark agreed.

"This is certainly the strangest mission I have ever been on," The Commander continued. "Let me tell you what we have been doing. When the UFO entered the atmosphere we were too deep to receive a warning from the Fleet. However, we heard it hit the water; lit the board right up. We acoustically followed it to this area. Initially it made a hell of a noise, which we believe was its hull cooling after being heated in the atmosphere. When it got into this area it slowed and we finally lost it among the bottom clutter. We were unable to pick it up on any of our passive arrays or even with an active sonar ping. Shortly thereafter a signal started from it, which you have seen. Then we received that second signal. Nothing has changed since then.

"Have you pinged it again?" Mark asked.

"No. We don't like to go active very often. Although it allows us to see better, it also gives away our position and allows everyone else to see us as well. There is always the possibility of a hostile nearby."

"Hostile?"

"We occasionally have..." the Commander paused, "...issues with foreign submarines. Consequently, I do not like to pinpoint our presence when they may be lurking around. As for the Bogeyman, it is much too deep for us. But we can certainly get you closer than you were on the surface. Then I guess we'll just have to wait and see."

'Don't go too deep on my behalf,' Mark wanted to add, but didn't. Instead he asked, "So when will we be in position?"

"About forty-five minutes from now," the Commander replied, consulting his watch. "I'll have you stay with me in the con when we approach. If you have any suggestions, let me know. Although from what you have been telling me, you appear to be as clueless as the rest of us. No offense."

"No offense taken. And I would say more clueless. Remember, I'm ex-Army. All this ocean and traveling underneath it is all very foreign. At home in Pensacola I liked to go boating, but rarely out of sight of land."

"Welcome to the Pacific; the deepest part of the planet," the Commander said with a chuckle. Getting up he concluded with, "I need to get back to the con. If you want to stay here, you may; I'll have someone get you when we get closer."

"I would really like to see the head and perhaps trouble you for a quick snack?"

"I'll send someone in to take care of you," the Commander said as he exited. In a minute a seamen entered and escorted him first to the head and then to the galley, where he was served a sandwich, before being escorted back to the con. Where the *Ronald Reagan* was filled with seemingly hundreds of miles of corridors and stairs, the submarine seemed cramped and claustrophobic. The numerous watertight hatches were reminiscent of every submarine movie he had seen, most of which involved people being trapped in flooding chambers, unable to open the hatch. Mark struggled to force that image out of his mind. This UFO business was scary enough, without his rampant movie fueled imagination making him claustrophobic as well. When Mark entered the con, the Commander gave him a quick tour of the screens he was watching. "This is our passive window of the bottom. It is still several thousand feet deeper than we can go. Here," he pointed at a spot on the screen, "is where we believe bogeyman is located based upon the last acoustics we received from it when it arrived. It is also the point where we believe the signal is originating. We are pulling a passive array so we will go over it and then circle around. We have done that several times already with no response. We'll see if anything different happens now that you are aboard. We'll start our pass in about ten minutes."

Mark watched the progression on the screen as the minutes dragged slowly by. It took some 30 minutes to make the pass and start circling back. Nothing changed. Another hour went by with no change. The Commander walked over to Mark. "Any suggestions?"

"I'm just a visitor here," Mark replied, shrugging his shoulders.

"True, but you were invited by our friend down there."

"Maybe he needs a lawyer?" Mark winced as he tried a joke to relieve the tension.

"Awful lot of trouble just to get a lawyer," the Commander responded to Mark's relief.

"You would think that..." Mark's comment was interrupted by one of the crewmen's report. "Sir, the Bogeyman's signal has stopped." The Commander quickly stepped over to the crewman's station. "Signal just stopped," the crewman repeated. "Here is the last location. I can't pick it up at all now." The Commander looked at the screens. "Jefferson, you getting anything?" the Commander asked.

"No, Sir."

"Bradley, you?"

"No, Sir."

Silence followed while the Commander considered his next move and the sonar men studied their screens. A few minutes later Bradley reported, "Got something. Signal is moving, heading two-seven-niner, and rising, speed thirty knots. This heading places it on an intercept course with us."

"I confirm," another voice reported, then added, "no screws, no engine noise, only rushing water - like a biological."

"You sure it is Bogeyman and not a biological?" the Commander asked.

"Yes, Sir. It's not acting like a biological."

The Commander and the XO leaned over the plotting chart.

"Sir, it's really picking up speed, rising straight towards us at forty knots!" another sonar man reported. One thousand yards, coming in fast, forty-six knots, on a collision course!"

"Right full rudder..." the Commander started his reply when Mark's head seemed to explode. One moment he was watching the screens and listening to the reports and then a ball of colored light seemed to burst inside his head. He grabbed his head and fell to the deck screaming.

The Commander did not have time to deal with Mark's outburst. He was too concerned about the incoming Bogeyman. He turned hard and released a noisemaker, standard tactics to evade enemy torpedoes. The disadvantage, of course, was that it created too much clutter to accurately track anything. He made another sharp turn and then went silent, bracing for impact. A corpsman was tending to Mark, first trying to gag him so that his screams would not be heard outside the submarine. Long minutes slowly stretched by as the crew collectively held their breath. They all recognized the maneuvers and did not need to be told there was a potential threat. A silence stretched throughout the ship, which made Mark's muffled moaning sound incredibly loud.

The sonar man strained as he scanned his instruments, trying to locate Bogeyman. Finally, he motioned to the Commander. "There it is," he whispered, pointing to his display. "Ten-thousand yards and leaving, it's heading back down to the bottom." The Commander looked at the display and breathed a sigh of relief. After checking the course and condition of the submarine he went over to the corpsman treating Mark. "How's he doing?" the Commander asked.

"He's unconscious, but I don't know why," the corpsman responded. "All vital signs are elevated: pulse, blood pressure, respiration. What happened to him?"

"I don't know," the Commander responded. "One moment he was standing there, the next he was on the deck holding his head screaming. I assume he panicked."

"Barring any other explanation, I would say he was in shock," the corpsman replied. "Is he psychotic?"

"Don't know, why do you ask?"

"Well, before he passed out, he was crying: 'Get out of my head, get out of my head,' over and over."

This last report gave the Commander a cold chill. Enemy submarines, torpedoes, these were threats he had trained for. What he was facing now was totally unknown.

CHAPTER 6

Mark regained consciousness slowly. The early morning light gently seeped through his closed eyelids, as he lay curled up in a wonderfully comfortable bed. He resisted awakening so he could enjoy the comfort for a few more minutes. But comfort was eluding him. The light was getting harsher, the bed harder. His mind started asking, 'Where am I?' and his consciousness slowly returned in an attempt to answer that simple question.

He was at home in bed, his alarm probably about to go off. But then he remembered a jet ride to an aircraft carrier. That meant he was in his bunk on the carrier. But wasn't there something about a submarine? And a burst of images. A jumble of sights, sounds and smells, all flashing in his mind like multiple disjointed movies played at high speed and in random order, too fast to understand. Try as he might, he could not recall anything else.

Still not ready to open his eyes, he concentrated on his senses. He was lying in a fetal position on a thin mattress, cold metal rails pressing against his knees and back. A light blanket lay over him. Reluctantly he opened his eyes, only to be blinded by harsh fluorescent light.

Stiffly, he rolled onto his back and heard a moan, vaguely realizing that it was from him. A corpsman materialized at his side.

"Have you decided to wake up?" the corpsman asked, before calling over his shoulder to the doctor. A moment later a woman swam into his vision. Mark fixated on the Silver Oak leaf and medical caduceus on her collar. She checked the monitors over his head and then his eyes in that impersonal medical manner all doctors seem to have. "Are we awake?" she asked.

'What a stupid question,' Mark thought. He hated the royal we of the medical profession. Somehow resisting the urge to say, "I don't know? I am. Are you?" he instead asked, "Where am I?" His words came out in a raspy type of croak. A look of concern flitted across the doctor's face.

"You don't know where you are?"

Mark felt irritation welling up within him. 'No, I just asked that for the fun of it,' he thought. 'And they joke about lawyers asking stupid questions.'

"What do you last remember?" she was asking.

"Just tell me where I am," Mark interrupted, his voice still raspy, but already getting better. His throat was so raw, it felt like he had been yelling.

"You are in sick bay on the *USS Ronald Reagan*," the doctor answered reluctantly. She started saying something else, but Mark wasn't paying attention. He could not remember coming back from the submarine. Had the submarine been a dream? He was starting to question his memory when the doctor's words registered.

"... remember being brought back from the submarine?" the doctor was asking. 'Okay,' Mark thought. 'So I was on the submarine. Everything did happen. But what ever happened with the UFO?' He needed more information. He needed to talk to the Captain. He certainly wasn't going to get anything from the doctor. He started to sit up, but the spinning room forced him to lie back down.

"Where do you think you're going?" the doctor asked.

"I need to speak to the Captain."

"You need to stay here. You have been out for a long time."

"How long?"

"About twenty-four hours," the doctor answered, again in a reluctant manner.

"Twenty-four hours!" Mark repeated, shocked. "I need to call my wife. She'll be worried sick."

"The Captain is on his way," the doctor continued. "He left orders to be notified the moment you woke up."

By the time the Captain arrived, Mark was feeling stronger. The hospital bed was raised so he was sitting up, and the room no longer spun. Mark smiled when the Captain walked in. "I seem to have been sleeping on the job," Mark said as the Captain asked how he was doing. The comment brought a smile, replacing the Captain's concerned look.

"You are a civilian, after all. Lost all your military training," the Captain replied to the joke. Mark smiled. He liked this guy. One of the few 0-6's who had not been ruined by the military, still had a sense a humor.

The Captain looked around the room. "Thank you doc, I'll call if you're needed." The doctor paused as if about to object, re-thought it, then left the room. "So what happened?" the Captain asked, serious now.

"Tell me what happened on the sub first," Mark asked. "I need to make some sense out of my memory. The last thing I remember is the UFO approaching and Commander Hastings taking evasive action."

The Captain nodded, "Commander Hastings told me that when Bogeyman was closing, you grabbed your head and fell to the deck screaming. I'm afraid he thought you were panicking and was a bit irritated with you at the time. Actually, he said something about a civilian losing it, jeopardizing his boat, and that he would have shot you on the spot if he had a gun. After all," the Captain explained, "Hastings thought he was under attack and you were making a lot of noise. Anyway, you were subdued by a corpsman, while Hastings took evasive action. The whole event lasted less than fifteen minutes. When they finally relocated Bogeyman, it was heading back down to the bottom of the trench. You were unconscious. A corpsman said that before you passed out, you were repeating: 'Get out of my head, get out of my head.' That last line was a bit unnerving to Commander Hastings. He stayed on station for another hour, but when it became apparent that the corpsman could not do anything for you, he surfaced and you were transferred back here by helicopter. That was about," he paused as he looked at his watch, "twenty-three and a half hours ago. The flight surgeon could not find anything wrong with you, although she tells me you had elevated vitals and increased brain activity on the EEG. They would have to explain to you the significance of the EEG. All I understood is that your brain was very active. But even they cannot explain why or what is going on. Which is why I am wondering if you can?" the Captain asked.

Mark closed his eyes and ordered his thoughts while the Captain waited patiently. Finally opening his eyes, he responded, "I remember the UFO approaching. Commander Hastings was ordering some maneuver. Then I was attacked. My mind suddenly exploded with sights, sounds, tastes, and feelings; but all too fast and jumbled to make any sense. Like watching a movie at fast-forward, but worse. It was... painful. Intrusive. A violation. Like someone was shoving their consciousness into my brain. It was overwhelming. I tried to fight it, but didn't know how," Mark paused, overwhelmed by the memory of the attack.

"Did they say anything?" The Captain asked.

"I don't know," Mark responded dejectedly. "I don't remember any words. I really don't remember any specific details. It's like I was overloaded. It's all jumbled and confused; like trying to remember a dream."

"Are you sure you were attacked?"

"No, not really." Mark admitted. "It felt like it at the time. But... I don't know what happened. But I don't think I panicked down there," Mark added, seeing the look on the Captain's face.

"Can you describe any details?"

"No, sorry. It's all a blur."

"Well, get some rest and we'll decide what to do next," the Captain concluded.

"I've rested. What I need now is something to eat. And I need to call my wife."

"You can't tell her what is going on, you know," the Captain stated.

"I know. I just promised to call. Let her know I'm okay," Mark agreed.

"Okay. If the doc is willing to release you, I'll send your escort down to get you," the Captain offered as he turned to leave.

"I wish I could give you more information, Mark said.

The Captain paused in the doorway, "It's a confusing business. We'll figure it out yet. I hope," the Captain added, more to himself as he left.

While the Captain exited to talk to the flight surgeon, Mark slowly got out of bed and tested his legs. He was quickly getting stronger. By the time the doctor came in, Mark had found his clothes and was dressed. "Thanks for your hospitality," Mark said, trying to preempt the doctor. She still insisted on taking vitals one more time. As she was finishing, Sgt. Jeffreys knocked on the bulkhead door.

"Captain says you need a tour guide," Sgt. Jeffreys said in mock seriousness.

"Yes, Sergeant," Mark matched his tone. "We need to conduct an inspection of the nearest galley. I'm starved."

"This way, Sir," Sgt. Jeffreys said as he led the way out of sickbay.

Mark walked confidently out of sickbay and made it around the first turn before he staggered and had to hold the wall. Sgt. Jeffreys hurried back and held him up. "Perhaps we should go back to sick bay," Sgt. Jeffreys suggested worriedly.

"No," Mark protested. "I'm just a bit tired and very hungry. Besides, I need to get out of that place. Doctors just want to treat you like a specimen."

"Okay," Sgt. Jeffreys agreed, although clearly not convinced. "At least let me help you. It's really not very far," Sgt. Jeffreys said as he took Mark's arm and helped him down the corridor. The corridor seemed to stretch on forever, but they finally reached the galley. Surprised at how tired he felt, Mark sat at a table near the door, while Sgt. Jeffreys went to get him some food. Mark's stomach growled as the aroma of the food wafted over him and he debated pushing to the front of the line. 'Or I could steal it from that guy at the next table,' he thought as he watched a hefty sailor sitting down with his tray covered with huge helpings of steak and potatoes. 'No,' he cautioned himself. 'He's probably a Navy seal and would eat my arm off!' Mark's thoughts were interrupted when Sgt. Jeffreys sat down, pushing a steaming tray towards him. "Got you a little bit of everything," he said as Mark hungrily grabbed up his knife and fork.

"Thanks," Mark said as he hurriedly cut a piece of steak. "I'm starving." He took a bite of the steak and gagged as a horrid taste filled his mouth. He spit the steak out, almost throwing up in the process. Mercifully, the familiar syrupy taste of his Coke washed most of the horrid taste away, barely saving him from the humiliation of vomiting on the table.

Sgt. Jeffreys looked up from his meal. "Are you okay?" he asked.

"Yea," Mark croaked as he quickly swallowed some more Coke. "Just swallowed wrong," Mark lied as he sat their breathing heavy, sweat standing out on his forehead. "How's your steak?" he asked Sgt. Jeffreys after his gag reflex subsided.

"Its great. One thing they really know how to cook is steak," Jeffreys responded enthusiastically.

Mark stared down at his plate. The steak looked fine. He cut another piece and sniffed it. The aroma was perfect. Making sure his Coke was nearby he carefully tasted the meat. He was relieved by the wonderful flavor of a perfectly cooked steak. 'What happened?' He carefully continued to eat, hoping that his food would continue to have its expected taste.

Laughter enveloped him as a group of seamen walked into the galley and jostled into the line. He listened to one of the sailors complaining about his current duties and smiled at the normalcy of the conversation. It was a conversation you could probably overhear anywhere in the world in a myriad of different languages. Some things are universal, he thought. He glanced up to catch the reply.

A bright light filled the room as four alien creatures materialized in front of him.

Mark jumped back with a cry, almost falling out of his chair. Sgt. Jeffreys looked up startled and the sailors at the next table glanced over. Mark looked back at the aliens, but they were gone, the complaining sailors standing in their place. "Sorry, bit jumpy today," Mark mumbled as he pretended to concentrate on his food. 'What was going on?' he wondered. 'Am I going nuts with all this talk of aliens?" He surreptitiously glanced back to make sure the aliens had not reappeared. He glanced around the room filled with sailors eating their meals. No one else had noticed, so it had not happened. 'But it had been so real,' he thought.

The aliens were not exactly like ones he had seen in movies, but rather a combination of many. Humanoid, definitely: tall, thin, almost gangly, with large, bald, somewhat triangular blue-gray heads. Huge, black, oval eyes were set at an angle beneath a prominent, flared ridge bone, which met close to the nose, or where the nose should be since they didn't have noses. A bright green, skintight jumpsuit, like a warm water dive skin, covered the rest of their bodies. 'This is too detailed to be my imagination,' Mark thought. 'Yet, they clearly were never there. So I must be imagining them.'

He glanced up and noticed that Sgt. Jeffreys was staring at him intently. "I'm feeling a bit... queasy," Mark lied. "Why don't you take me back to my room?" He thought sickbay was probably more appropriate, but he wouldn't voluntarily go there. 'I just need to lie down and rest,' he tried to convince himself.

"How about sick bay?" Sgt. Jeffreys suggested instead.

"No, I just need to lie down. Rest. I'll do that better in my bunk. You never get any rest around doctors." Mark got up shakily from the table and walked hesitantly towards the door. Once in the corridor Mark leaned heavily on Sgt. Jeffreys as they headed to his room. 'This could be just like an alien ship,' Mark thought as they walked through the endless corridors. That was a mistake.

Mark blinked. The familiar gray corridor was gone. In its place was a larger, tube-like passageway, lit by harsh, unnatural looking light. Colors flowed in odd combinations along the walls. The hatch at the end was obviously an airlock, although Mark couldn't say how he knew that.

Mark was too tired to react, which was probably good since Sgt. Jeffreys would certainly have dragged him to sickbay. Fortunately, when Mark looked back the corridor had reverted to Navy regulation gray with all the usual markings, including the obligatory 'you are here' diagram on the wall. The trip seemed to take forever, but the corridors stayed Navy. After an eternity he was able to collapse in his bunk.

"I'll be right outside your door if you need me," Sgt. Jeffreys stated as he stepped out of the room.

Mark lay back and closed his eyes. 'What is happening to me? No one else is seeing aliens, so they can't be real. Therefore, I must be hallucinating. Am I going crazy?' He thought about that for a while. 'No, I don't believe I'm crazy. Of course, what does it feel like to be crazy?' he asked himself cynically. 'The submarine is the key. Without that I would need to be checking in to that padded room right now. Great,' he thought, 'I've decided that I'm not crazy. That means space aliens are invading my mind. What a relief,' he told himself sarcastically as he walked over to the sink to splash water in his face.

Large black eyes stared at him from a triangular, blue-gray face.

Mark leaped back from the mirror with a yell, tripping over a chair in the process and falling to the floor.

The door opened and another alien rushed in and grabbed him.

Screaming, Mark flailed his arms wildly until the alien transformed into Sgt. Jeffreys. Sgt. Jeffreys pulled a radio from his belt and called for assistance, restraining Mark until the corpsman arrived. Aliens continued to flicker in and out of Mark's sight until the flight surgeon administered a shot, which put him to sleep.

Mark awoke dazed and disorientated. Opening his eyes, he recognized sick bay as the memories of the last couple days flooded back. His throat dry and medical personnel nowhere in sight, he started to get up. The hospital cot creaked as he shifted his weight. "Where do you think you're going?" Sgt. Jeffreys demanded from behind him.

"Just getting a glass of water," Mark replied weakly.

"I'll get it, you stay here."

"But I..."

"No buts. You stay or I will tie you down."

Mark laughed. "You have some bedside manner, Sergeant."

"I'm a Marine. We expect to be obeyed and get downright nasty if we are not."

"Yes, Sir! I will behave," Mark said, raising his hand sluggishly in a poor imitation of a salute. Sgt. Jeffreys left and was back in a second with a glass of cold water that Mark sipped carefully, hoping that it did not turn into some disgusting alien brew. It didn't. "So how long was I out this time?" Mark asked as he sipped the water carefully.

Sgt. Jeffreys checked his watch. "Only about five hours. The flight surgeon wanted to fly you to Guam. But the Captain said you were needed here. He would decide in the morning whether to fly you out."

"What time is it now," Mark asked.

"Zero-three-twenty.

"What time does that make it in the States?" Mark asked.

"That would be about one-twenty, Monday afternoon, Eastern time," Sgt. Jeffreys calculated.

"Monday! Beth is going to kill me," Mark groaned.

"I guess I should tell the doc you're awake," Sgt. Jeffreys said. "The Captain told her to notify him when you woke up."

"Wait a minute," Mark asked. "I need a few minutes to rest and collect my thoughts. I'll make much more sense in a few more minutes," he added when Sgt.

Jeffreys seemed to hesitate. "You probably think I'm crazy."

"Doc thinks so," Sgt. Jeffreys said, avoiding the question. "But I don't think the Captain does."

"What about you?"

"I don't know. You are certainly acting odd, but I don't know what is going on. So I haven't formed an opinion yet."

"But you stayed here. Did they order you to?" Mark asked.

"Yes," Sgt. Jeffreys admitted reluctantly. "They wanted someone here who could subdue you if you had another... episode."

"Is that what they call it? Episode. What a cute word. How about terrifying hallucination? That would be more accurate." Mark said. "Let me tell you what it's like and you tell me if it sounds like an 'episode.'" Mark continued, getting mad.

"You don't have to," Sgt. Jeffreys replied.

"No, I want to. I want your honest opinion." Mark explained. He also thought it would be a more honest opinion than the doc's, but didn't say it. "What do you know so far?" Mark asked. "No need for me repeating too much."

"Not much really," Sgt. Jeffreys admitted. "There are lots of rumors, but that's all, just rumors."

"What are the rumors?"

"Well, rumor has it that two fighters were scrambled to intercept an incoming bogey. Some say it was an intercontinental missile, others that it was a satellite falling out of orbit. Whatever it was, it splashed and sank. It must be important, because ever since it hit, we have been patrolling this area. Our mission had been to go to the South China Sea after stopping and replenishing at Guam. They now say that we are doing some training maneuvers here first, but no one believes them. We think they're trying to find the bogey. They're even trying to reroute the turtle over here."

"The turtle?"

"Yes. It's a two-man submersible that the Navy uses to service underwater equipment. It can go real deep. Rumor has it the Captain is madder than a hornet over some delays in getting it here."

"What about me? Any rumors about me?" Mark asked curiously.

"No. Not really. They think you're either a scientist or just some civilian VIP on a tour."

"Well let me tell you what is really going on," Mark said. "And I warn you, this will be the strangest story you've ever heard." Mark then proceeded to tell Sgt. Jeffreys what was going on, starting with the NORAD report, through his recruitment in Pensacola, the events on the submarine and ending with his 'hallucinations.' As he explained the hallucinations to Sgt. Jeffreys, he started to notice a pattern. "So," Mark concluded, am I crazy?"

"Man, your story is so, so..."

"So crazy?" Mark interjected.

"Yes, it makes the craziest rumors reasonable in comparison."

"I had trouble believing it in the beginning also, sometimes still do. So I'll make this deal. Don't answer me yet. Think about it and tell me later whether I should be locked in padded room. Okay?"

"Sure," Sgt. Jeffreys replied dubiously.

"Thank you," Mark replied. "By the way, everything I just told you is top secret, so if you want to keep those stripes, you better not repeat it," Mark added, feeling a little guilty for spilling confidential information to the Sergeant.

"You think I'm going to repeat that story?" Sgt. Jeffreys said with a laugh.

Mark smiled. "You better tell the doc I'm awake. I need to talk to the Captain, and," Mark added, "if I have another 'episode' in the meantime, make sure to tell the Captain exactly what I told you about these hallucinations."

The Captain arrived in sickbay within 10 minutes of receiving the call that Mr. Williams was awake. He was frustrated. It was going on five days since the alien had landed and they were no closer to figuring out what was going on. His task force had been on station since then and soon he would probably start attracting unwanted attention, despite the cover story that Washington was trying to sell. He certainly did not want to be competing with the Chinese or the Russians, while trying to deal with a suspected alien. He was pretty well convinced that this was an alien encounter, no matter how much he wished for another explanation. What this thing was doing could not be explained by human technology, and now their hope to communicate was dimming, as Mr. Williams seemed to be going crazy. With these glum thoughts, the Captain entered sickbay and headed directly to Mr. Williams' room. When he saw that Mr. Williams was alert, he turned to the flight surgeon and Sgt. Jeffreys saying, "Thank you, that will be all."

Both immediately turned to leave, but Mr. Williams asked Sgt. Jeffreys to wait. Turning to the Captain he said, "I need Sgt. Jeffreys to stay. I'll explain in a moment. But I've already told him what is going on, so you'll probably have to up his security clearance."

The Captain suppressed his irritation and merely nodded, 'What is done is done,' he thought.

"I think I'm starting to figure out what's going on," Mr. Williams started to explain; probably noticing the Captain's no nonsense attitude. "Not with the UFO, I still don't have a clue what he is doing here." The Captain wondered if Mark's use of the term "he" rather than "it" when referring to the UFO was significant. Mr. Williams continued, "I mean what is happening to me. Having these dreams, or hallucinations, or episodes, if you want to use the flight surgeon's terms. I think they are alien thoughts or memories that were somehow transmitted to me when I was on the submarine. I think they were trying to communicate, but I just couldn't receive, not clearly anyway. It's like they downloaded a bunch of information, but I don't know how to access it. So when I was in the galley, I started to access random bits of information. It was triggered by what I was doing.

When I was eating my steak, it triggered an alien memory of eating... something. The memory was so vivid that I actually felt and tasted alien food. It was revolting and I almost threw up in the galley. Then some sailors came in and I heard them talking about work and it triggered another memory and I saw four aliens standing in the galley.

"All of these came in short flashes. I had Sgt. Jeffreys take me back to my room to rest. On the way one of the ship's corridors turned into an alien corridor. When I was in the room, I looked in the mirror, and an alien looked back at me and when Sgt. Jeffreys ran into the room I saw an alien running in. Each time was without any warning. And each alien memory was related to something I was seeing or doing. These aliens are unlike anything I have ever seen. Not that I have ever seen an alien," Mr. Williams added quickly. "I mean they are not some alien from a movie I watched. They are totally different. Unique. That's why I say it is like I have alien memories that I am accessing at random. I hope that makes sense," Mr. Williams ended. "Because that's the best that I can explain it."

The Captain thought for a long while. "You're seeing aliens on board this ship, but you think they are memories they transmitted to you?"

"Yes."

"Sgt. Jeffreys, did you see anything," the Captain paused, "out of the ordinary?"

"No, Sir."

"In any other context what I just said would get me locked up in a padded room," Mr. Williams continued. "But you're the one who invited me to this party. So here it is. I am seeing things, alien things. They seem real to me when I see them because I see, hear and even taste this 'memory.' But they are only in my head. But I am seeing them as if they were really here, or as if I were there. This is so hard to explain. I see what the alien sees, taste what he tastes, and feel what he feels. I have no control over them. I'm just receiving, just watching. It was like if you gave me a memory of yours. I would see it from your eyes, from your ears; like a movie, but one in which I saw, heard, tasted and felt what you did - a movie in which I am the main actor. But I can't control it. I am just passively watching and feeling what the actor is doing. I was the alien, or in the alien. Which is why I think it's a memory. A past memory, it's not something that is going on now. But yes, to answer your question, I think these memories were transmitted to me on the sub. Why else would I be having them now? And in such detail? It's either that, or I am going crazy," Mr. Williams added, half jokingly.

The Captain wondered if Mr. Williams was cracking under the strain. He had seen it before. But that still did not explain the Bogeyman, and he knew that it existed, whatever it was. "What are they trying to communicate to you?" the Captain asked.

"I don't know," Mr. Williams answered. "It's probably just a portion of what they intended to communicate. I probably have not accessed the rest.

These memories, or at least my access to them, are very random right now, so I don't even know what they sent, let alone why they sent it. And I have never heard any words, only senses - sights, sounds, smells and taste - never thoughts or feelings. Just the five senses." After a long pause Mr. Williams asked, "So, do you believe me, or do you think I'm crazy?"

"It's an incredible story," the Captain replied slowly.

"It is," Mr. Williams responded. "And I didn't believe in UFO's when they told me in Pensacola and was still rather doubtful when I first got here. But now...? Either I have gone crazy, for no apparent reason," Mr. Williams added meaningfully, "or this is really a UFO and they have contacted us, or at least are trying to in their own way."

The Captain considered before responding. "Yes. This whole thing has been hard to believe," he finally said. "We have been searching for a man-made explanation for what we have seen and tracked. And so far there isn't one. We do not have anything that could have entered from space and maneuvered as this vehicle maneuvered before entering the water. And its' movements underwater are beyond our technology. So that leaves only one other explanation, albeit an incredible and unbelievable explanation. So, to answer your question," the Captain paused, making up his mind, "I guess I have to believe you."

"Thank you," Mr. Williams said with apparent relief in his voice. The Captain wondered if Mr. Williams doubted his own sanity. The Captain only smiled in response. "So, have you received any transmissions since I left the sub?" Mr. Williams asked.

"None," the Captain replied.

"So now what?" Mr. Williams asked.

"We send this one upstairs," the Captain replied. "This one is clearly above my pay grade," he added with a laugh.

"I think it's above the President's pay grade also," Mr. Williams replied.

"You're probably right, but he's stuck with it."

"In the meantime, can I get out of here? I don't care much for doctors and I am still starving."

"Let me see what I can do. Unless there is a medical reason to keep you here, I don't see the harm. Just don't overdo it."

"I won't. I've had enough excitement for a little while."

"Are you willing to keep trying to access these memories?" the Captain asked curiously.

"I haven't intentionally accessed them yet," Mr. Williams admitted. "But I don't think I have a choice about unintentionally accessing them."

"No. Perhaps you don't. Do you think it might be better to stay here where you can be monitored?"

"I really don't like hospitals. And since these visions are only in my head, they can't hurt anything."

"For now we can give that a try," the Captain agreed tentatively. "But you have to have someone with you at all times to make sure you stay out of trouble."

"Okay," Mr. Williams agreed.

"Very good," the Captain continued. "Sergeant Jeffreys."

"Sir?"

"He's in your charge. Take good care of him. You have a radio?"

"Yes, Sir."

"Good. Make sure to stay in touch. Report to me or the XO directly as the situation warrants. Right now this mission is top secret. The flight surgeon is not clear except for medical needs. No one else without my express permission. Do you understand?"

"Yes, Sir."

"Very good, Sergeant. You take care of our civilian here, while I drop this into Washington's lap. I'm sure they will have a few questions for you." With that the Captain turned and left.

CHAPTER 7

Mark managed to get a quick bite to eat before he was taken to communications, where he could call home. A Lieutenant was assigned to monitor him to make sure he didn't blurt out any classified information. Ironically, the Lieutenant wasn't briefed on Mark's involvement, so the only prohibition he gave Mark was not to talk about their location and their mission.

"Hey honey," Mark started when they finally got the call through. "How are you doing?" Mark finished lamely, knowing what would follow.

"How am I doing?" Beth said. "How are you doing? Where are you? What's going on? You haven't called in two days! Are you all right?"

"I'm fine," Mark answered when Beth paused for a breath. "Sorry I didn't call earlier…"

"I've been worried sick," she interrupted.

"I know," Mark said apologetically. "The schedule here is very… erratic. And it's not easy to arrange a call through, particularly during the daytime; your daytime," Mark added.

"So how have you been doing?" Beth asked, her tone sounding somewhat mollified.

"I've been sleeping a lot, jet lag," Mark answered.

"Have you found anything?"

The Lieutenant looked up as this sounded like it was asking about the mission. Mark smiled at the Lieutenant before answering. "No, nothing that we didn't already know. Although I think this is going to take a bit more time than anyone expected. Can you call the office and make excuses for me?"

"Sure, but for how long?"

"I don't know," Mark answered. "I'm losing track of days over here. What day is it anyway?"

"It's Monday," Beth answered, concern creeping into her voice.

"Well, let's say for the rest of the week," Mark said. "Tell them I have the plague, or something. Or kill off one of my relatives, perhaps Cousin Fred, I never have liked him," Mark chuckled. "And don't worry if I don't call on any schedule. Like I said, things here have a life of their own."

"Are you getting to meet any foreigners?" Beth asked. "I know how anxious you were to meet someone new?"

Mark had to suppress his smile. Beth had clearly been planning on how to get around the censorship issue. "Not yet," Mark answered. "But I am trying to figure out the best way to get to know them. You know I'm not good with languages, never have been."

"But you are trying, you have an opportunity to learn there, don't you?" she asked.

"Oh yes," Mark replied. "It's just a bit difficult. But I'm going to keep trying. I'll tell you all about it when I get home," Mark promised. "How is everything at home?" Mark tried to change the subject as the Lieutenant was starting to appear worried about the direction of the conversation.

"Are you safe?" Beth asked, undeterred by Mark's attempt to change the subject.

"Right now I am probably the safest person on the planet," Mark laughed. "You can only imagine the amount of protection around me," Mark added, thinking of the entire carrier task force surrounding him.

"Okay, but be careful," she replied.

"I will."

"Some people have been around asking questions about you," she added.

"People? What people?" Mark asked.

"Two men came by wanting to know all about you. They said they were with the government."

Now Mark was concerned. "Did you check their I.D.'s?"

"Of course I did," Beth said. "They were from the NSA, National Security Agency."

"What did they ask you?" Mark asked, surprised by this turn of events. Why would the government be checking up on him with his wife?

"They wanted to know all about you," Beth answered. "But they didn't get far. I told them they could ask you whatever they wanted and to get off my property before I called the police."

Mark laughed, imagining Beth sic'ing the dogs on the agents. "Did they leave?"

"Oh yes, they left promptly. But why are they checking up on you?"

"I don't know. Paranoid, I guess," Mark replied. They talked a little more before Mark reluctantly ended the call, promising to stay out of trouble and to call back when he could. After that, Sgt. Jeffreys escorted Mark back to his room. Mark lay on his bed staring at the ceiling, running the events of the past few days through his head. What were the aliens trying to send him? Why couldn't he understand them? For that matter, why didn't they just send text or video messages? The airwaves were full of all sorts of message traffic. So how come the aliens could not translate it? As advanced as they were, translation of the spoken word must be child's play. And then the biggest question: Why me? The ceiling didn't provide any answers. When he couldn't take the silence any longer, he called out: "Sergeant Jeffreys."

The door opened and Sgt. Jeffreys poked his head in, "You called, Sir?"

"Yes."

"Are you okay?"

"Yes. I just need someone to talk to. The events of the last few days are bit overwhelming. I thought it would be nice to have just a normal conversation with someone for a change. Would you mind?"

"Don't mind at all," Sgt. Jeffreys said as he walked into the room and sat in the only chair.

"So, do you think I'm crazy?" Mark asked.

Sgt. Jeffreys hesitated. "You want the truth?"

"I don't want a yes man. Give it to me straight."

"Okay. Your story to me earlier was true. Although, if I did not hear the Captain confirm it, I would have said you were nuts," Sgt. Jeffreys answered.

"That is certainly understandable," Mark responded. "I didn't believe it until the President himself told me."

"But," Sgt. Jeffreys continued. "I have some real concerns for you with these continuing hallucinations. I could see them driving you nuts."

"You and me both," Mark agreed. "I just wish I could figure out what they're trying to send. If I could control what triggered the visions, maybe they wouldn't shock me so much and I could concentrate on understanding them. I don't know. Why is an alien trying to talk to me anyway? There must be millions of people who would love to talk to an alien. Why didn't they choose one of them? But no, they have to choose me. And then they have to do it in a way I don't understand, and which makes me feel crazy. Now how fair is that?"

"Do you really expect me to answer that?" Sgt. Jeffreys asked.

"No. Just ranting and raving."

"I would be ranting and raving as well," Sgt. Jeffreys agreed.

"Thanks," Mark replied. "So, I have a random question. Why is it that every time I've had an escort, it's been you? Are you the only Marine on the ship?"

"No. And you have had other escorts standing by your door. It just happened that every time something interesting was happening, it was during my shift. Of course, now that you've spilled your guts to me, I suspect I'll be working overtime. I don't think the Captain wants any one else to hear your story. Heck, the flight surgeon isn't even cleared."

"Sorry about that," Mark apologized.

"Don't apologize. I wouldn't miss this for the world. You don't know how boring it can be assigned to an aircraft carrier. Not always, mind you. But it's hard to get into town when you're in the middle of the Pacific. And somehow I don't think this trip is going to be boring. Not anymore, anyway."

"Certainly not boring," Mark agreed. "Terrifying, perhaps. Exhausting. But not, boring."

After a period of silence, Sgt. Jeffreys added, "Are you okay?"

"What?"

"Are you okay?"

"Yes. Why, what happened?"

"You kind of zoned out there for a few seconds," Sgt. Jeffreys explained.

"I had another one of those visions," Mark said. "But this time it didn't shock me. I guess I'm starting to get used to them."

"What did you see this time?" Sgt. Jeffreys asked with interest.

"Four aliens sitting at a table talking," Mark answered slowly.

"What were they saying?" Sgt. Jeffreys asked, leaning forward attentively.

Mark thought for a moment. "Actually, they weren't saying anything. I just assumed they were talking, I didn't hear any words. I guess they looked like they were talking. It was all very quick, maybe just a couple of seconds and then we were back. How long was I out?"

"Just a couple of seconds is what I noticed," Sgt. Jeffreys answered. "What did they look like? What did they do?"

"Sorry," Mark replied. "It's hard to remember that you didn't see it when you were sitting right here. Let's see. There was a sort of table about this high," Mark continued, holding his hand up at waist level. "It was black and shiny with a lot of colored lights across the top of it. I was sitting, or maybe standing, off to the side watching. There were four aliens sitting around that table, sitting on stools. One legged stools. They looked like the other aliens I've seen."

"You've never described them to me," Sgt. Jeffreys said.

"Oh, sorry," Mark replied. "Let me try. They are humanoid, in the sense that they have a general outline like we do; head, torso, two arms and two legs and walk on two legs. After that, they are not human at all. Their heads are weird. I don't know how to describe them."

"Why don't you sketch it?" Sgt. Jeffreys suggested.

"I can't draw to save my life," Mark objected.

"I'm not bad, why don't you describe them to me," Sgt. Jeffreys said.

"We can give it a try," Mark said. Sgt. Jeffreys found a sheet of paper and a pencil. "Okay," Mark continued. "Their heads are shaped like an exaggerated human skull; big on the top, with the jaw area narrow. Try starting with a big triangle standing on one of the points and then round off the points. This will be looking at their face. Their face is fairly flat, with two oversized, jet-black, oval eyes, located about the same level as ours." Sgt. Jeffreys drew two large round eyes. "No. Not like ours. They are more oval. Draw them about two inches high and four or five inches long. They almost touch in the center and then angle up about thirty degrees to within an inch of the temple. The eyes are brownish near the center of the face; the rest of the eye is jet black. That's it.

The forehead is like a flattened triangle that slopes back slightly. It looks like all bone. There is a bony ridge over the eyes that is really pronounced near the temples where the bone kind of flares out and down, like it is protecting the side of the eye. Almost like they had horns curling down in their evolutionary past. Between their eyes, starts a bony ridge that runs down to the chin. On your picture it would be about two inches wide. No, taper it down as you get to the chin. That's right.

Now, the mouth is a small horizontal slit half way down. I don't know if they have a nose as such. I didn't see one. I didn't see any ears either, although there is some type of bony ridge where our ears would be, but you can only see it from the side not the front. They have prominent cheekbones that run vertical, rather than horizontal. That's real good," Mark finished, looking at

Sgt. Jeffreys' sketch. "If you ever get out of the Marines, you should be an artist."

"That is some weird looking dude," Sgt. Jeffreys said, looking at his sketch. "Is this really what they look like?"

"It's pretty close," Mark said. "Their skin is a kind of bluish-gray, hairless; like smooth leather. The back of their heads is composed of three lobes, rather than the one that we have. They are divided by two creases that run from the top of the head down to the neck. They all wore a sort of bright greenish mesh jumpsuit, skin tight, like a warm water dive skin that started at their necks and outlined their bodies. They are tall, thin, kind of gangly."

"Want me to draw the bodies too?" Sgt. Jeffreys asked as he reached for another piece of paper.

"I don't think I could describe it accurately for you," Mark objected.

"Why not, you did a real good job with the face," Sgt. Jeffreys said.

"That's because I have seen the face several times, including in my mirror. So that image is seared in my brain. It was so weird. The rest was kind of overload, so I can't tell you any more details. Except for their hands; they were doing something with their hands on the table. I'm not sure what. Their hands, very strange; four fingers, I'd say two elongated, multi-jointed fingers, with two opposable thumbs, one on each side, which were almost as long as the fingers."

"Two thumbs?"

"Yes. It was like your thumb and little finger were both thumbs. And then put two fingers between them," Mark explained.

"That's weird," Sgt. Jeffreys exclaimed.

"This whole thing is weird," Mark countered.

"No dispute there," Sgt. Jeffreys agreed.

"Well, I guess this is an improvement," Mark added. "I'm not screaming or flailing around anymore. Maybe now I can concentrate on what they are trying to send me. It's amazing how tired it makes me though. I guess I'll try to get some sleep."

Sgt. Jeffreys headed for the door. "I'll be out here, or my relief will be, if you need anything."

As Sgt. Jeffreys left, Mark walked over to the sink to brush his teeth. He glanced hesitantly in the mirror, wondering what he would see. But it was his familiar face staring back. When it did not change, he wondered if he could force the change. Holding the sink firmly to steady himself, he stared in the mirror and concentrated on the alien face he had seen before, trying to remember every detail. But try as he might, his face continued to stare back at him. 'Okay, so that's not it,' Mark thought as he headed back to his bunk. He would have to try something else later. But first, he was going to try to get a little more sleep before the morning's briefing.

Mark woke up late in the morning, surprised that he had not been awakened earlier. After a quick shower and shave, he opened the door to find Sgt. Jeffreys standing nearby. "Don't you ever sleep? You haven't been here the whole time, have you?"

"No," Sgt. Jeffreys admitted. "I left after you went to bed and caught a quick nap."

"I missed the morning briefing," Mark stated. "Why didn't you wake me up?"

"When the Captain heard you were still asleep, he told me not to wake you. He does want to see you after you've had breakfast."

"After breakfast? I knew I liked that guy," Mark responded enthusiastically. "Let's get breakfast. I am so very tired of getting interrupted halfway through a meal."

"The Captain suggested that you eat here. I can order whatever you want."

Mark started to object, but then realized the suggestion was probably a good one. He ordered a bagel and orange juice, which arrived within 10 minutes. Shortly thereafter, Sgt. Jeffreys took him to the bridge for his meeting with the Captain.

"Got some sleep after our last visit?" the Captain asked sincerely.

"Actually, very good. Slept like a baby. And no alien visits. Well, I did have one while Sergeant Jeffreys and I were talking that only lasted a couple of seconds: very quick images of aliens sitting around a table, perhaps talking. The good thing is that the vision didn't scare me, so maybe now I can concentrate on trying to understand them." Mark answered. "I did intentionally try to access one of the alien memories in front of my mirror. I thought if I concentrated I might be able to re-create an earlier memory. But it didn't work. I'll have to try to figure something else out."

"So no new information then?" the Captain asked.

"I'm afraid not," Mark answered, shaking his head.

"Washington wants you to try again," the Captain responded.

"Try what again?" Mark asked puzzled.

"The submarine. They want you to go back down in the submarine and see if the alien attempts another contact," the Captain explained.

"The submarine," Mark repeated after a long pause.

"It worked once. They think it may work again," the Captain continued. "I know you don't like it down there. But maybe this time you'll be ready for it. At least, that's their reasoning." When Mark did not respond, the Captain continued, "You know I can't order you to do it. But it does make sense."

"It makes sense," Mark reluctantly agreed.

"And?" the Captain asked.

"You're right, I don't like it. I am not a submariner. I like dry land. If not that, I want to at least be on top of the water," Mark stalled. "Any messages from our friends downstairs?"

"None since you were on board the *Louisville*."

"The last time they wanted me on the sub, they asked," Mark said, stalling for more time before he made his decision.

"That's true," the Captain agreed. "Washington thinks the ball may be in our court now."

"Who in Washington?" Mark asked.

"I don't know who is making the decisions," the Captain admitted. "But, I bet it 's safe to assume that nothing is happening over there without the President being involved. Not with something like this."

Mark let the silence stretch out before finally answering. "I'll do it."

The Captain smiled, "We will contact the *Louisville* and arrange the transfer. It will probably take a couple hours to set it up. We'll keep you posted."

Exactly two and a half hours later Mark was once again struggling into the bulky Gumby suit as a Seahawk warmed up on the carrier deck. A cold wind was whipping across the flight deck, which chilled Mark's already cold mood. "This would have been a lot more fun twenty years ago,'" he complained. As they finished zipping up his suit, the helicopter took off. "Isn't that my helicopter?" Mark asked the sailor helping him. Even though they were standing next to the tower, he had to yell to be heard over the noise on the flight deck.

The sailor turned and looked at the departing helicopter. Turning back he yelled, "Yes, Sir. It is."

"Don't you think someone should tell them that I'm not on board?" Mark yelled back.

The sailor stepped through a bulkhead door and reached for the radio on the wall. After yelling a conversation on the radio, the sailor came back to Mark. "Change in plans," he said. "They want you in the CIC conference room." He helped Mark take the bulky Gumby suit back off and Sgt. Jeffreys escorted him up to the now familiar briefing room. The conference room was empty. Sgt. Jeffreys spoke into his radio before turning to Mark. "They want you in sonar. Follow me."

He led Mark to sonar where they found the Captain and the XO studying a display. "You sent for me, Captain?" Mark asked.

"Yes," the Captain responded. "We have a new development. Sonar picked up a signal rising up from the trench. They first picked it up a couple hundred feet underwater. Now it's floating on the surface. We think our friends downstairs sent it. It's a pulsating signal crossing several frequencies. Not something any of our standard equipment will do. I sent the Seahawk out to investigate. They should be on station in a couple minutes. *Louisville* picked it up also. They were near the surface when it first appeared, getting ready for the transfer. Their acoustical array does not work as well on the surface so they went back down to see what they could discover."

They waited silently as the minutes slowly ticked by, each lost in their own thoughts. Finally, the radio broke the silence. "Sea Dog, this is Fisherman."

"That's the Seahawk," the Captain explained to Mark.

"We are over the target. It appears to be a round white object, perhaps a meter in diameter. Floating. It looks like a ball or balloon. Video is on. Instructions please."

The Captain walked over to another monitor where the helicopter's video feed was displayed. In it they could see the waves and a bright white object bobbing on the surface.

"Looks like a big white beach ball," Sgt. Jeffreys whispered to Mark, who nodded in agreement.

"Can you think of any reason we should not pick it up?" The Captain asked Mark.

"No, Sir," he responded.

"XO?"

"No, Sir," the XO responded. "I think the Bogeyman sent it up for us. We might as well see what it is."

"I agree," the Captain stated as he picked up a microphone. "Fisherman, this is Sea Dog. You are authorized to retrieve the target. Be careful."

"Roger, Sea Dog. Retrieving target." They were able to watch the retrieval from the bridge as the helicopter dropped a rescue diver into the ocean, and then lowered a basket. The diver approached the ball carefully and maneuvered it into the basket, before raising it up into the helicopter. Close up, it still looked like a big white beach ball. "Sea Dog, this is Fisherman. Returning home with target."

The Captain turned towards the air commander. "Secure an area away from the tower for Fisherman to land. No one goes near them without full biohazard protection. Let's inspect this cargo before we bring it in any farther. I want a full biohazard drill on this one. Check it for radiation and anything else you can think of." The air commander turned to his support personnel and gave the appropriate instructions.

When the helicopter landed and shut down a team approached wearing full biohazard suits. After several minutes they reported back to the commander that all was clear. The helicopter was lowered on an elevator and taken to a secure corner of the ship. Mark and the Captain were present when a crewmen carefully removed the white object and placed it in a wheeled cargo container.

Mark noticed armed Marines standing off to the side and hoped this would not turn out to be one of the scarier scenes from one of the *Alien* movies. Chiding himself, he noted that the white object really looked more like a beach ball than some alien egg. 'Of course,' he asked himself, 'What does an alien egg look like?' Trying to shake his increasing uneasiness he joked, "Are you sure this is the object transmitting the signal? Or did you just do a full biohazard screen on a floating beach ball?"

"That would be funny," the Captain responded. "But I already checked. And it is still transmitting," he added as he held up a receiver for Mark to see. "The signal you see displayed on the screen is coming from the object," the Captain explained.

"Just thought I'd ask," Mark said, still uneasy. "It does look like a big beach ball."

"The question now is what to do next?" the Captain said.

Mark resisted the urge to say, "Play ball." A moment later everyone jumped as a loud snap, like an electrical arc, filled the air, followed by the smell of burning ozone. The sailor nearest the container looked in and exclaimed, "It's gone." The others approached and looked inside the container. The beach ball was gone, but on the bottom of the container rested a black cube about 2 inches in diameter.

"What the heck is that?" the Captain asked.

Mark looked down at the cube.

His vision shifted and he was again looking at a cube, but this time it was sitting on an alien control panel, its surface shimmering with multiple colors. He watched as "he" reached out with an elongated forefinger and touched the cube. The colors swirled and then "he" was walking in the jungle...

The vision ended and Mark was once again looking down at the cube at the bottom of the storage container. "It's a memory cube," Mark answered, quickly recovering from his vision.

"A what?' the Captain asked.

"A memory cube," Mark repeated. "I've seen them before. The aliens store memories on them, like a thumb drive for a computer, or a DVD. They touch them to access the memory."

"It's activated simply by touching it?" the Captain asked, eyeing the cube suspiciously.

"That's how the aliens do it," Mark explained.

"Let's get this thing to a secure location first," the Captain decided. He then proceeded to give the crewmen instructions on how to transport the cube to the briefing room without touching it. Once there they secured the room and set up a video link with Washington. Present were the Captain, Mark, Sgt. Jeffreys and five other officers, whom Mark did not know. The XO was watching from another location, it having been decided that if something went wrong they did not want to take-out the two highest-ranking officers on the ship. Who was watching on the video link was unknown, but Mark imagined they had quite some audience.

Mark repeated what he had seen during his brief vision. "Oddly," Mark finished. "This cube is solid ebony. The alien's cube in the vision had swirling colors on it. I wonder if this cube is different, or turned off, or if the aliens see in different wavelengths than we do."

After an endless debate with the observers in Washington, it was finally decided that someone should touch the cube. Mark thought he would be the logical choice, but the people in Washington overruled it, saying he was too valuable an asset to risk on the first touch. 'Nice being an asset,' Mark thought sarcastically. At least he knew where he stood.

Sgt. Jeffreys, the only enlisted present, volunteered and was granted permission. He strode to the front and slowly put his finger towards the cube, almost as if he was touching a hot burner. A puzzled look came across his face when he touched the cube. He pulled it back and looked at Mark, "All you have to do is touch it?" he asked. Mark nodded. Sgt. Jeffreys touched it again and held his finger against the cube. "I'm not getting anything." One by one the rest of the individuals in the room did the same thing, with the same result. After some further debate, Mark walked up and touched the cube.

Huge ferns towered over him as he walked down a jungle path. Alien sounds surrounded him. He stepped out in a clearing and looked across a vast prairie sloping down to a huge lake or perhaps an ocean inlet. He adjusted his vision (somehow) and the view zoomed closer. He waited. After a while he spotted movement in the tall, grass-like vegetation. Watching carefully he noted several areas where the grass swayed in a manner inconsistent with the light breeze. He continued to wait and watch. A pattern emerged, several parallel lines of movement heading towards a common point. As the lines slowly got closer, a creature in front of the approaching lines trumpeted in alarm and bolted away. From the lines jumped three creatures that roared as they chased the first. Too late. The intended victim had a head start and quickly outdistanced the attackers. Looking down at his hand, he watched a long, blue-grayish "finger" enter a sequence on an instrument affixed to his other wrist. When the sequence was finished, he turned and reentered the jungle.

Mark "awoke" with a start, breathing heavy and sweating, his heart pounding in his chest. He staggered back and was caught by Sgt. Jeffreys.

The Captain was staring at him with concern. "What happened?" he asked.

"It worked," Mark answered breathlessly. "It's a memory cube. Like our DVD's or flash drives." Catching his breath, Mark continued, "Only the difference between this and our technology is like the difference between..." Mark searched for a comparison, "say, watching Charlie Chaplin in a silent movie and then watching *Avatar* in 3-D. It was just like the visions I've had before, but much more intense. It was real. Other than the fact that I'm in an alien body, there is no way to tell the difference between my experience here and my experience in the cube." He went on to explain what he had seen and whom he had been.

When he had finished describing what he had seen, the Captain asked, "You saw all of that just now?"

"Yes."

"How long did it take?" some voice from Washington asked.

"Long? I guess the whole thing probably took about forty-five minutes to an hour? Why? Did you time it?" Mark asked.

There was a profound silence that Mark found unnerving. "What?"

"You jumped back the second you touched the cube," Sgt. Jeffreys answered for the group.

"I wasn't touching it for forty-five minutes or more?"

Sgt. Jeffreys merely shook his head no.

A general conversation broke out amongst the observers as to what this meant. Mark was pelted with questions: What did the animals look like? What did the vegetation look like? What did the alien look like? What planet was it?

"Whoa," Mark interjected. "One at a time. The animals were a blur in the undergrowth, so I have no idea what they were. Fast and loud, and big; perhaps the size of a horse." Mark paused to consider the vision. "But that is assuming the plants were six to eight feet tall, which is a huge guess on my part. They could just as well have been one foot or thirty feet tall. I had no reference points. I guess I could have been looking at ants in grass, but just real close up. The plants; they appeared to be large ferns, huge trees, jungle like. Nothing I have ever seen before. The planet; no idea, again, didn't look like anything I have ever seen. Oh, the alien: the only thing I saw was a long thin blue-gray finger. I have no idea the size, because again, there wasn't anything familiar around to compare it to. And his other "wrist" had a silvery green suit on it, so I never saw flesh. And before you ask," Mark continued. "I have no idea what the instrument was, it was just a confusion of small lights."

"So you see all this," one of the attendees asked, "but you can't here their thoughts?"

"Correct," Mark said. "The five senses only; sight, sound, touch, taste and smell, but no thoughts."

"So why are they sending this? What are they trying to communicate?

"I don't know," Mark replied.

The questioning continued, but Mark was unable to provide any further details. Eventually, everyone in the room touched the cube again to see if it would now work for them, but it didn't. "I guess you're our sole alien interpreter," the Captain said to Mark. "Any idea why?"

"No. Just lucky I guess," Mark responded to the Captain while the video attendees argued some point. 'This is getting us nowhere,' Mark thought as the discussion became repetitive. 'But now that I know what to expect, I'll try to maintain contact. There must be something in there that they want us to see.' Having decided that, he walked over and very deliberately touched the cube.

He strode with long, quick steps down a narrow, circular corridor towards an open air lock. Ducking through the airlock he emerged into a large common room filled with aliens. The aliens glanced over at his entrance and then went back to their business. Some were eating; some were huddled around small tables intently studying their contents. 'Almost like watching a chess game,' Mark thought. Others appeared to be engaged in some type of exercise. Mark's alien, or "host" as Mark was beginning to think of him, ignored them as he strode quickly across the room to enter another airlock that took him through another cylindrical corridor. 'This is like walking around in a gerbil cage,' Mark noted. He passed through other corridors before entering another room, this one containing several more aliens working on what appeared to be some type of instrumentation. His host walked over to a blank wall and touched it with his forefinger. Symbols flashed in the air, which his host studied for some time, touching various symbols as they popped up. Finally, he walked over to a flat table top, which lit up upon his arrival. He rested each hand on the table.

Mark watched with amazement as his fingers sank into the solid looking table. His host locked his knees and remained in this position as seemingly random symbols flashed in the air in front of him. His host remained standing for several hours, the only movement being minor twitching of his fingers inside the console. He did not sway or tire. The only sound was a faint hum from surrounding stations. The other aliens were silent as they worked on their adjoining projects. As the hours dragged by, Mark tried to control some of the memory. He tried moving the alien's eyes, head, and arms, all to no avail. 'Like trying to change a movie,' he thought. He would just have to wait. He tried to make sense of the symbols flashing in front of him, but again to no avail.

After what seemed like an eternity, his host unlocked his knees and pulled his hands out of the table, before proceeding back down the corridor towards the common room. However, this time he turned into a side corridor and entered a room that looked like a beehive lying on its side. Row upon row of octagonal openings about two feet in diameter stretched from floor to ceiling. An alien head popped out of an opening about seven rows up. The new alien looked down, then leapt in one fluid motion, landing lightly next to his host. They touched fingertips for a brief moment before they left through the airlock Mark had entered.

'Not again,' Mark thought when the two aliens went back to the last room. 'Not another several hours of standing, doing nothing.' Fortunately, the aliens went to another section of the room where they faced a blank wall and rested their hands against it. As before, their fingers melted into the seemingly solid material. Once again symbols and lights whirled in front of them. But this time the symbols remained in the bottom half of the wall while the top half became opaque as objects materialized. At first it appeared to be more random designs, but upon closer inspection the designs began to coalesce until finally resolving into something that looked like railroad tracks twisting and floating in space. The view ran "up" the track as if taken from a train, only to stop at one of the railroad ties. The tie changed color and disappeared, only to be replaced by another tie. Then the train proceeded up the floating, twisting track, only to stop at another tie, which also was replaced. Mark longed to see what type of train he was in, but the view never looked back, only forward. The process continued for some time before the train tracks suddenly receded, as if his train had fallen off the tracks. There was a blur of movement as unrecognizable images

rushed past, finally replaced by the view of what looked like an egg floating in space.

At this point the aliens pulled their fingers out of the console, which immediately turned black and solid looking. Mark's host went back to the honeycomb room. He placed his hand against the wall and looked up to see a bar slide out next to a hexagonal opening about 10 rows above him. Without hesitation, he leapt up, grabbed the bar and spun feet first into the opening, which was just a little longer than the alien. The host touched a glowing dot on the inside wall and the entrance way spiraled shut. 'This must be a sleeping chamber.' Mark realized as the vision faded.

Mark staggered back from the cube. He would have fallen had Sgt. Jeffreys not caught him. As it was, his legs crumpled and Sgt. Jeffreys lay him gently on the floor. Mark managed to give Sgt. Jeffreys a weak smile before consciousness eluded him.

CHAPTER 8

Once again Mark woke up in sickbay. 'This is getting to be a habit,' he thought. He lay still, giving himself time to take stock of the situation before medical personnel asking stupid questions besieged him. Mark recalled finding the cube, touching it, and the resulting visions, which came back to him in vivid detail. He remembered staggering back after touching the cube the second time, vaguely recalling seeing Sgt. Jeffreys before he lost consciousness. He stretched his body; stiff, but otherwise fine. 'These mind trips are exhausting,' he thought, 'but at least I don't have a headache like the first time. I wonder how long I was out?'

Opening his eyes, he looked around the now familiar sickbay. He was back in his "private room" off to the side of sickbay. For once Sgt. Jeffreys was not in sight; he had finally awakened during Jeffreys' off shift. He was surprised how weak he felt as he struggled to sit up. An I.V. pulled on his arm. 'That must be supper,' he thought wryly. A myriad of other leads were attached to his body, monitoring pulse, oxygen saturation, blood pressure, and who knew what else. He hated being tied up with all these tubes and considered pulling the needle out himself, but squeamishness stopped him. Instead he disconnected the pulse monitor, chuckling when the alarm went off. 'That should get their attention,' he thought with amusement. It worked. Within five seconds three medical personnel ran into his room. They were not amused when they saw him sitting up on the bed, dangling the pulse lead in his hand.

"What do you think you're doing?" One of them asked him angrily. "Now lie right down..."

He didn't finish his sentence before Mark interrupted, "Let's get one thing straight. I am not your guinea pig. I appreciate you taking care of me while I was... asleep. But now that I'm awake, I can take care of myself, so if you'll kindly take this stuff off me."

"You can't take that off," one of them started to say.

"Oh yes I can. You forget, I'm not military. I'm a civilian. And my body is my own to do with as I wish. And my wish now is to get all this stuff off me. So, the only question is: Are you going to do it, or am I?" Mark reached down to the I.V. on his forearm. When the medics did not assist him, he pulled off the tape holding the needle in his arm and then, clenching his teeth, jerked the needle out. This brought an unexpected response from the three medics. Two rushed over and grabbed him, while the third shouted, "Hold him, I'll get the restraints."

Mark struggled ineffectively in their grip. "You can't do this against my will!" he objected, and then froze.

An elongated blue-gray finger reached out and touched the third cube on the console. His vision changed... A cold blue-gray alien looked down, as he lay vulnerable on his back. Restraints held him. Overhead lights glared painfully in his eyes. The blue-gray was reaching towards him with a short rod, clearly some type of weapon. Rage welled up within him and he felt his lithe, muscular body tense in anticipation. He flexed his body, letting his claws slide out, thin, sharp and deadly. He summoned the energy in his core, let it coil, and grow, until in a focused burst his arms and legs whipped out with his deadly claws. The blue-gray alien jumped back in shock as the restraints parted and he was free...

The third corpsman was picking up the restraints when Mark froze. He turned back to assist, restraints in hand, when Mark reacted. One moment Mark was sitting on the hospital bed with a corpsman holding each arm, the next there was a blur of movement and the two corpsmen were falling back against the wall. The third corpsman took another step towards Mark before he was struck in the solar plexus and fell to the ground gasping.

A doctor and a Marine entered the room and stopped in the doorway. Mark was standing next to his bed, clad only in a hospital gown; while around him lay three corpsmen gasping for breath. Mark's rage dissipated as quickly as it came. He glanced up at the newcomers. Calmly, he addressed the Marine; "Corporal, would you be so kind as to call Sergeant Jeffreys and tell him I'm awake. And perhaps tell the Captain I would like to see him, if he has a moment." Addressing the doctor, who was looking at the three men on the floor, Mark explained, "I believe you will find they are slightly out of breath. Just a small disagreement over the improper use of restraints. Now, if you'd be so kind as to tell me where my clothes are so I don't have to greet the Captain naked." Mark motioned to his flimsy hospital gown. "In the meantime, I need to go to the head." With that, Mark stepped over a stunned corpsman and into the head, closing the door behind him.

'What was that?' Mark asked himself when he had safely closed himself in the head. "Did I just beat up three corpsmen? This is not going to go over real well! Why did I do it? Sergeant Jeffreys was right, these visions are going to drive me crazy. Now I'm beating people up. And what alien was that?' Mark never saw his host, but the feel was totally different than before, much more powerful, and feline. Complete with claws. He had seen a blur of "his" arm right at the end of the vision and it appeared to be covered with silvery fur. This was new, the blue-gray aliens appeared to be hairless, at least what he had seen of them. And the emotions! It was the first memory that contained emotions. Still no thoughts, but strong emotions, rage, anger. Surprisingly, no fear. It was apparently a prisoner of the blue-gray alien and from the 'feel' of it, probably intelligent. So how did the blue-grays get this memory? How did he get this memory? It was not from the cube; at least he didn't think so. Was it one of the cue based visions he received on the submarine?

However, the real question was, did he strike the corpsmen of his own will, or did the vision cause it? He had never been in a fight before, not as an adult anyway. Was he being manipulated? That thought was terrifying. He had been mad when they grabbed him. But mad enough to fight? He didn't think so. The vision had come so quickly. When it ended, he knew he could get free, so he did. No thought, just reaction. And what was that force and how had he focused it to get free? He had disabled three men in a matter of seconds. When the corpsmen were down and more people were arriving, he was suddenly calm. Was it the realization that he could not fight the entire ship or was the influence of the vision wearing off? How would he explain this to the Captain? He couldn't mention the influence of the vision. They probably had a brig on a ship this size and it was certainly not a place he wanted to be. Nor did he want to be restricted to sickbay.

After contemplating his actions as long as he dared, Mark opened the door of the head and stepped out. The room was filling with corpsmen, some tending to the three dazed corpsman, others milling in the doorway. Mark considered trying to walk out into the hall, wondering if he could do so unnoticed, but thought that unlikely since he was the only one wearing a hospital gown, the type which exposed your backside. Deciding an authoritarian approach would work best, Mark addressed the nearest standing corpsman, "Are you the one getting my clothes?" When the corpsman only looked at him confused, Mark continued in a hushed, yet firm manner. "The Captain will be here any minute and I can't meet him like this. Where are my clothes?" The confused corpsman muttered something about a closet in the outer room. "Good, take me there."

As Mark exited the room, another corpsman looked up and said, "Hey, you can't..."

"It's okay," Mark interrupted. "He's just showing me where my clothes are so I can get dressed for the Captain. He'll be here any moment now." Mark figured that continued mentioning of the imminent arrival of the Captain should work wonders. He hurriedly dressed, finishing just as the Captain arrived, while the rest of the sick bay remained a study in confusion. The Captain smiled when he saw Mark. "I see you're awake."

"Yes, and feeling much better," Mark said, then leaned forward so he could talk privately to the Captain. "That last vision was intense, I have a lot to report." Over the Captain's shoulder, Mark observed a corpsman pointing at him, while speaking to the doctor. Fearing the impact of the doctor's report, Mark quickly continued in a hushed manner, "If we can get to a secure location before I forget any of the details..."

"Are you well enough to travel to the CIC conference room?" the Captain asked.

"Sure, but you'll have to lead. I still don't know my way around this ship of yours."

As the Captain turned to escort Mark out of sickbay, the doctor and several corpsmen spilled into the room. "Captain," the doctor said. "May I have a word with you?" At that moment, Sgt. Jeffreys ran into the room and abruptly halted when he saw the Captain, adding to the confusion.

"It will have to wait," the Captain said as he turned and led Mark out of sickbay, with Sgt. Jeffreys falling in step behind.

Taking a cue from his courtroom experience, Mark wanted his version of events presented to the Captain first.   "I should tell you there was a small misunderstanding down here a few minutes ago. Shortly after I woke up I tried to get up to go to the head and a couple of the corpsmen grabbed me and tried to put restraints on me.   You know how I tend to be claustrophobic. I'm afraid, I objected. They're okay," Mark added hastily. "And I'll be glad to forget the whole thing if you'll ask them not to repeat it," Mark added in a very forgiving manner.

"I'll talk with the flight surgeon about it," the Captain replied as he climbed a staircase.

Mark motioned to Sgt. Jeffreys to catch up. "Am I glad to see you," he whispered. "I'll tell you the details later. Right now I need you to help me make it up to the conference room before I pass out in front of the Captain."   They followed the Captain, Sgt. Jeffreys' surreptitiously assisting Mark up the staircases. On the way Mark asked Sgt. Jeffreys to bring him up to date.

"Do you remember touching the cube?" Sgt. Jeffreys asked.

"Yes, both times," Mark whispered back. And then I think you caught me and I passed out the second time. How long did I touch it?" Mark whispered, not wanting the Captain to hear.

"The second time you touched the cube about 5 minutes," Sgt. Jeffreys responded.

"Only five minutes?" Mark asked incredulously. "Wow! It lasted several hours. How long have I been out?"

"Better part of 12 hours," Sgt. Jeffreys whispered back as he helped Mark up another flight of stairs. "We're almost there."

In the briefing room Mark gratefully collapsed in a chair. "Give me a minute to catch my breath," Mark asked.

"Sure," the Captain said. "We also need to get some people online. Our little show has gotten rather popular." A number of people walked into the briefing room and a video link was established with Washington. Mark noted that two new medical looking personnel also entered the briefing room and Mark wondered if there was going to a problem from the earlier incident. "This is Dr. Smith and Dr. Ballenger," the Captain introduced them to Mark. "They've been flown in to assist. I'll give you more details after the briefing." Mark shook their hands, wondering what their presence implied, but deciding he would deal with it later.

A few minutes later the briefing started with the now familiar, "This is a secure, top-secret briefing, all unauthorized individuals are instructed to leave now." One of the new doctors pointedly looked at Sgt. Jeffreys, who at Mark's request was sitting nearby and was the only enlisted in the room. "He's been cleared," Mark told him.

The briefer continued: "As everyone should know, we made contact with the alien artifact at 1445 hours, Pacific time, yesterday. At 1730 hours, Mr. Williams touched the artifact and then touched it a second time at 1840 hours. The second time he passed out after being in contact with the artifact for four minutes, thirty-six seconds. He has just recently awakened."

'And beat up three corpsmen while possibly under the influence of an alien vision,' Mark thought ruefully. 'I hope they miss that part.'

"Mr. Williams," the briefer concluded, introducing Mark. 'Well here goes,' thought Mark as he turned towards the video camera, 'show time.'

"Pardon me if I remain sitting, these..." he paused to consider the correct word, "...visions, are exhausting. To avoid any suspense, let me start by telling you what I do not know. I do not know what these aliens want, or why they are sending this information, or why they have chosen me to receive it. I have not received any communication from them in the sense of speech or thoughts. What I am receiving, as best as I can describe it, appears to be alien memories or experiences. I received several very short, random visions after the first contact in the submarine. These appeared to be linked to what I was doing at the time: eating, talking, walking through corridors." He neglected to mention the fight vision; no sense bringing that up. "Now two visions while touching the memory cube, which is what I call the alien artifact," Mark added. "These visions, or memories, are extremely detailed and fairly long, lasting thirty minutes to several hours, although apparently my physical contact with the cube is very short." He then proceeded to describe what he had seen the day before. Despite attempting to provide as much detail as he could, there were a flurry of questions when he finished his narration.

"What did the aliens look like?"

"What did they eat?"

"What were they doing?"

"What planet were they on?"

"How do they interact?"

"Did they have weapons?" 'That last question had to be from a military observer,' Mark thought with amusement. "The answer to most of your questions is: 'I don't know.'" Mark responded. "However, let me answer what I can. The aliens all wore some type of jumpsuit, so the only parts of their bodies that I could see were their heads and their hands. Of course, I was an alien, so to speak, so I could feel how they moved. I told you about the ridges I saw on their heads. Now I know that is how they breath, through the ridges. I described their hands as having four fingers, or two fingers and two thumbs. That's true. They also have an extra joint or knuckle. Their fingers are long and thin and have a pad at the end, instead of a fingernail. I still don't know how tall the aliens are. I am assuming my height, but I have no frame of reference to measure them against. They are tall and thin and surprisingly agile. They move fast. One jumped what appeared to be twenty or thirty feet. Again, I have no frame of reference. I should say it jumped five or six times its height. They sleep singly, but in a hive structure.

Whether this is typical to their species, or just necessary for the particular structure I was in, I don't know."

"Speaking of the structure, it did not appear to be moving, so I do not think it was on anything; say like this ship on water. But it did appear to have airlocks, so it could have been some type of spaceship. There was gravity, which felt normal to me. But, I am feeling through the alien's senses, so I do not know what the gravity would've felt like to me as a human. But there was clearly no weightlessness. That would mean that we were on a planet. Unless their science has created artificial gravity. All of the corridors were circular and what I saw of the rooms, all were curved. It seems like where our buildings and rooms are all based on squares or rectangles, theirs appear to be based on curves or, in the case of the sleeping room, hexagons."

"Oh, back to the aliens, they walk funny. They have an extra joint in both the arms and legs. It's like each leg has two sets of knees and each arm has two elbows, so they are very flexible. Their arms and legs are about the same length, although I have not seen them walk on all fours, it's always upright. There's something odd about their knees. I think one set works backwards, maybe like a chicken. Same for the elbows; one set bends one-way and the other set the other way. And they can lock their knees. We stood in one position for what seemed like hours and I clearly felt him lock his legs when we started. I say 'him.' That's habit on my part. I don't know if they are male or female, or something else for that matter."

"I'm afraid I'm rambling here. There is so much to describe, but it is also very frustrating as there is so much I didn't understand. I have no idea what they were doing in the common room. I call it a common room because it had the same kind of characteristics as a common room would have here, with people apparently just hanging out. I can't figure out their technology at all. And there is still no conversation. You recall, I told you two aliens touched fingers. At the time I assumed it was a greeting, like shaking hands. But now I wonder if it was communication. They may be telepathic. Or they may touch to be telepathic. The more I experience these visions, the more I think one of the channels is missing. It's like watching a movie, but having the sound turned off. Here I am living the movie in all respects, sight, touch, taste and sound, but no speech, no thoughts, no communication. It could be that the memory cube cannot record speech or thoughts. Or, perhaps more likely, since we are not telepathic, I cannot hear or understand that part of the memory. Whichever, it makes this very frustrating."

"You are sure that this is a memory, and not a current vision?" someone from the video asked. "Maybe a real time feed from the UFO?"

Mark considered his answer. "I can't rule out the possibility that it is real-time. If it is... What size is that UFO? Thirty meters?"

"Thirty meters wide, about six high, but oblong shaped," some voice answered from the video.

"Those are rough estimates," another voice objected.

"Well, that's roughly ninety feet," Mark continued. "If I'm watching what is going on in the UFO, then they are a lot smaller than us. The corridors and rooms I traveled through would take up much more than ninety feet if they were our size. But my feeling is that these are memories. I have seen the cubes used in past visions. So to answer your question, I believe this memory cube is more similar to our flash drive, than a phone. I think its past."

"What about the science room?"

"What were they doing on the train track?"

"What about the egg?"

"What did they look like?"

'This sounds like a press conference,' Mark thought as he was bombarded with questions. "I'm a lawyer, not a scientist," Mark answered. "Science room is my guess; it seemed like they were using a microscope. I have no idea what they were doing. Why were they replacing the railroad ties? Where were the floating train tracks going? How did they stay on them as they spun and twisted in space? What was the egg doing there? It was all just a visual picture that I don't understand. They could just as well have been on some alien Google, flashing on random sites and ended up on an egg. Or playing a video game. I don't know. That's why I am trying to describe everything in such detail to you so that you can come up with your own conclusions. I can tell you what my 'guesstimate' is, but without being able to access speech or some form of communication, I am just guessing based upon my personal experiences. For all I know, these creatures could be six inches tall and addicted to video games."

"In which case that ship of theirs could hold thousands of them," another voice on the monitor observed.

"It could be a colony ship," someone else added.

As the comments swirled around, Mark turned to Sgt. Jeffreys and whispered, "Do you still have the sketch you drew?" Sgt. Jeffreys nodded and pulled a piece of paper out of his pocket and handed it to Mark. Turning back to the camera Mark announced, "This might help." The conversations stopped as everyone focused their attention back on Mark, who was holding the piece of paper up for the camera. "This is a pencil sketch that Sgt. Jeffreys made for me when I described the alien to him. It is a fairly accurate representation of the alien's head." Mark went on to point out the features on the alien's head.

"What about the rest of the body?" someone asked.

"I don't have a sketch of the rest of the body," Mark explained. "At the time, I had only glimpsed the body, so I didn't have a clear memory of it. But I can describe it for you now. As I have described before, they are generally humanoid in the sense that they have two arms, two legs, a torso and head, and walk upright. They are thin. I would say gangly. The arms and legs are the same length and have an extra joint. Again, very thin. But they move fast and feel strong. They feel very light, but whether they are light or it's just low gravity, I don't know. I already described their hands. The only exposed parts are their hands and head. I have never seen their feet. Their bodies are covered with a skin tight suit, like a dive skin."

"If it's skin tight, you can describe their body structure," someone interrupted.

"I don't know," Mark said. "I've thought about that and I don't know if the suit is skin tight to them, or if they are wearing some type of body armor. But what I saw," Mark continued as someone tried to interrupt him, "...looked very strong. This is tough to describe. Their torso is wider at the chest than at the hips. There is what looks like a bony prominence that runs down the center of the torso from the base of the neck down to the pelvis. In the chest area, there are three, flat ribs, if you will, that run from that bony structure out and slightly down. On a human, the top 'rib' would be at our collarbone and it would angle slightly down to our shoulder. On us, it would be about two or three inches wide and flat. Then there is a slight groove or depression and then the second 'rib' runs parallel beneath it and then the third rib. That makes up their chest. The abdomen just has the vertical bony ridge running down the center with the sides kind of hollowed out. The alien's back is the same, except the vertical bony prominence is missing. Just the ribs are there. The hips look a lot like ours, but narrower. Their arms and legs are thin and somewhat angular. It's like their bones are more prominent, like our skull, rather than buried inside flesh. Again, whether this is their actual body, or some type of suit or armor, I don't know."

"Why do you say armor?" a voice asked.

"Because it looks so strong, that's all."

"But if you are one of them, can't you tell whether it is their body or not?"

Mark paused as he considered the answer. "This is tough to describe. I can feel what they feel. I feel a strong chest, but whether that is their chest, or they are wearing body armor that I feel, I don't know. They have never run their hands across their chest or taken their suits off during my visions. So I am really only going by visual."

The conversation continued, but Mark was unable to provide any further details. Finally, someone on the video link called a recess. "How long has this been going on?" Mark whispered to Sgt. Jeffreys. "I seem to have lost my watch."

"About three and a half hours," Sgt. Jeffreys responded after consulting his watch.

"Dealing with Washington, you're lucky it wasn't longer," the Captain interjected with a chuckle, having overheard the whispered conversation.

"You're probably right," Mark laughed. "So before they decide to reconvene, can we get something to eat?"

"That seems to be all that you do, sleep and eat," the Captain observed.

"This is a cruise I signed up for, isn't it?" Mark asked, feigning a shocked manner. "Isn't that what all the brochures say; come and relax and enjoy our food and entertainment? I'm still waiting for the floor show."

"Civilians," the Captain muttered. Well, we certainly do not want to lose our Frommer's rating. Do you feel up to dining in the galley or do you want to have some food delivered?"

"I think the exercise will do me good," Mark replied. "I'm getting a bit stiff sitting here. Sgt. Jeffreys will keep me out of trouble." 'I hope,' Mark added seriously to himself as he remembered the consequences of the last vision.

"OK," the Captain said and turned to Sgt. Jeffreys. "Sergeant, take this tourist down to the Officer's Mess before he starves to death."

"Aye, aye, Sir," Sgt. Jeffreys responded, snapping to attention.

CHAPTER 9

Mark managed to get to the Officer's Mess without incident. Once safely ensconced in a corner table, Sgt. Jeffreys commented, "You certainly are getting to be an alien expert."

"Not much of an expert." Mark's exasperation was evident. "I can't even tell you how tall they are. You know, they really could all be the size of a flea for all I know. Then there would be an entire world of them on that ship. The problem is that I don't have anything to compare them to."

"You have the cube."

"I thought of that. But the question is whether they constructed the cube for our use or not. If it's the same cube, then they are about our height. But what if they constructed it so that it would be in the same proportion to us as to them? In that case we would still not have any idea how big they are."

"So what do you do next?"

"Keep touching the cube, I guess. Until I figure out what they are trying to send."

"You think you can keep doing it? I mean physically; it takes a lot out of you."

"I don't know any way around it. I just hope it gets easier."

"I wonder how many terabytes it holds?" Sgt. Jeffreys added, as he dug into his food. The question hung in the air as they both ate in silence.

When they got back to the conference room, the video link was off and the Captain was talking to the two doctors who had been introduced to Mark earlier. "Mark, you remember Dr. Smith and Dr. Ballinger?" The Captain asked as he motioned to the two men standing nearby. Mark merely nodded. "They have been sent here to assist us in our communication efforts. Evidently they are some type of UFO experts," the Captain added in a tone that Mark thought was odd.

"Extraterrestrial intelligence is our specialty," Dr. Smith pronounced as if on a stage. Mark took an immediate disliking to him. "We have prepared several protocols for First Contact. Protocols that will assist us in overcoming communication barriers and preventing inadvertent biological cross-contamination."

"As we have been explaining to the Captain, proper protocols have not been followed here," Dr. Ballinger interrupted Dr. Smith's introduction. "In fact the absolute failure to follow any protocol in the handling of this contact..."

Dr. Smith resumed his introduction. "...is why we are here. We intend to establish protocols for resumption of this contact. You have been lucky so far. No offense Captain, but recovering the artifact without first establishing a contact protocol was reckless in the extreme. Fortunately, the ocean cleansed the alien artifact..."

"Which is no doubt why the extraterrestrials sent it in that manner. To protect us from any inadvertent cross-contamination," Dr. Ballinger interrupted again. "But now we will not have to rely upon them to protect us. We will establish our own protocols." Dr. Smith finished.

Mark couldn't believe what he was hearing. As if this wasn't complicated enough without the government sending some administrative bozo's to really screw things up. "What do you intend to do?" he asked as neutrally as possible.

"We will set up a homeostasis environment for further contact with the artifact. We will monitor your body's response to contact. Electroencephalography. Cardiac. Respiratory. Endocrine. All systems. We will run full labs to establish a baseline and monitor chemistry changes. We will also run various tests to identify any possible changes."

"Tests? What tests?" Mark interrupted.

"Basic physical tests. Cardio, stress tests, lymphatic systems..."

"And of course a full battery mental examination," Dr. Ballinger interjected.

"You mean an MMPI?" Mark asked, referring to the standard psychological exam.

"That, of course. And others."

Mark would have walked out had he not been on an aircraft carrier in the middle of the Pacific Ocean. 'I should never have taken this job,' he thought. Aloud he said: "Since I'm evidently your new guinea pig, I wonder if you would answer some questions for me?"

"We can try," Dr. Smith offered hesitantly. "But I'm not sure you'd understand all of it. We are scientists and have spent years studying."

Mark smiled in response. It was a smile that opposing counsel in court had learned to dread. "I imagine with all of your training and knowledge, you will be able to dumb it down enough so that even I can understand." The sarcasm of the remark was lost on the doctors, but not on the Captain who appeared irritated, probably by their criticism of his recovery of the artifact, Mark reasoned. Like he had time to put together protocols while a two-foot wide white ball was floating away in the waves in the middle of the Pacific Ocean. It would be washed up on the Chinese mainland before they finished with their protocols.

Mark sat in a front row chair while the two doctors stood in front of him. As if on cue the Captain and Sgt. Jeffreys sat down as well, forming an audience for the doctors. "Before you explain this to me, perhaps you can give me some background. You say you are scientists. Are you also medical doctors?"

"Oh, yes." Dr. Smith answered with an air of pride. "We have PhD's and MDs."

"Are you practicing doctors, medical doctors that is?"

"We are researchers."

"And your experience with extraterrestrials?"

"We have studied this area intensively. We've worked with SETI, have written extensively on the subject and have been involved in numerous societies and working groups dedicated to this subject. We have written numerous protocols covering this area."

Mark recognized nonsense when he heard it. Time to pin these so-called experts down. "Have you ever seen an alien?"

"No, but we..."

"Have you ever heard one?"

"No, but we anticipate that soon..."

"Have you ever seen an extraterrestrial object or artifact before today?"

"No."

"So today is your first contact with anything alien."

"Yes."

"And therefore, all of your protocols and procedures are by necessity, completely theoretical."

"Yes. But they are based upon years of studying..."

"They are based upon guessing what an alien encounter might be, correct?" Mark finished his cross-examination.

"It is based upon theoretical constructs..."

"Never mind," Mark waved off his answer. "And the physical tests you intend to conduct on me are?"

Mark listened as they listed a battery of physical and psychological tests, many of which he recognized from doing medical malpractice litigation. "And all of these tests are to obtain a baseline for future studies?"

"Yes, basically." Dr. Smith answered, pleased that Mark understood what they needed to do.

Mark smiled again. "Would you excuse us while I talk with the Captain, please?" The scientists exchanged looks and then walked out of the conference room. When the door closed Mark turned to the Captain. "What planet did they find these bozo's on? I cross-examined them into oblivion. They wouldn't even be allowed to testify in court." The Captain merely shook his head in disgust. "Who sent them?" Mark asked.

"Someone in Washington," the Captain answered. "All I know is that they arrived while you were," he paused, "... sleeping. And I have orders to assist them with what they need."

"Assist? Does that mean you will force me to comply with their tests? Because I'm here to tell you, those bozos aren't touching me. You heard them; they're not even practicing doctors. They probably can't even find a vein."

The Captain looked troubled. He turned and glanced at Sgt. Jeffreys, who was sitting behind him. Sgt. Jeffreys caught the look and headed for the door. When the door closed, the Captain turned back to Mark. "I have orders to assist, which means to provide them with the space and materials they need. As you so eloquently pointed out to me before, I do not have jurisdiction over you. I could put you in the brig if you were threatening my ship or mission, but I can't force you to do something against your will."

"I appreciate your position."

The Captain nodded his head in acknowledgment. "But we are stuck with these... bozo's, as you put it. So I would appreciate it if you would comply with their requests to the degree that you feel comfortable."

Mark considered for a while. "They are shooting in the dark, you know." The Captain nodded. "Okay. They will have to explain the nature of the tests to me before hand. I will allow them to do non-invasive monitoring, like the EEG, when I am in contact with the cube, but they can forget the invasive tests and the psych nonsense. And your doctor has to supervise it."

"I thought you didn't like my doctor."

"I don't. But she's the lesser of the two weevils."

"Weevils?"

"Never mind," Mark laughed. "Bad joke. Although Captain Aubrey would have appreciated it."

"Captain Aubrey?"

"A fictional British sea captain during the Napoleonic wars," Mark answered as he rose from his seat. "I guess we need to get this show on the road. If their protocols are ready, I'm ready to have another go at the memory cube."

Fifty-five minutes later Mark was sitting up on a stretcher with electrical leads attached to his chest and head, while nearby monitors plotted his brain waves, heart rhythm, pulse, respiration and oxygen saturation. He ultimately had allowed all the monitoring equipment they requested, but had steadfastly refused an IV. In fact, the protocols would have taken longer to setup, particularly as the doctors wanted to seal the room and install a separate air exchange system. Mark objected to the delay, threatening to contact the memory cube whether they were ready or not, sarcastically noting that it had not killed anyone so far as it had been "cleansed by the ocean." Even with Mark's impatience, it still took almost an hour to set up the equipment. 'Here we go,' Mark thought as he finally reached over and touched the cube.

Mark mentally screamed as he swooped several hundred feet above the treetops. He was skating through the air over the jungle, the wind blowing across his face, as he studied the jungle below. Mark caught a glimpse of "his" alien feet resting on two pads, like skateboards, that he moved like skates through the air. Occasionally, he could see through the broad leaves of the jungle canopy to the ground below, which must have been at least 300 feet further down. The jungle was unlike anything he'd seen before. The leaves, the colors, the variations in the shapes, all were strange. Everything had a brighter, more vivid appearance than he was used to on Earth. Alien symbols materialized in thin air in front of him, spun and blinked in and out of existence, replaced by an infrared type image of two creatures somewhere ahead. His momentum slowed and then stopped as these images moved to the center of his view.

'They must be below us,' Mark thought as he continued to watch. He slowly descended, deftly angling between the giant tree branches that formed a massive vivid green canopy. He stopped again about 100 feet above the ground. Below him he saw the two creatures that had been displayed. As he watched, two more creatures crept into the clearing, to be greeted by the first with a

snarl. The creatures were lizard like, about 3 feet tall with sharp looking teeth. They walked primarily on their back legs. 'Dinosaurs,' Mark thought. He wanted a closer look at the creatures, to look at their feet to see what type of claws they had, but his host was more interested in the display floating in front of him and in surveying the distance through the trees.

Another display materialized with a different type of creature highlighted, still a lizard type, but walking on all fours and much broader and possibly much bigger, although Mark could not tell from this perspective. More symbols whirled in the air in front of him as his host did... something? Mark could only watch and wait. Mark's host looked down again and Mark was surprised to see that there were now seven of the large lizards beneath him, still seeming to pay no attention to the alien floating 100 feet above them. They appeared to be agitated now, circling, growling and snapping.

His host touched the device attached to his wrist and the creatures settled down and headed off single file in the direction of the other larger creatures. His host skated through the air after them, keeping the creatures in view either visually or by the infrared-type sensor, until they emerged from the jungle into a vast valley filled with dense ferns about six or eight feet tall. The creatures fanned out into the undergrowth and disappeared from sight, although Mark was able to follow their progress with the infrared display as they moved forward. Looking ahead, Mark could make out three of the larger creatures.

'This certainly looks like carnivores versus herbivores,' Mark thought as the creatures repositioned to cut off any escape, stealthily crawling through the undergrowth. The three prey animals, which is how Mark considered them, appeared unsuspecting as they grazed, *their positioning subtly changing until one of them was separated from the other two. The predators quickly picked up on this new positioning and reformed their approach to box in the lone prey. But before they completed their encircling maneuver, one of the prey rose up and bellowed a warning. All three prey looked up, startled.*

Mark expected the predators to either give up - their plan having been discovered too soon - or to rush their intended target in hopes of overcoming it by sheer numbers. Instead, the predators started hooting to each other. Three of the predators veered off to attack the two larger prey while one rushed at the separated prey from the other direction. The two groups of prey began backing up in panic, which further separated them from each other. The predators jumped and roared and made a fearsome display at their targets, but never actually made contact, their intent clearly being to drive them farther apart from each other. The prey were confused and scared, hollering and roaring, but still backing away from the threatening predators. When they were separated by about 100 yards, the remaining predators, which had stayed hidden during this attack, swiftly jumped out onto the unsuspecting lone prey. The attack was vicious and incredibly swift. One moment the prey was backing, standing 20 or 30 feet tall and the next there was a blur of bodies jumping across it and it lay on the ground with huge gashes across it. Mark realized they had first jumped to take out what in a human would be the hamstring, effectively crippling the creature and then jumped for the throat, mortally wounding it. The whole attack was over in seconds and the creature was dead before its two companions could decide to help.

A second incredible thing occurred. Rather than stopping to eat, as Mark would expect a lion or other creature to do, the predators disappeared into the undergrowth. This caused even further consternation with the remaining prey, as they no longer knew where their enemies were located. A moment later a predator jumped up in front of the prey causing them to step back in alarm, only to be cut down from behind by the rest of predator pack, which once again attacked the hindquarters first and then attacked their heads and throats with killing blows. Only then did the predators converge on the carcasses to eat. Mark's host watched a few moments longer before skating back to the jungle.

Mark woke on the hospital gurney. He was exhausted, but managed to stay conscious. Sgt. Jeffreys was the first to notice that he was awake. Mark smiled weakly. "Water," he managed to say. He had to drink through a straw, while an orderly held the cup, as his arms were too heavy to lift. When he wanted more, they gave him Gatorade to give him more energy. "Let me rest for a while," he managed to whisper. "Then I'll tell you what I saw." He lay back and closed his eyes, but did not sleep. Instead, he pondered over what he had witnessed.

The vision had not lasted long at all, probably less than an hour. The jungle appeared to be the same one he had seen in the earlier vision, made up of huge trees and fern like plants. Huge compared to his host, Mark reminded himself. A blade of grass would tower over an ant like a redwood. But these plants appeared huge. They were like nothing he had ever seen before. And then the animals; clearly they were dinosaurs, or dinosaur like, he corrected himself. He didn't know anything about prehistoric flora, but the animals could have been from any dinosaur movie he had ever seen. They could have come straight out of *Jurassic Park*. If only he could have seen whether the predators had the famous velociraptor toe claw. They had left some grievous slash wounds on the herbivores. If this was a scene from the Jurassic era, then Stephen Spielberg would certainly be jealous of the filming technique.

Could this be a view of Earth long ago? The thought shocked him. What if they were showing him scenes from Earth's past? But if they were, that meant the blue-grays, or their race, were millions of years old. But that did not make any sense. If the blue-grays were that old and had such advanced technology hundreds of millions of years ago, shouldn't they have progressed by now to, what, godlike proportions? Look how fast we have progressed in the last fifty years, Mark reasoned. Just assuming the same growth rate would place the blue-gray's civilization in a plane that would be virtually unknowable to us. Did they stagnate? Did they hit an evolutionary dead end? The less mind-boggling explanation was that these were scenes from another planet, which would explain the brighter colors of the sky and plants. But why were they showing this to him? What were they trying to tell him?

The more Mark thought about it, the more confused he became by what he had seen. Having more questions than answers, he finally decided he must face the upcoming inquisition. He would let others try to figure this out.

CHAPTER 10

After three hours of constant questioning, Mark was convinced the meeting had long passed the point of productivity. In all that time, they had not come up with anything more than Mark had already figured out and now the questions were becoming repetitious, with no new suggestions or insights. 'There should be a rule that no meeting runs over three hours,' Mark thought. After that the brain gets foggy and time is wasted. 'Perhaps one hour for government meetings,' he thought with an audible chuckle. He turned to the Captain. "You don't need me here anymore. How about if I get something to eat? You can call if you need me."

The Captain nodded his head in agreement. "I would go with you if I could," he whispered conspiratorially. "I'll cover for you. Just make sure that Jeffreys keeps his radio handy." With that Mark stood up and walked out of the conference room, with Sgt. Jeffreys on his heels.

"Where to boss?" Sgt. Jeffreys asked as they exited the conference room.

"Away from this endless meeting," Mark responded as he walked down the corridor. "Do you have any exercise equipment around here? I need to get my blood pumping and I don't feel like doing laps around the flight deck."

"They're doing flight ops now, anyway," Sgt. Jeffreys answered as he led Mark down some stairs into a new set of corridors. "The skittles would have a fit if you went up there now."

"Skittles?"

"The crewmen on the flight deck."

"Why skittles?" Mark asked, still confused.

"Oh, you've seen them," Sgt. Jeffreys explained. "Everyone has a different colored jersey. Looks like a bag of skittles."

"If you say so," Mark said unconvinced.

"Just go with it. You're in the Navy now."

"How could I forget, I'm surrounded by gray."

"Hey, gray's a great color. Matches everything," Sgt. Jeffreys laughed as he led Mark into a room filled with exercise machines.

"This is more like it. All I have been doing is sleeping and eating," Mark said. "The only exercise I get is virtual exercise during the visions. After that, I'm either passed out or sitting through those endless debriefings. Back home I was pretty good about hitting the gym fairly regularly. Here I've done nothing but sleep and eat."

"What about the miles of corridors and endless stairwells that you constantly complain about?" Sgt. Jeffreys asked.

"Ok, you got me there," Mark conceded. "I have walked and done the Navy's version of a stair master."

"How about these?" Sgt. Jeffreys asked as he walked over to a wall lined with free weights.

"No, that is too much like exercise. You can play with those. I'm going to bike. Maybe I can bicycle home and forget about all this nonsense."

"Good luck. If that worked, we would all be on those bikes."

They worked out in silence, Mark riding the stationary bike, while Sgt. Jeffreys used the free weights in the corner. As Mark pedaled, he replayed the visions in his head, trying to figure out what they meant. What was he missing? Why were they sending these to him? The more he thought about it, the more convinced he was that a channel was missing, that he wasn't receiving the entire message. He felt emotions with the cat creature, as he referred to the second alien, but not with the blue-grays. Why not? Was the cat more primitive, something he could understand, while the blue-grays were too advanced? That brought him back to the cat vision. What happened there? He still wasn't sure whether he started that fight or the vision prompted it. He knew the Captain would be talking to him about it before long. Hopefully, his earlier explanation would be sufficient. He was not about to tell anyone about the cat vision. Not until he figured it out anyway.

Several sailors came into the exercise room. Loud and boisterous, they headed to the free weights where Sgt. Jeffreys was working out. Mark watched absently as he continued to pedal, noting that the bike was approaching another incline on its random setting and his heart rate was still only 124. The sailors were wearing civvies, so there was no telling rank. Lower enlisted, Mark guessed by their age and immaturity. They were just kids, 18 or 19. Certainly not much older. He watched as they pushed and shoved each other and showed off with the weights. He tried to remember what it was like when he was 18, but fortunately those memories were buried by time. Certainly, he hadn't been this immature.

There were five of them, each one trying to out do the others either in the weights they were lifting or in their attitude. One of them walked over to where Sgt. Jeffreys was working out and snatched up some weights that Sgt. Jeffreys had been setting up. It was only then that Mark realized that Jeffreys was wearing civvies as well, having been called suddenly while off duty. Mark watched irritation flash across Jeffreys' face and wondered what the Marine would do to these kids. Jeffreys glanced at Mark and then moved on to another weight set. A Marine with self-control? Mark's opinion of Sgt. Jeffreys went up another notch. Mark glanced down at the bike's monitor, as the pedaling got harder. He was at the top of a four bar incline. He considered turning the level down, but then chastised himself. 'You wanted some exercise,' he told himself as he leaned into the bike, watching the rpm and his heart rate increase.

A commotion across the room made him look up. Three of the sailors were harassing Sgt. Jeffreys, yelling at him to finish his set and move on, while making fun of his light weight. Five against one, they could afford to pick a fight, Mark thought. But Sgt. Jeffreys was not rising to the bait. Mark leaned into the bike, one more bar left to this incline. 'Perhaps we should leave after that,' Mark thought as sweat poured down his face, although the thought of being forced out by these punks was irritating. Sgt. Jeffreys finished his set, got up off the bench and was headed to another weight set, when one of the sailors pushed him from behind. He whirled around...

Trapped, he watched helplessly as five blue-gray aliens encircled his mate and advanced, weapons ready. His mate crouched, ready to spring, her claws already extended and fur bristling. She snarled and barred her fangs, her body tensed. A blue-gray alien behind her aimed at her and a bolt of lightning shot out, striking her in the back...

Mark did not remember coming off the bike. His first conscious thought was overwhelming rage as he rushed over to the group of sailors, who were now all facing Sgt. Jeffreys, daring him to react. "Stay out of this old man," Mark vaguely heard one sailor say before he waded into the group, fists and feet flying. Mark dropped four sailors before they knew a fight had started and then turned to the remaining one who had jumped back in fright. A snarl escaped Mark's lips as he dropped into a fighting crouch, one arm slightly extended, the other back, fingers curled into a claw. A hand touched his shoulder.

"Sir, don't..." Mark spun, barely managing to pull back his arm before he back slashed Sgt. Jeffreys' face. "Sir, it's okay. It's over..." Sgt. Jeffreys' words finally registered. Breathing heavily, Mark dropped his arms and slowly stood up from his crouched position. Seeing Mark relax, Sgt. Jeffreys turned to the sole standing sailor. "You and your friends won't bother us anymore, will you?"

"No, Sir," the sailor managed to stutter as Sgt. Jeffreys turned to the four sailors on the floor, who were starting to painfully sit up.

"You guys really stepped in it this time. You have no idea who you are messing with. Now I might, just might, be able to keep this from the Captain," Sgt. Jeffreys said as he held up his radio. "You better pray that I can. And you had better not breathe a word of this to anyone or it will really hit the fan. Do you understand?"

Mark didn't know if the sailors were now more afraid of Sgt. Jeffreys' threats or of him. They mumbled assurances of silence and staggered out of the room.

"What was that?" Sgt. Jeffreys exclaimed when the sailors had left.

"What?" Mark answered, stalling for time. He knew full well what Sgt. Jeffreys was talking about and was really freaked out that he had succumbed to another cat vision. His only consolation was that the sailors were not hurt, just banged up. But if he kept losing control, what would happen next?

"You charging in and beating up those kids?" Sgt. Jeffreys said.

"It was five against one."

"You were protecting me? From them?" Mark nodded his head, afraid to say anything else. "I'm a

Marine. And they are straight from High School. Nothing was going to happen."

"Sorry," Mark managed to say. "I thought you were in trouble."

"And I'm trying to keep you out of trouble. I appreciate you trying to help me," Sgt. Jeffreys added. "I just think it was a bit of an overreaction."

'You think it's an overreaction. You have no idea how much of an overreaction that was,' Mark thought. His heart was racing and his breathing was still pretty heavy; which Mark hoped Sgt. Jeffreys would attribute to the work-out bike and not realize it was from the adrenalin rush he received from the last vision.

"I don't think those sailors will tell anyone," Sgt. Jeffreys was saying. "So if you are good with it, I think it would be best if we don't mention this to the Captain."

"I'm good with that," Mark mumbled, still feeling shaky after having lost control. "How about taking me back to my room? I need to take a shower and change. Then we can find something to eat."

"This way," Sgt. Jeffreys said as they exited the exercise room. They walked to Mark's room in silence; Mark still trying to figure out what was going on and how to control it. When they got to Mark's room, Sgt. Jeffreys said, "I'll wait out here. By the way, you didn't tell me you knew Kung Fu. What style was that?"

"Style?"

"Your fighting stance."

"Oh, that," Mark hesitated. "Tiger claw."

CHAPTER 11

Mark breathed a sigh of relief when he was alone in his room. What was going on? The blue-gray alien visions were simply visions, exhausting, but only visions. But these cat visions were controlling him. They had one of the missing channels: emotion. Still no thoughts, but the emotions were overwhelming. He would have to get control before he really hurt someone. Or he would have to tell the Captain. Then he would certainly be confined, either in the brig or in sickbay. Neither option was very appealing.

Mark stripped down and stepped over to the shower, hesitating before getting in. 'What? Afraid to get wet?' He stepped into the shower and reached for the shampoo, mildly surprised that his fingers did not end in claws. He couldn't seem to shake the last vision. Lathering up, he was surprised when his hand brushed against skin, not fur. Shaking his head, he turned the water on cold, hoping the shock would clear his mind. By the time he got out of the shower he had shaken most of the alien vision, although he still felt an underlying rage for the attack on his mate. He would have to be careful to control that. A knock on the door interrupted his thoughts. "Come in," he called out.

Sgt. Jeffreys poked his head in the door. "The Captain called. Wants to know if you would come to the conference room."

"Tell him I'm getting out of the shower," Mark answered. "I'll be there as soon as I get dressed. By the way, what time is it?"

"Four fifty-eight in the morning," Sgt. Jeffreys replied.

"Doesn't anyone sleep around here? What day is it, anyway?"

"Thursday."

"Boy, my bio-rhythms must be real off. I've been up all night," Mark said.

"But you slept all day," Sgt. Jeffreys pointed out.

"This whole business is really screwing up my schedule," Mark noted. "What time is it back home?"

"About midnight."

"Okay, I'll see the Captain, check out the memory cube and then when I sleep that off, I should be able to call my wife," Mark planned.

When Mark arrived at the conference room, the only people present were the Captain, Dr. Ballenger and Dr. Smith. The Captain glanced up as Mark entered. "Mr. Williams," the Captain stated, and Mark wondered about the use of the formal greeting. "The doctors here have a new protocol they wish to utilize during your next encounter with the memory cube. I thought you would want to hear their proposal so you can consider it before the next session."

"Sure," Mark said noncommittally while he took a seat, wondering what the Captain was trying to warn him about. The Captain sat as well and nodded to the doctors.

"Well, yes..." one of the doctors started.

"Yes, the new protocol," the second continued. "We have decided to enhance your perceptibility to the alien artifact. Your consciousness is probably blocking your ability to receive the, ah, missing channel as you put it."

"This new protocol will make you more receptive to the missing channel," the first doctor completed.

"You mean with a drug," Mark said.

"Of course."

"What kind of drug?"

"I'm sure you're not familiar with it."

"Try me."

Mark did not recognize the chemical name of the drug, but had a sneaking suspicion as to what it was. "Is that a psychotropic drug, by any chance?" he asked.

"Why yes," Dr. Smith answered, apparently surprised by Mark's insight.

"I thought so." Mark took a deep breath as anger welled up inside him. He wasn't sure whether his anger was from the cat vision or rage at their audacity, using psychotropic drugs on him. He took a few moments to calm down before answering, "No."

"No?" The doctors seemed genuinely surprised.

"No. You will not be administering any drugs on me. I have allowed you to monitor, but you will not be administering any drugs."

"But these drugs will enhance your ability to…"

"No!" Mark shouted as he stood up, his rage barely contained. "I draw the line at any drugs. You don't have a clue what you are doing and I don't intend to be the poor guinea pig that you test your protocols on. Now I intend to go back and visit the memory cube before I go to bed. If you want to monitor, that is fine. But that is all you will do." With that, Mark got up, turned to the Captain and said, "At your convenience," and left the room.

An hour later Mark was hooked up to the monitors in sickbay. The two UFO doctors, as Mark referred to them, and the ship's surgeon were present along with Sgt. Jeffreys. The Captain had been unable to attend due to an incident that required his attention. Leaning back on the hospital bed, Mark reached over to the bedside table and placed his finger on the memory cube.

Mark was running down a corridor of the alien habitat. Other blue-grays were running in and out of side rooms, some carrying containers. Mark's host ran into the science room where he placed his fingertips on one of the tables. Small gold lights flickered in a random order on the tabletop. As the host stared at the flickering lights, Mark could hear frantic activity in the outside corridor as numerous blue-grays continued to run down the hallway. After several minutes, the flickering lights went out and his host pulled his hand away from the tabletop. Mark watched as a couple dozen memory cubes rose up out of the seemingly solid surface of the table. His host quickly picked up each cube and carefully placed it on top of a solid looking tube, where it disappeared into the surface. Once full, he closed the container, picked it up, and quickly exited the science room.

As he entered the hallway, it began to bend and stretch. The light strips changed color and took on a halo effect. His running slowed, while the other aliens in the hallway became distorted, like watching them in an amusement park mirror. 'What is going on?' Mark wondered. He had never had anything like this occur during a vision. They had always been sharp and lifelike. This was like a bad dream or watching an old VHS tape that had been left in the sun too long. Or how movies depicted someone who had been doped. 'Doped! That's it,' he realized. 'The doctors drugged me.' He was furious. As his host ran his distorted way down the corridor, Mark frantically tried to pull his hand off the cube. But all his senses were alien senses. He could not feel his human body, nor figure out how to control it. Although distracted by his attempts to release the cube, he realized that his host was approaching an open airlock, which he had not seen before. His host stepped out of the airlock and looked around.

Despite the distortion, Mark realized it was the jungle world he had watched before. His host looked back and Mark saw that the alien habitat was in fact a number of circular buildings connected by tubes, sitting in a clearing surrounded by jungle. The host looked up and Mark saw a number of objects streaking up into the blue sky. The distortion was too great to make out anything but blurry shapes. His host turned and ran across the clearing to another structure, which was distorted beyond recognition. The dash across the clearing seemed to take forever, like running through molasses or quicksand, while everything around him distorted into bizarre shapes.

Finally, he entered the other structure, secured the container of memory cubes and jumped up a shaft that ended in a small room containing a single seat, which enveloped his body as he sank into it. Or was that more distortion? A panoramic view materialized above his head. The view became less distorted and Mark recognized the alien habitat from his new vantage point about 20 feet up in the air and perhaps 100 yards away. He watched as several blue-grays exited the structure, some running towards him, while others ran off-screen in another direction. The view shifted, now showing the sky. Mark's vision blurred again as the drugs coursed through his system.

Mark opened his eyes and the sick bay materialized in front of him. He was not sure whether the vision had ended or he had managed to break contact with the cube. Although the vision was over, the drugs were still in his system. The lights sent out odd colors and were surrounded by halos. He turned his head and the room lurched sickeningly. The room was crowded with the two UFO doctors, the ships surgeon, the Captain and Sgt. Jeffreys. They appeared to be having a rather heated argument, but their words were distorted and their movements jerky. Mark tried to lift his arm, but was unable to move it. Exhausted, he let his head roll back and passed out.

Mark woke up, eyes bleary, mouth feeling like parchment. Gratefully, the lights seemed to have regained their natural color, although everything seemed a bit fuzzy. He noticed Sgt. Jeffreys sleeping in a chair in the corner of the room. He tried to call out his name, but only a moan came out. It was enough. Sgt. Jeffreys jumped up and came to his side. "Water," Mark croaked, the word inaudible even to him.

"You want water?" Jeffreys asked. Mark tried to nod. Jeffreys was gone for only a second before he came back with a cup of water and a straw, followed by the ship's doctor. Jeffreys looked at the doctor for permission before placing the straw in Mark's mouth. The cool water ran down Mark's parched throat, while the doctor checked his vitals.

"I'm very sorry. I couldn't stop them," the doctor was saying as she checked Mark's pupils. "However, the effects should be wearing off. Most of it appears to be out of your system already."

"They drugged me," Mark whispered, more a statement than a question.

"Yes," the doctor acknowledged. "I placed an I.V. as a precaution as you appeared to be reacting to this vision stronger than the past ones. Dr. Smith administered the drug in the I.V. when no one was watching. I saw him remove the needle from the I.V. tube, but of course by then it was too late. I pulled the I.V., but not before you received some of the drug. I could only monitor you after that." The doctor appeared to be genuinely remorseful.

"How much longer will it affect me? Mark asked.

You have metabolized most of it. Probably another eight to ten hours to be safe, then it should be completely out of your system. But," the doctor glanced around to make sure no one else was there but Sgt. Jeffreys. "They have no concern for the Hippocratic Oath." Mark looked at her quizzically. "No concern for the patient or his rights," she explained. "They plan on doing it again. They pulled rank on the Captain. They have orders straight from Washington, Joint Chiefs or Department of Defense. Someone way up the food chain." She paused, and then added, "I've got to call the Captain. He left orders to call him when you woke up."

"The Captain was furious when he found out," Sgt. Jeffreys continued the story after the doctor left. "I thought he was going to personally throw them off the flight deck. Then they made a call to someone in Washington, who pulled rank on the Captain. The Captain didn't take that very well. He let them know what he thought about it. They dressed him down pretty good, even threatened to relieve him. That didn't slow him down any, though. They may have his relief on the way now."

"How do you know?" Mark asked.

"Heard it. We enlisted know how to be invisible. Just stand at attention in the corner and we disappear. Its amazing what you learn that way."

'Leave it to the government to make a bad situation worse,' Mark thought ironically.

The Captain arrived a few minutes later. "That will be all," he said tersely to the doctor and Sgt. Jeffreys, both of whom beat a hasty retreat from the room. "I'm sorry," he said to Mark sincerely. "I did not know they were going to do that. I should have been here. I gave you my word that you could decide." The Captain let the apology hang in the air.

Although Mark was furious about the drug, he realized neither the Captain, nor the doctor was to blame, and both were as upset as he. He managed a weak smile. "Not your fault," he whispered, noting that his voice was getting better.

"So, how are you feeling?"

"Like my brain was run over by a truck."

The Captain nodded. "Doc says the drug should almost be out of your system."

"I hope so, that was really bad. If that is what tripping is like, I can't imagine wanting to do it a second time."

"You know I will not be able to protect you anymore?" the Captain said after a pause. "They intend to drug you again. I can't stop them. They pulled rank on me and if I interfere, they will just replace me with someone who will obey them."

"I'm sorry you were put in this position," Mark responded. "And I appreciate your efforts to protect me."

"Didn't do much good."

"So how high did they go? The President?

"I don't think so," the Captain answered after considering for a moment. "He may know, but probably not. I was talking to an Admiral. But they were not his orders. Someone had leaned on him pretty hard. I don't know where it is coming from. He mentioned the SECDEF. Secretary of Defense," the Captain added when Mark looked confused. "But I don't know if it originated there or somewhere else."

"Who are these guys? What agency?" Mark asked. "I just thought they were incompetent, conceited idiots. I didn't think they actually had power."

"I don't know," the Captain conceded. "They never have said. I was just informed to expect them and to cooperate. I wasn't given any other information on them."

"This is like one of those movies where someone in the government is out to get you," Mark observed. "I enjoyed watching them, but I never wanted to be in one."

"The government has a lot of layers. Unfortunately, some are not as friendly as others," the Captain remarked.

"Are any of them friendly?"

"Sure, and many are competent too."

"Yea, and I believe in the tooth fairy," Mark responded dryly.

"Speaking of layers, or bureaucracy, are you ready for a debriefing?" the Captain asked after a moment of silence. "It's been about six hours since you touched the cube."

"Not yet. Can you stall them? Have the doctor, your doctor that is, say I'm not physically up to it yet."

"Sure. For a while anyway."

"I need more time to get these drugs out of my system so I will make sense." Mark added. "Oh, and keep those two doctors," Mark said 'doctor' with a sneer, "away from me until the briefing. I can't guarantee I will be polite when I see them."

"You do have a way with medical personnel," the Captain responded with a knowing smile.

Mark decided to let the comment go. No sense trying to explain that one. After the Captain left, Mark considered his position. How was he going to get out of this? He was furious that they had drugged him. The nerve of them! And who knows what they would do next. It was hard enough coping with the alien contact. It would be just too ironic to have his own government ruin his brain with their incompetent experts. But how could he stop it?

It clearly violated his personal and patient rights; you didn't have to be a lawyer to figure that out. But what good was that? He was dealing with the government. And you didn't have to read many spy novels to believe that the government could and would do whatever it thought was best, regardless of the individual's rights. All you had to do was read the newspapers about Guantanamo Bay, the CIA black ops prison cells, or the NSA, to realize that sad truth. So any argument about patient's rights would fall on deaf ears.

He could refuse to touch the cube again, unless they promised not to drug him. But that wouldn't work. They had already demonstrated they would do anything they wanted once he was unconscious. And he could not rely upon the Captain or anyone else to protect him. They would simply replace the Captain with someone who would be obedient. Maybe if he refused to touch the cube at all. But if he refused, they would simply tie him to the hospital bed and force him to touch the cube. Maybe he could refuse to tell them what he saw? Mark thought about that for a while. No, that would not work either. They would just administer some more drugs, Sodium Pentothal or something, and get what they wanted. By the time they finished with all their drugs, his brain would probably be fried forever.

They can't do this, Mark argued with himself. He was an American citizen. Right, Mark answered sarcastically. The government will do anything they want to me since I'm only one person and the fate of the world rests on my ability to contact the aliens. That's the way the government would justify it. They would not care if at the end he was locked away in some sanitarium, a drooling idiot.

Who could protect him? His partner? His partner didn't know what was going on. His wife? But what could Beth do against the government? He ran several scenarios in his head before realizing that she couldn't do anything either. The government would deny any involvement with him. They could stick with their cover story that they spoke to him about a court-martial and after he left they never saw him again, just another missing person. Beth's story about him being flown to the *Ronald Reagan* at the request of the President would be ridiculed as soon as she mentioned the UFO sighting. After that, only the *National Enquirer* would run the story. No, he would have to figure out how to get out of this himself.

'Think! Think,' he told himself. 'You're a lawyer. But I need to be a spy, or something,' he thought. 'But you are a lawyer, so think like a lawyer. What argument will win this case? Who's the decision-maker here? What are their goals? What arguments would sway them? We know individual rights is a non-starter. What would work?' Mark lay back, running scenario after scenario in his mind, trying to figure out which argument would be the most effective.

Finally, he called for Sgt. Jeffreys. "I need to talk to the Captain."

"I'm ready," he told the Captain a short time later. "But this last vision was very different. Something's happening. The President needs to hear this first hand. He needs to be on the video link."

The Captain looked at Mark quizzically. "Ok, but Washington will want a summary before they commit the President to the briefing."

Mark considered the Captain's remark. He couldn't provide a summary as it would defeat his plan, but he needed the President there. "Tell them there is a crisis going on in the vision which needs immediate action."

"I'll see what I can do."

Two hours later Mark, assisted by Sgt. Jeffreys, walked into the familiar conference room where technicians were setting up the video link with multiple screens. This time one of the screens was reserved for the President. The Captain, Dr. Ballenger and Dr. Smith were already in the room. Mark walked up to Dr. Smith, noting Sgt. Jeffreys tense up by his side and the Captain turn to watch as he did. "That was a very interesting drug you administered," Mark commented nonchalantly. "It made a huge impact."

Dr. Smith puffed up with pride. "We knew it would. Couldn't understand what all the fuss was about. We were right all along, of course."

"You have other drugs as well?" Mark asked innocently.

"Oh yes, there are several very promising combinations that we can use."

"I thought so," Mark said, somehow resisting the impulse to shove the doctor's glasses down his throat. Instead, he walked over to his usual seat next to the Captain, surprised by how fatigued he felt.

Finally, the screen blinked and the President appeared with the accompanying announcement, "Ladies and Gentlemen, the President of the United States." Mark wasn't sure whether they were supposed to applaud or stand at attention. Exhausted from his past vision and still a bit put out by the whole drug episode, he remained seated. He noted that the President was wearing a polo shirt, rather than a suit and tie. Belatedly, Mark realized that it must be around midnight Eastern Time. So he probably had either awakened the President or was keeping him from going to bed. He better make this worth it, Mark thought.

The Captain, being the senior officer present, started the briefing. "Mr. President, as you are probably aware, Mr. Williams made contact with the alien artifact at zero-seven-forty-eight, ship time, which would have been four-forty-eight p.m., your time. His contact lasted thirteen minutes and he has been… indisposed, until about two hours ago, at which time he requested that you attend this briefing. With that, I will turn this over to Mr. Williams," the Captain concluded and sat down. The cameraman turned the camera to Mark, who remained seated.

"Mr. President, I appreciate your attendance." The President nodded and Mark proceeded. "This vision was very different from the previous ones," Mark started, noting with irritation the pleased smiles on the faces of Dr. Ballenger and Dr. Smith. Ignoring them and consciously trying to keep the irritation out of his voice, Mark continued. "I believe this was a key vision, perhaps the one the blue-grays have been leading up to." 'That got their attention,' Mark noted, as the audience seemed to lean forward. "This vision was back in the alien habitat. I now know it is an alien base, located on a planet. The blue-grays were alarmed and appeared to be evacuating the base."

"Let me start at the beginning. My host was the same blue-gray alien from my last vision. This time the vision started with him running down a corridor into the science room. All around him other blue-grays were running around as well, many carrying various objects. My host ran into the science room where he collected about two-dozen memory cubes, before running down a new corridor and exiting the habitat. The habitat is on a planet, the same planet that the jungle visions come from. When my host ran out of the habitat, I could see that it was located in a huge clearing in the jungle. And in that clearing were several spaceships." Mark paused, noting that his audience, including the President, was spellbound. Mark paused a moment longer for dramatic effect before continuing. "And then the vision changed dramatically. And it was all due to the efforts of two men." Mark looked over at the two doctors, who seemed to swell up with pride. "Mr. President, do you know Dr. Ballinger and Dr. Smith?" The cameraman hastily swung the camera over to the two doctors, who haughtily stood up and bowed, oblivious to the slight look of annoyance on the President's face by this interruption of the story.

"No, I don't think I do," the President replied, to Mark's relief.

"They were sent here by someone in Washington," Mark explained, realizing that he had made it past one very important hurdle, "possible the Secretary of Defense, to assist in the contact. You see, they are self-proclaimed UFO experts. They administered a psychotropic drug to me while I was in contact with the memory cube, basically unconscious. Actually, they did it after I expressly forbid them to." Mark paused again, hoping the doctors would take the bait. They couldn't resist.

In the silence that followed Dr. Ballinger proudly pontificated, "Well, we knew that the drug would help and once you realized the benefits of the drug…"

"We knew you would be glad that we had administered it," Dr. Smith finished. "As you said, the effects were dramatic. Laymen always have such a negative preconception of the benefits of medication management in the psychological arena."

"Yes," Mark said, drawing the cameraman's and the audience's attention back. "Mr. President, these two so-called doctors and the people who sent them here have unilaterally jeopardized, perhaps irretrievably, our contact with the aliens."

The announcement was met with a shocked silence. Finally, the President broke the silence. "Mr. Williams, perhaps you would like to explain?"

"Certainly, Mr. President. I was telling you how this vision was very dramatic. The aliens were evacuating their base, almost in a panic. Like an alarm had gone off. And they were fleeing to their spaceships. It was at this point that these," Mark paused, "gentlemen, surreptitiously administered a psychotropic drug to me. And as they said, the effect was dramatic: I lost the rest of the alien's message." A hushed silence followed before Mark continued. "From that point on, everything became distorted. Colors changed, shapes blurred and twisted, time seemed to expand and contract. For the first time I got to see an overview of the outside of the habitat, a view of several spaceships, and I was at the controls of an alien spaceship about to launch." Mark paused again as the audience waited for his next words. "And I can't give you any details, because my view was too distorted by the drugs they gave me!"

No one spoke as each listener considered the ramifications of the potential loss. Sputtering objections from the doctors finally interrupted the silence. "We are experts in this field... We know what is best.... We're trained…"

"Mr. President," Mark interrupted the doctors' ranting.

"Yes, Mr. Williams."

"I came here at your personal request, and I am willing to keep trying to communicate with these aliens. But I can't do it with people I do not trust. People who evidently have their own agenda, which obviously is not in the best interest of the country." To himself he added, 'or mine.' "Sir, I would request that you have these two gentlemen removed from this ship immediately and that they not be replaced by anyone, unless you approve them personally. I cannot communicate with the cube while people are experimenting on me with psychotropic drugs or while worrying about what someone may do to me while I am incapacitated. It interferes with my ability to concentrate on what the aliens are trying to send. I lost contact with the cube just as we were about to launch."

There was silence while the President considered the request. Finally, he asked. "Is there any reason I should not grant Mr. Williams' request?" Mark held his breath. This was just like in court, but now the stakes were much higher and more personal. The doctors started to voice an objection, but were cut off by the President. "Other than from either of you." When no one else voiced an objection, the President continued. "Mr. Williams. Your request is granted. Captain Hastings."

"Yes, Mr. President."

"Take the necessary steps to have them removed from your ship immediately."

"Yes, Mr. President," Captain Hastings said as he motioned to Sgt. Jeffreys, who jumped up and quickly escorted the sputtering doctors out of the room.

The President turned his attention back to Mr. Williams. "Mr. Williams, obviously I have been briefed routinely on your progress and I would like to thank you for your continued efforts, despite the physical and mental hardships that you are incurring. And I personally apologize for the actions of these men. I had no knowledge that they were there or what they were doing, but I can assure you, that it will not happen again." The latter part of this statement seemed to be directed off camera.

"Mr. President," Mark interjected. "Two final things, if I may?"

"Yes?"

"First, Captain Hastings was not involved in this incident. In fact, when he found out, he was furious, but was evidently overruled by someone in Washington. They threatened to relieve him if he did not comply with the doctors' future requests. I would ask that you issue orders right now to Captain Hastings, in front of all involved, providing him full authority to protect me from any further interference. I will gladly discuss suggestions for future contact with anyone, but ultimately

I have to decide under what conditions I continue to make contact."

"Agreed," the President said after a moment's consideration. "Captain Hastings."

"Yes, Mr. President."

"You are to protect Mr. Williams. If anything like this comes up again, you are to report directly to me, understood?"

"Yes, Mr. President."

"You said two things, Mr. Williams," the President added.

"Yes, sir. The Navy Flight Surgeon believes that this drug won't clear my system completely for another eight to twelve hours. I don't dare touch the cube until I am clean, since the drug disrupts my ability to perceive the visions. I don't want to lose anything and so far the cube has never repeated itself. So if I miss it, it may be gone for good. I just wanted to let you know that I wasn't shirking my duty when there is a delay in my next report."

"That's fine," the President agreed. "And rest assured, Mr. Williams. I am going to give this my personal attention. I will not allow first contact with an alien race to be jeopardized by the unilateral actions of a few individuals."

"Thank you, Mr. President." With that the President signed off and the conference ended, no one thinking about continuing the debriefing after Mark's bombshell.

As they were leaving the conference room, the Captain took Mark aside. "Thank you for that. You probably just saved my command."

"It's only fair. You went out on a limb for me. I couldn't leave you hanging."

"I appreciate that," the Captain said. "By the way, you must be a pretty good lawyer."

"Why do you say that?"

"That was one heck of a good argument you just presented. I thought we were both goners." Mark smiled in response. As they walked into the corridor a sailor gave the Captain a status report on the doctors. The Captain listened and turned to Mark. "Sergeant Jeffreys is still tied up with the doctors. When he is done, I will give him the same orders the President gave me. You don't mind if he becomes your personal bodyguard from now on?"

"No, Sir. I would welcome it. And speaking of orders, the one I would like to make now is at the Officer's Mess."

"Now I know you're feeling better," the Captain laughed. "You still think you're on a cruise ship. Well, I suppose the least we can do is make sure you're well fed. I will have another escort assigned to you until Sgt. Jeffreys is available. Try not to tell him everything you know."

"Yes, Sir," Mark responded to the rebuke. "I will try to refrain from compromising your entire crew." The Captain smiled. "In the meantime," Mark added. "Can you have him escort me to communications? I haven't talked with my wife in two days and she will be worried sick."

"Sure," the Captain agreed. "Just remember to keep your comments general. It is a non-secure line on her end."

By the time Mark's call got through it was almost 2:00 a.m. back in Pensacola, although it was only 5:00 p.m. ship's time. "Sorry to wake you up," Mark started when a sleepy voice answered the phone. "It has gotten so hard to coordinated calls with the time change difference, that I figured it was just better to call you now."

"That's okay," Beth answered, already sounding more alert. "Are you alright? You haven't called in two days. Is everything working out?"

"I'm fine," Mark responded. He had been planning on how he could explain what was going on within the confines of the censors, so when he was certain she was awake, he continued. "Have you had a run-in with those two government men again?" he asked.

"No, I haven't seen them since we last spoke," Beth answered.

"Well, I have," Mark said. "Although probably not the same two. Two men joined our..." he paused, worried about the censor, "...our tour group here. Said they were doctors and wanted to give me a physical. Very pushy types."

"What happened? What did they do?"

"Nothing at first," Mark continued. "I just ignored them. But then they got really pushy about it. Wanted to conduct..." Mark paused again, realizing he was getting too detailed. "You know how they want you to take every immunization in the world, even when you are just traveling to Europe?"

"Yes?" Beth answered, her tone clearly suggesting that she was trying to follow.

"Well, these guys were like that. And they wouldn't take no for an answer. I finally had to contact the president of the tour group to get them kicked off the tour."

"Really? It got that bad?"

"Yes. I'll tell you the details when I get home. But now they are gone, so it doesn't matter. But I'm glad you gave me a head's up. I don't know if they were from the same group you talked to, but it wouldn't surprise me."

"So what is going on now?" Beth asked.

The censor's head came up as a warning. Mark smiled and mouthed "no problem." Aloud he said, "Nothing new. I should have taken a Rosetta Stone course before I came out here. You know how bad I am with languages. It takes me a long time to learn a new one."

"Certainly other people can help you," she responded.

"The only way I can learn is by doing it myself," Mark answered. "So right now I am trying to teach myself. I just have to be patient." They talked a little longer, Mark asking how things were going on at home and the office, before he reluctantly signed off. Once again promising to call when he could. By then Sgt.

Jeffreys had arrived and Mark asked him to take him to the galley for something to eat.

CHAPTER 12

By the time Sgt. Jeffreys escorted Mark down to the Officer's Mess, the recent events were catching up with him. Looking at the line, he said, "I don't think I can do that line. Do you mind if I just sit here at this corner table and let you get the food?"

"No problem. What would you like?"

"Anything will do. How about bacon and eggs, grits and some OJ?"

"It's supper time," Sgt. Jeffreys replied.

"Well my system thinks it is breakfast time," Mark replied.

Sgt. Jeffreys went to get the food, while Mark gratefully collapsed in a chair, resting his head in his hands and replaying recent events. The session with the President had gone better than expected. Hopefully, the President would do a little housecleaning and Mark would not have to worry about a repeat performance. It was hard enough dealing with alien visions without also having to deal with government intrigue. The ship's doctor had taken a blood sample from him that was being flown to Guam for further analysis. Once he received a clean bill of health they would expect him to contact the memory cube again.

'What was going on in the cube?' Mark wondered. With the drug issue, he never really had an opportunity to reflect on the events in the cube. 'The base was being evacuated, and in a hurry too. Not only the base, but also the planet. But what was so important, or so scary, that they would up and run? Could it be an earthquake? But there's no warning for an earthquake. Well, at least we have no warning,' Mark corrected. 'They might. Could it be a tsunami? Or perhaps a hurricane? But hurricanes gave plenty of warning. It really could be anything.' He finally decided he would just have to wait and see what happened next.

His thoughts were interrupted by Sgt. Jeffreys' arrival with two steaming trays of food. 'This is more like it,' he thought. However, before he had a chance to dig into the food, three young officers approached his table. "I told you they were sneaking in," one of the officers was saying to the other. "We can't let them get away with this." Mark looked up at the three, noting the single gold bar on their collars and the gold wings on their chests. 'Great,' he thought. 'Aviators. The only thing more obnoxious than an aviator, was one right out of flight school.' He had lived next to several aviators on Pensacola Beach and they tended to be obnoxious and overbearing. These three were no exception. Sgt. Jeffreys was trying to explain to the three that they had permission from the Captain to eat in the Officer's Mess, but the officers were either not listening, or not buying the explanation.

"I can't take this again," Mark said to Sgt. Jeffreys, fearing a repeat of the exercise room incident. "Not after what I just went through."

Sgt. Jeffreys looked at Mark with concern. "It's okay, I'll take care of it, Sir. No need for you to get involved." Sgt. Jeffreys turned his attention back to the aviators. Fearing another cat vision and its effect, Mark bolted from the table, heading for the corridor. The aviators chased after him into the corridor, where they grabbed him and threw him against a bulkhead.

Leaping through the closing airlock, he broke free of the trap, landing lightly on all four padded feet as he broke into a run, his claws making scratching noises on the metal deck. He rounded a corner, only to be confronted by two more armed blue-grays. He leaped sideways as they fired, the arcing energy of their weapons singeing his fur, but otherwise missing him. Twisting, he bounced off the wall directly at the two, his claws extended. The first alien dove to the ground, just out of reach. The second was not quick enough. He felt his front claws dig into the alien's scalp, jerking the blue-gray backwards off his feet, while his hind claws reached for his neck. This blue-gray was going to die…

Sgt. Jeffreys ran after the three officers. He saw them catch Mark and push him against a bulkhead. He saw Mark tense, an absent look in his eye. Sgt. Jeffreys knew what would happen next. The three Ensigns didn't stand a chance. They thought they were about to chew out some enlisted for sneaking into the Officer's Mess. How would he explain to the Captain why Mark beat up three Ensigns? And he was supposed to be protecting Mark, even from himself. All these thoughts went through Sgt. Jeffreys' mind as he turned the corner. He leaped between the officers, crashing into Mark and falling onto the deck, holding Mark tightly in a bear hug. Mark thrashed in his grip, almost breaking free, while Sgt. Jeffreys kept repeating: "It's me, Sgt. Jeffreys, I've got you, relax." After a few frantic seconds, Sgt. Jeffreys felt Mark relax in his hold.

"I'm okay," Mark whispered.

Sgt. Jeffreys loosened his hold. When nothing happened, he let go and rolled to his knees. "You okay now?" he asked Mark. Mark nodded and then closed his eyes. "Seizure," Sgt. Jeffreys said to the three confused Ensigns standing above him. "I need to take him to Sick Bay."

"You need help?" one of the Ensigns asked, clearly confused by the change in events.

"No, I have this." With that Sgt. Jeffreys pulled out his radio. "This is Sgt. Jeffreys. We've had another seizure incident. We need corpsman outside of the forward Officer's Mess. Bring a stretcher." With that he turned to the Ensigns. "Thank you, Sirs. I can handle it from here. That's why they have me escorting him." When the Ensigns wandered back to the mess hall, Sgt. Jeffreys turned to Mark. "Can you walk, or do you want me to call Sick Bay for a stretcher?"

Mark was still lying on the floor. He looked up confused. "Didn't you already call?"

"Oh, that," Sgt. Jeffreys laughed. "Didn't press the mic button. Faked it to get the butter bar's off our backs."

Mark managed a weak laugh. "Help me up." Once standing, Mark added, "I'd like to go back to my room. Maybe I can stay out of trouble there."

"Sure," Sgt. Jeffreys agreed. "Wait a minute," Sgt. Jeffreys called to a passing sailor. "There are two trays of food on a corner table on the left. I need you to get them and follow us. I can't carry them while assisting this VIP." The sailor complied and the three of them marched their way down to Mark's room. When they finally arrived, Mark collapsed on his bunk, relieved that no further incidents had occurred.

"Do you want company, or do you want me to wait outside?" Sgt. Jeffreys asked after placing the trays of food on the small table and dismissing the sailor.

"Are you kidding?" Mark asked in disbelief. "After all that you think I'm going to send you out in the corridor? Sit down and eat. You deserve it."

Despite his hunger, Mark was having trouble eating. He couldn't get his mind off the last vision and its probable consequence for the aviators had Sgt. Jeffreys not intervened. He couldn't tell anybody about the visions' impact on him or he would be locked up. But he could not, not tell either. The potential dire consequences were too great. He could not live with himself if he really hurt someone. Blaming it on the drugs was one idea. But that wouldn't work as the warning would go unheeded once the drugs wore off. A compromise position came to mind. "I appreciate you helping me out at the mess hall," Mark voiced tentatively.

Sgt. Jeffreys looked up from his meal. "I think I helped out the officers. I think they were about to get their butts whipped."

'I think they were going to get killed,' Mark thought, but did not say. Instead, he said, "They were going to get hurt. No question about it. I need your help with this. I am usually very laid back. But these visions have been wreaking havoc with my system. Everyone knows how exhausting they are. What no one knows, except perhaps you, is how hard they are on my self-control. My temper. I seem to get enraged very easily."

"I noticed."

"Yes. Well, you did exactly the right thing today. You protected me and protected those arrogant aviators. Although they'll never know it. I need you to keep doing that."

"Did they turn into aliens, like I did the first time?"

"Why do you ask?"

"Because it looked like you had one of your visions right before I tackled you."

"I still get some quick flashes or glimpses," Mark extemporized, not wanting to admit the influence of the cat visions. "Some so quick, I'm not sure what they are." Mark added. "Anyway, I appreciate your help."

"That's my job." After a few moments Sgt. Jeffreys added, "Perhaps we should order room service from now on rather than subjecting you to the crowds."

'Or the crowds to me,' Mark thought, but instead merely agreed. He would still have to be very careful with these cat visions. He also needed to tell the debriefers about these other aliens, perhaps after the next cube contact. He would tell them about the alien cats, but not let them know what triggered the visions or their consequences. 'So which alien was sending the visions?' Mark wondered. He had always assumed it was the blue-grays. But now that he was experiencing the cat visions, he wondered. He still didn't have an answer when he finished his meal and lay down on his bunk. "I think I'll rest for a while. It's been a long day."

"It's almost nineteen hundred hours," Sgt. Jeffreys replied. "You've been up all day. Except for your nap of course."

"My drug induced nap," Mark said irritably. "Was that just today? Seems like ages ago. But I'm beat. You can make yourself comfortable here, if you want. You don't need to stand outside."

Despite everything on his mind, Mark fell asleep. He dreamed about aliens and dinosaurs and driving trains through eggs, but it was all disjointed, nothing made sense. When he awoke, it took several minutes to shake the dreams from his consciousness. The last thing he could remember was a train traveling up a spiraling track in the sky with an egg as the sun. He lay in bed a while longer, letting his mind wander. Suddenly it clicked. He knew the answer. He sat up in bed and looked around. Sgt. Jeffreys was sitting in the corner reading a book. "I need a computer," Mark stated.

"A computer, what for?"

"I need to get on the Internet."

"You can't send any e-mail or get on any chat rooms, it's blocked when we're on maneuvers."

"I don't need to. I just need to get on Google to do some research. I think I figured something out, but I need to check it first."

"Okay. Let me see what I can do."

Twenty minutes later Mark was sitting at a computer console typing in a Google search, while Sgt. Jeffreys sat nearby watching. After an hour of research and printing several pages, Mark turned to Sgt. Jeffreys. "I can't believe I didn't get this before. It's so obvious."

Sgt. Jeffreys looked at the printed pages. "You think that's what they are doing?"

"It looked just like that."

"So what's it mean?"

"I don't know. But this is a start." After a moment, Mark added, "You think the Captain is available. I probably should tell him. See if he can come here so I can show him on the computer. But let him know it's not an emergency, just something I would like to show him if he has the time."

Mark was surprised when the Captain joined them within ten minutes. "I didn't mean to disturb you, but I think I figured something out."

"You're not disturbing me. There is an entire carrier task force sitting here in the middle of the ocean because of our friends downstairs and so far you are the only one who can contact them. So, no. I wouldn't say you are disturbing me." The Captain laughed. "So, what have you found?"

"I think I figured out what the aliens were doing in one of my visions," Mark responded excitedly. "Look at this. I found a picture on the internet of the railroad tracks I saw in the blue-gray science room."

The Captain looked at the printed picture. "This is what you saw in your vision?"

"Not exactly, but really close to that. It has to be the same thing."

"This is a very odd railroad track. What is it?"

"The caption's on the second page," Mark answered.

The Captain turned to the second page and read: "Electron Microscope View of DNA."

"That's why I didn't recognize it," Mark explained. "Most pictures that we see of DNA are simply models. Smooth double helixes. But that is what it really looks like. Actually, this view is flattened because of the way the slide has to be prepared for the electron microscope, but the irregularities and striations are accurate. I was watching the blue-grays gene-splice. They were traveling up a DNA strand, changing its composition. That has to be it. I told you I thought I was looking in a microscopic view by the way the scene blurred. I'll bet you anything that the egg in the vision was being gene spliced."

"Whose egg was it?" the Captain asked.

"That I don't know. It could've been theirs. They may be egg laying creatures."

"So why were they gene-splicing?"

"Hey. You only get one answer today. I didn't say I solved the whole thing. I just figured out one part. You have to wait a while longer for me to figure out the rest of it. Or, are you someone who reads the end of a book first to find out what happens." Mark responded.

"I'd like to jump to the back of this book," the Captain retorted.

"So would I," Mark agreed. "But it probably wouldn't make any sense unless we went through it chapter by chapter. It's not like the end will say: 'The butler did it.'"

"You're probably right," the Captain agreed. "Can you write this up in a format I can send off to Washington?"

"Already working on it," Mark answered, pointing to a document on the screen. "Give me a few more minutes to clean it up and you'll have it."

"Thanks. By the way," the Captain added. "When you're done, you may want to swing by Sick Bay. The Doc is talking to Guam. She may have an update on your blood work for you soon."

"I'll do that."

CHAPTER 13

It took over an hour for Mark to finish drafting his report on the DNA findings and get down to Sick Bay. He was greeted by a corpsman that he did not recognize, who curtly informed him that sick call was at 0600 and unless he had an emergency, he would have to return at that time. Laughing, Mark turned to Sgt. Jeffreys, "Why is everyone being so friendly today?" Turning back to the corpsman he said, "Please tell the doctor that the Captain sent Mark Williams down here and if she has a free minute I would like to speak to her."

Predictably, it did not take long before Mark was ushered into the doctor's office, while Sgt. Jeffreys took station outside her door. Mark got right to the point. "The Captain said that you were talking with Guam. I was wondering if I had a clean bill of health and if I can contact the cube again?"

"The last blood work was clean," the doctor stated. "You should be okay. However, I can't guarantee there will not be lingering effects. These drugs are not completely understood and, of course, I have no idea how the cube works or what it does."

"They did brief you about the cube?" Mark asked.

"Yes, after you showed up here unconscious, they had to."

"So when can I resume contact?"

"That's really between you and the Captain, isn't it? Now that Doctors Ballinger and Smith are gone." Mark noted that she said 'doctors' grudgingly.

"I know that we kind of got off on the wrong foot," Mark replied. "Which was probably my fault. I try to avoid doctors. But as I do end up down here every time I touch the cube, I might as well start here. I also appreciate your concern when those bozos administered that drug. Anyway, I guess what I am saying is, if you have any suggestions on how to continue doing this, I am willing to listen."

The doctor considered for a moment. "I really do not know what they were looking for with all that monitoring."

"I don't think they knew," Mark interjected.

"Probably not," the doctor conceded. "But from a truly medical perspective, I do not need all of that monitoring. It probably wouldn't hurt to monitor basic vitals. That could give us a warning if something odd was occurring. In an abundance of caution I might suggest that we keep a vein open in case of an emergency. But I know your dislike of IV's and I can't say it's a medical necessity."

Mark winced at the reminder of the corpsman incident, but chose to sidestep the issue. "You're right, I don't care for needles."

"That's all I can think of. I don't believe the monitoring provided any useful information. But of course, I'm not a UFO expert." They both laughed at that.

"Thank God you're not. I would really worry if you were. Okay, I'll check with the Captain. I would like to make contact again as soon as possible. I can't wait to find out what happens next."

An hour later Mark was lying on the hospital bed hooked up to some basic monitors, with the doctor, the Captain and Sgt. Jeffreys in attendance. "Well here goes; wish me luck," Mark said as he reached over and touched the cube.

He was enveloped in the pilot's chair with several new overlapping views floating in thin air above him. One showed blue sky above him, marred only by white, wispy, cirrus clouds. Every few seconds a spaceship would shoot up and disappear in the distance. A second view showed the habitat, which still had a few blue-grays running from it carrying various containers. A third view materialized, dark, with alien symbols scrolling down one side. His host moved his fingers slightly and lines appeared, accompanied by more symbols. There appeared to be a dark round object in the center of the view. The view pulled back and more symbols appeared along with another round object. A line connected the objects and more symbols appeared next to the line. Yet a fourth view materialized, overlapping the others. It was covered with alien symbols that flowed and flashed. His host was moving his fingers and toes slightly, almost like typing, as the symbols continued to flow. Mark longed to look down at 'his' feet to see what they looked like, but of course he could not control the memory.

Without warning or any sense of motion, the habitat receded as he took off. In seconds, he was soaring above the ground, staring down at the shrinking continent. His attention was torn between the view of the sky, which was quickly going from blue to black as altitude increased, and the view of the receding planet. The planet was beautiful; bright green forests against a dazzling blue ocean, more water than land. There was a giant plume of smoke in the distance, perhaps a fire or maybe a volcano. The view of the sky filled with stars as they exited the atmosphere, while the planet filled the view on the other screen. Another view blinked into existence, showing undecipherable symbols against a view of the sky.

Giving up on trying to understand the symbols, Mark turned his attention back to the planet, which almost completely filled the second view. An object appeared in the upper right portion of the view, headed down towards the planet. Another spaceship? Mark wondered. But it did not look like any of the ships he had seen taking off. It was roughly circular, although pockmarked and tumbling. It was quickly engulfed in a blaze of fire as it encountered the atmosphere and streaked towards the planet, leaving a long fiery trail before it impacted.

The resulting explosion was like watching a nuclear bomb go off, but much bigger. A giant cloud began to form at the impact site, while concentric circles of force raced across the water and land, destroying everything in their path. He continued to watch, mesmerized, as the mushroom cloud grew, covering an enormous expanse. As the planet receded in the view screen, the mushroom cloud continued to grow, larger and larger, still visible from this distance.

As the view drifted, Mark noted another meteor flare as it entered the atmosphere, streaking towards the planet. This one appeared even larger than the first. The impact will be gigantic, Mark realized. Then another object, much closer and very bright swung into the view screen, and the vision ended.

Mark opened his eyes and the Sick Bay materialized in front of him. "Oh my God," he gasped, before passing out.

CHAPTER 14

Mark woke up slowly, feeling drugged, and momentarily panicked at the thought. Opening his bleary eyes, the room came into focus without any of the distortions from the previous drugs. He saw Sgt. Jeffreys sitting in his usual chair, reading a book. Mark glanced at his arms, no IV's. 'Probably just exhausted,' he reasoned. As usual, his throat felt like parchment. He tried to speak, but only a moan escaped his lips. Sgt. Jeffreys was at his side in an instant, a glass of water and straw in his hands. Mark gratefully felt the cool liquid slide down his parched throat, licked his dry lips, and drank some more. "How long?" Mark whispered.

"You've been out about six hours," Jeffreys replied, glancing at his watch. "It's fourteen-twenty hours, Friday afternoon."

The doctor walked in and glanced at the monitors. "How are we feeling?"

Mark was too tired to be irritated by the royal we. "Drugged."

"No one drugged you," the doctor replied emphatically.

"Figure of speech," he explained. "How about, like I've been run over by a truck."

"We haven't done that to you either," the doctor replied. Mark smiled. Perhaps he had been too hard on the doctor earlier as it appeared she had a sense of humor. "Would you like some Gatorade or Jell-O?" the doctor was asking. "That will get you going until you're ready for a real meal." Mark nodded. "I'll send some in. Now, I've got to notify the Captain that you're back with us."

Mark gasped as the details of the vision suddenly rushed back to him. "I need to talk to him now."

He hadn't fully recovered when the Captain arrived a few minutes later. "How are you doing?"

Mark waved aside the question. "Okay," he answered absently. "The vision, I need to tell you about the vision," he added urgently. "They were escaping the planet. Asteroids, huge asteroids, were striking it. The explosions. Huge explosions! That's what the blue-grays were escaping from. Oh my God!" The words tumbled out.

The Captain glanced at Sgt. Jeffreys with a look of concern and then back at Mark. "Okay, calm down. Take it easy." Mark took a deep breath and tried to relax. "Now, slow down and tell me what you saw," the Captain instructed.

Mark took another deep breath and forced himself to speak slowly. "The vision started where the other one left off. I was in the pilot seat of a spaceship, sitting on the ground next to the habitat. It was still being evacuated and other spaceships were taking off all around me. We launched and I watched as we took off. I saw the habitat, and the jungle and the ocean and finally I could see the entire planet as we entered space. It was a lot like Earth, blue oceans, white clouds, and green land. The continents were not exact, but they were pretty recognizable. We launched from what looked like North America, but it wasn't quite right. The middle was under water. And Mexico did not attach to South America. Africa was perfect, but Europe was flooded. I don't know. It looked so much like Earth, but then it didn't. No sign of civilization.

"And then something shot past us in space, heading down to the planet. It was huge. I think it was an asteroid. It blazed into the atmosphere and hit. On Earth it would be in the southern part of the Gulf of Mexico. There was a huge explosion, like the largest nuclear bomb you could imagine. We were already in space, traveling fast, so the view kept getting smaller. But I could still see the blast wave and the mushroom cloud expanding. By then it had covered the entire Gulf of Mexico and was still expanding. As we sped away, another asteroid was streaking down, this one even bigger. It was going to hit somewhere in the Pacific, near Asia, if we use my Earth analogy. The vision ended as we were passing another planet, it looked like a moon, barren, white and pockmarked. No atmosphere. My God, I watched a planet being destroyed and I think it was the Earth!" Mark ended, getting agitated again.

The Captain looked shocked, but managed to keep his voice calm. "Relax, we're still here. You watched a scene from the cube. The Earth hasn't been destroyed."

Mark lay back, trying to catch his breath.

"Was this the same jungle with the dinosaurs?" Sgt. Jeffreys asked.

"Yes, but I…" There was a long pause. "Dinosaurs," Mark repeated, lost in thought. "Weren't they wiped out…"

"… by an asteroid," Sgt. Jeffreys finished. "I studied everything about them when I was a kid," he explained.

"Dinosaurs were millions of years ago," Mark objected.

"About a hundred million years ago," Sgt. Jeffreys corrected.

"We need to get this new information to Washington," the Captain stated. "Are you up for a conference call?"

"How long will it take you to set it up?"

"Probably an hour or so," the Captain estimated as he glanced at his watch and calculated the time difference. "Maybe a little longer."

"I'll be ready. But first I need to call room service."

"Right," the Captain laughed. "You're lucky we are not charging you for these meals. You'd owe the Navy a fortune by now." As he left, he turned to Sgt. Jeffreys, "I'll call you when I have the conference call scheduled. Take care of him. Probably should keep him here. Have whatever he wants delivered." He turned to Mark, "I think it's better if you conserve your energy right now. This will probably be a long session."

"No complaints from me," Mark agreed, but for an entirely different reason. He was more afraid of the possibility of another cat vision incident in his exhausted condition.

As it was, it took two and a half hours to set up the conference. The break allowed Mark to finally eat a leisurely meal and recover from his last vision. It also gave him some time to ponder the implications of what he had seen. When the conference finally started, he still had not figured it out. "Let me describe for you what I just saw," Mark stated and then explained in as much detail as he could what had transpired in the last vision, ending it with his concern that it looked a lot like Earth, although a slightly different Earth. Silence followed, broken finally by a myriad of voices, all asking questions. One voice, which Mark considered the moderator, overrode the others and brought order to the conference.

"Are you sure it was the Earth?" the first person asked.

"I'm not sure. The characteristics of the continents were very similar, although with the differences I noted. But it was immediately recognizable at first glance as the Earth. It was only when you looked closer at the details that you realized they were a bit off."

"Are you certain that the planet was the same one that had the dinosaurs?"

Mark thought for a moment before responding. "I cannot say that it absolutely was. But I am assuming it was." He held up his hand to stop the objections that started with the last comment. "Let me tell you what I base my assumption upon and you can decide for yourself whether it's valid. First, my host in the dinosaur visions feels like the same host in the habitat systems. Remember, I am seeing through his eyes, so I cannot see him. But it feels like the same host. Now granted, I have only been in a limited number of visions, but the others felt slightly different. So I'm assuming it's the same alien in both sets of visions.

"Second, the jungle I viewed in the dinosaur visions appears to be the same type of jungle when we left the habitat. Again, I was not able to analyze it, so I cannot conclusively say it was the same. But it did appear to be the same. Third, and this is probably the weakest scientific reason, these visions feel like they are coming in a chronological order. The sequence goes as follows: first, the dinosaurs hunting and failing to capture their prey. Second, the blue-grays are apparently gene-splicing an egg. I'm now assuming it is a dinosaur's egg. The next sequence shows another set of dinosaurs, presumably the offspring of the gene-splicing experiment, hunting in a pack and this time using very sophisticated and coordinated hunting techniques. We then have the blue-gray aliens evacuating the base just before it is destroyed. That's the chronology."

"You're making huge assumptions that are not supported by what you have seen. There is no evidence that these were dinosaurs, that they were gene-splicing or that this was even the Earth."

"It's a bunch of rubbish," another voice added. "Just fabrication."

Mark took a deep breath to quell his irritation before he responded. "I don't mind if you disagree with my interpretation, but I take offense at the suggestion that I am making this up," Mark responded as calmly as he could. "I have been very careful to tell you exactly what I have seen, and qualified my observations when I was not sure of the details. And I have also been very careful to tell you when I am interpreting or theorizing about events, so you know it is my personal opinion, rather than something I actually saw. Remember, I didn't ask to come to this party. I was invited, rather emphatically at that. I'm not some nut case off the street yelling the sky is falling. So when you can explain how a lawyer, with no engineering background, built a spaceship, launched it into space without anyone detecting it, then maneuvered it back down to Earth while NORAD watched, streaked down to the ocean, stopped and hovered, and then out-maneuvered one of your hunter-killer subs, then you can call me a liar."

An uncomfortable silence followed, broken finally by a new voice from the video. "Gentlemen, perhaps I can shed some light on this."

"Yes, Dr. Benson, why don't you introduce yourself and present your findings?" the moderator instructed.

"Ahh, right. My name is Dr. Gerald Benson. I'm a paleontologist and professor at the University of California, Berkeley. I was asked to attend this meeting based upon your description of the dinosaurs in your earlier... visions. I was provided transcripts of your prior conferences and asked to provide my theory on the type of creatures that you were describing. I was told that they were probably an alien species, but they figured my expertise with our dinosaurs would provide me with a good basis to make assumptions about this new alien species. However, after this last vision of Mr. Williams, this request is probably moot. But since there still appears to be some disagreement over whether this is Earth, let me review a few points with Mr. Williams. Now, Mr. Williams, let me show you a few pictures. If the cameraman can get these. Can you see them?"

Mark looked at the screen. "Can you zoom in a little? Ok, there. I see it."

"All right, are any of these creatures the ones that you saw?"

Mark studied the pictures. "I would say it was the second picture. I can't say it was definitely that one. But it looks real close. I never saw the feet."

"What about the second group of dinosaurs, what you referred to as the prey? Any of these pictures match them?" the doctor asked as he presented several more pictures.

"It could have been any of the three on my right, your left. I really don't see much difference in them. The other two are not it."

"You have picked out dinosaurs from our late Cretaceous period, a period that ended sixty-five million years ago. The predators are in fact velociraptors. Their fossils have been found in Asia and in Montana; the

Montana ones being smaller, about three feet tall, while the Asian ones are about six feet tall. The fossil record puts their habitat in desert areas, though, not jungle. However, based upon our study of the fossil record, they did hunt in packs and probably communicated with each other rather extensively. The fossil record easily supports the first vision you recounted. The second vision I can't support or refute from the fossil record. Although it does seem to be too sophisticated for what we believe these creatures could do, particularly the last part where they cornered and killed the remaining prey before eating."

"That's where I wondered if the gene-splicing wasn't related," Mark suggested. "But I'm just trying to make sense out of all the visions."

"Perhaps. That is out of my area," Dr. Benson conceded.

"But that doesn't mean anything," a voice objected. "It's not proof."

"I agree," Dr. Benson stated. But this last vision provides further evidence that Mr. Williams was viewing Cretaceous era creatures." A number of angry retorts ensued, which Dr. Benson ignored. "Let me explain. Mr. Williams, can you tell me what the area around Texas looked like?"

"There wasn't a Texas. And Florida was missing too. But the east and west coasts were there with a giant lake, no it was connected to the Gulf, taking up the middle states. The west coast connected down to Mexico, but there was a gap before South America. And I definitely saw Africa and Greenland."

"Were there ice caps on the north and south poles?" Dr. Benson asked next.

Mark thought for a moment. "No. No, I don't remember seeing any ice caps. Just blue. No white except clouds."

"Hold on a second," the doctor said as he typed something into his laptop. After a few moments, he spun the laptop towards the camera. "Is this something like what you saw?"

Mark studied the display on the laptop. "Yes, that's it. That's it exactly!" he responded enthusiastically.

"That's a computer model of what we believe the earth looked like sixty-five million years ago, at the end of the Cretaceous period, before the continents moved into their current positions. The climate was warmer, there were no ice caps, and water covered much of North America and Europe.

"But why choose sixty-five million years ago?" someone asked.

"Because of the asteroids, the doctor explained. "Mr. Williams described seeing two asteroids hit the earth, one hitting in the lower Gulf of Mexico. It actually hit near the Yucatan peninsula, leaving a crater one hundred and ten miles in diameter." Dr. Benson paused while his comment sunk in.

"What? How do you know?" someone asked.

"Mr. Williams is describing the Chicxulub crater, which was discovered by Dr. Penfield in the late 1970's.

It is centered near the town of Chicxulub in the Yucatan Peninsula and isotope analysis dates the impact back sixty-five million years ago, the end of the Cretaceous period. It is estimated that the bolide, or meteor as laymen usually refer to them, was about six miles in diameter. This impact also coincides with the K-T extinction event, which was a mass extinction of half of all the plants and animals on Earth. It was also the end of the dinosaurs. The K-T event can be seen in the rock strata as a thin band of sedimentation and is found throughout the world. All of this is undisputed fact. It has been theorized the K-T extinction was caused by the Chicxulub bolide and its catastrophic effect on the planet."

Dr. Benson was in full lecture mode. "Some scientists, however, argue that Chicxulub was not big enough to cause such a mass extinction. In 2009, a team of researchers led by Sankar Chatterjee of Texas Tech University studied the Shiva basin, which is a large submerged depression west of India. He submitted a paper to the Geological Society of America theorizing that this was evidence of an impact from a bolide approximately twenty-five miles in diameter, about four times the size of the Chicxulub bolide, leaving a basin five hundred kilometers in diameter. He believes that this impact vaporized the Earth's crust at the impact point and created new plate tectonics in the region. He believes this impact coincided with Chicxulub and the two combined created the huge anomalies and climate shift that resulted in the K-T extinction. The Shiva basin research is still new, although it is gaining acceptance in the scientific community. What Mr. Williams witnessed," Dr. Benson concluded, "coincides with the K-T extinction line and provides, at least for me, sufficient proof that he was viewing dinosaurs of the late Cretaceous period here on Earth and then the Chicxulub and Shiva bolides."

Once again there was silence as the audience considered these shocking statements. Then the questions started. Fortunately, they were directed at Dr. Benson, so Mark just sat back and listened, while trying to make sense of the whole thing. It was nice to have someone else at the center of attention for a change, particularly when he was supporting Mark's reports rather than calling him a liar. Mark sat back and listened as the conversation flowed back and forth as proponents of various theories made their points, only to be shot down by the other listeners.

As Mark listened, he wondered if it would be better with fewer scientists in the audience and more science fiction writers. The scientists were so rigid in their analysis. They were unable to accept novel theories or facts if they could not immediately subject them to scientific proof. Whereas science fiction writers had been drafting theories about aliens for years and oftentimes were writing about technology that was only a few years out. Mark sat back and relaxed, really only half listening to the various conversations. One comment did catch his attention when a speaker noted that only two dinosaurs had shown up in the visions. 'I am going to have to tell them about the cat visions,' Mark realized, having forgotten that he never mentioned them to the group, of course for a very good reason. He would need to do it soon or they would wonder what else he might be hiding. He tried to figure out how best to reveal this information without anyone figuring out the incredible impact these visions had on him. The real danger there of course was Sgt. Jeffreys. After few moments he came up with a solution. Leaning over towards the Captain, he whispered, "If you have no objection, I would like to send Sgt. Jeffreys down to get me a sandwich. It looks like this meeting will last forever and I'm starving. Would you like anything?"

"That's fine. No thank you, I don't need anything."

Mark motioned over to Sgt. Jeffreys. "Would you run down to the Officer's Mess and get me a sandwich and a Coke, and whatever you may want?" Mark watched Sgt. Jeffreys leave and checked his watch. He probably had ten to fifteen minutes before Sgt. Jeffreys returned. He waited for a couple of minutes after Sgt. Jeffreys left so the timing of his comment would not obviously coincide with Sgt. Jeffreys departure, just in case the Captain had any further lingering suspicions about the corpsman incident. When there was a break in the conversation, he jumped in. "What I don't understand is why the two sets of visions I receive don't track?" That caused a pause in the conversation.

"What two sets of visions?" a voice asked.

"Well, one set of visions has been coming from the memory cube, which we have spent all our time talking about," Mark explained. "But the first set of visions came from my contact in the submarine. They started before we had these conference calls. Those visions used to really take me out, but as I got I used to them, they would come and go in a blink of an eye. They're very disjointed and only last a second or two. But what I mean about not tracking is that they do not appear to be in the jungle, or in the habitat. They are completely different. I've even seen different aliens in them. You would think they would send the same set of visions in the memory cube if..."

Mark didn't finish his sentence before someone interrupted, "What other alien, another blue-gray?"

"What?" Mark asked. "Oh, I've received glimpses of several other blue-grays, but also some type of cat creature." Mark noticed the Captain glance over at him as a barrage of questions was asked. "Okay, for those who don't already know," Mark continued. "I started receiving visions immediately after the submarine encounter. What I think occurred is that the blue-grays sent me a huge telepathic vision, for lack of any better term, while I was in the submarine. I couldn't receive it properly. In fact it knocked me out. Ever since then I have had very brief, one or two second, random visions that I believe are remnants from the submarine encounter. My face in the mirror turned into a blue-gray, a couple crewmen standing together in the mess hall turned into blue-grays, a corridor in the ship turned into an alien corridor, not the habitat corridor, but clearly alien. Like I said, the visions only last a second or two and have no relation with the visions I have been receiving from the cube.

"The most recent non-cube visions have involved a new creature, which I refer to as a cat since it has fur, four legs, a tail and claws. They are about the same size as a blue-gray and can walk either on two or four legs equally well. They appear to be captives of the blue-grays, but whether they are a sentient race or equivalent to, say a tiger, I don't know. In the very short visions I have seen them in, they have no clothes or other evidence of civilization, if you will. But they appear to be quite intelligent. How intelligent I do not know. They hate the blue-grays, though. I've seen them, I think twice. Both times they were trying to escape from the blue-grays. But now I'm giving you my analyses. This is what I saw.

"The first vision, which lasted about two seconds, started with two of these cat-like aliens. One had apparently been immobilized by the blue-grays. The second was crouched, ready to spring, claws extended. A blue-gray stepped up behind the crouching cat and raised a weapon, which looked like a metal rod about one foot long and about an inch thick. He shot the crouching cat with a lightening bolt. And the vision ended. I do not know what happened next. I don't know if the lightening acted like a Taser, simply incapacitating, or if it kills. It certainly sounded loud, like a transformer shorting out or high-voltage arcing. If it acted like it sounded, then it would have killed the cat.

"The next vision was a cat running down a corridor on all fours. It rounded a corner and met two blue-grays armed with those rods. One blue-gray shot at the cat, but missed. The cat jumped and sank its claws in the second blue-gray's head. The vision ended then. I suspect it tore the blue-gray's head off, judging by the speed, but I don't know. These cats do not look terrestrial. I say tiger-like only to give an impression. If you saw them on TV in no other context, you would think you were watching some type of science fiction movie. They resemble tigers only in the sense that they have four legs, tail, fur and claws. Their shape and movement are completely wrong."

The questions came quickly, which Mark answered, always avoiding providing any time frame for the visions. He did not want anyone to match them up to the fights, so he just left the time vague. He never mentioned the first cat vision in Sick Bay. No sense going there, too risky. He looked nervously at his watch. Sgt. Jeffreys would come back shortly and would most likely figure out the context of the visions. He answered the questions as quickly as he could, trying to satisfy each questioner without encouraging more questions, all the while watching the door for Sgt. Jeffreys return. They were still asking about the cats when Sgt. Jeffreys entered, so Mark tried to divert the group's attention back to the dinosaur question.

"But getting back to my initial question, why don't the visions track?" Mark interjected. "Since the blue-grays are clearly aliens, I always assumed the dinosaurs were also. Obviously, I've had a lot of time to think about the dinosaurs. Before this last vision, I concluded that the dinosaurs were aliens on an alien planet. After all, if the blue-grays were conducting gene-splicing on the dinosaurs sixty-five million years ago, then they would have had sixty-five million years of evolution before being here today. Look how much our technology has changed in the last fifty years. In sixty-five million years the blue-gray evolution and technology would be godlike. So why would they be lurking down in the Mariana Trench? It makes no sense.

"My second hypothesis, again assuming that the blue-grays were present 65 million years ago, was that they could time travel, perhaps in a wormhole or black hole. But there again, with the technological ability to do that, why are they at the bottom of the ocean? And why can't they communicate with us. Again, it makes no sense. So, I concluded that we must have been watching events from another planet. Of course, now that I've had this last vision and Dr. Benson has educated us about the K-T event, I have to rethink my hypotheses.

"There is another possible explanation, one that was mentioned after the first contact, that none of this is real. I'm watching the equivalent of a documentary, a movie. In that case it means the blue-grays are not over sixty-five million years old or time travelers and what I am watching is pure fiction. But then the question remains, why are they sending this?" The last question sent his audience arguing the pros and cons of the various theories, while Sgt. Jeffreys discreetly brought over his meal.

"Did I miss anything?" Sgt. Jeffreys asked in a whisper.

"Endless questions and arguments. I did tell them about the cats."

"Cats?"

"Didn't I tell you?" Mark tried to answer casually. "I glimpsed a catlike creature in one of those brief visions I still get after the submarine encounter. I'll give you the details when we get out of here." Mark bit into his sandwich, hoping that he had managed to provide the group with the cat vision, without jeopardizing his position by confessing the impact it had on him. The conference finally broke up with various individuals deciding to establish working groups to further consider the events.

"That was over three hours!" Mark complained as he and the Captain exited the conference room. "That was more exhausting than the vision itself."

"You've never worked in the Pentagon, have you?" the Captain responded.

"No. When the Army decided to bring me back stateside, I decided to get out instead. I can only take so much bureaucracy. I've been with small firms ever since."

"Must be nice."

"I've enjoyed it. Of course I don't get to play with Uncle Sam's toys anymore, like you do."

"Yes, there are some benefits," the Captain agreed. "Speaking of toys, are you intending to contact the cube this evening or would you like to wait till tomorrow. We have been going at this pretty long."

"I thought I would get some rest first. That conference was really taxing. I don't want to contact the cube already tired."

"That's probably a good idea. Go hit your rack. Let me know when you're ready to go again. I must admit, as confusing as this is, I can't wait to see what they send next."

"Me, too. Although I wish they'd send something that makes sense of it all."

"And soon," the Captain agreed. "If we stay on station here much longer, we're going to be getting a lot more attention, not all of it welcome. I would like to resolve this little mystery of ours, before some of the locals start snooping around."

"Locals?"

"It's a big ocean out here, lots of potential company. Russians, Chinese, Koreans, just to name a few."

"I hadn't thought of that. I've been so busy concentrating on our friends downstairs."

"You continue to do that. I get paid to worry about the locals, not you."

"You can have that job. I'll try to hurry my side up. I probably could get away with just a nap," Mark suggested.

"No. You're doing fine. Take all the time you need. You need to be well rested. I've seen what those visions do to you. Besides, we don't let our pilots fly without sleep. No sense treating our civilian passengers worse than that."

"Okay. I will consider it your direct order to go to bed."

The Captain laughed. "Let me know when you're ready. Now I've got to catch up on the work that meeting kept me from doing." With that he headed upstairs, while Sgt. Jeffreys escorted Mark back to his room.

Mark told Sgt. Jeffreys about the cat visions on their way back to his room, carefully omitting any reference to a time frame or how the visions affected him emotionally so Sgt. Jeffreys would not figure out what prompted the fights. As anxious as he was to see the next vision, Mark forced himself to at least take a nap before he tried the cube again. As he lay on his bed, he realized that he had not called home. He thought of asking Sgt. Jeffreys to set up the call, but then guiltily decided to call later. Sleep came quickly.

CHAPTER 15

Mark awoke slowly. He lay there in that wonderful dreamy neverland before life's demands start intruding on your consciousness. He opened an eye and experienced a moment of disorientation when he realized he was in a small, gray room, not his own comfortable bedroom. Events flooded in and he came fully awake. He glanced around the room. How can you tell what time of day it is without a window, he thought. The clock on the wall read 4:32. Was that a.m. or p.m., he wondered? Climbing out of bed, he opened the door to the corridor and a Marine snapped to attention. "Good morning, Mr. Williams," he barked.

"Huh, morning," Mark responded, not very officially. Okay, one question answered, morning. "Where's Sgt. Jeffreys?"

"He's off, Sir. But I have orders to call him when you wake up," the Marine responded as he reached for his radio.

Mark considered telling the Marine to wait until a more reasonable time, but he was wide-awake and figured he might as well get the day started. "Okay. Tell him I'm up and hungry. I need some breakfast."

"Yes, sir."

Mark stepped back into his room, amazed at how this trip and the cube was wreaking havoc with his biorhythms. One moment he was a night owl, now an early bird. When this was all over, he would probably have to sleep for a week before he got his rhythm back. Looking at the clock, Mark figured he probably had time for a quick shower before Sgt. Jeffreys arrived. As it was, he was showered, shaved and dressed, before he heard a knock on the door. "Entrez," he called out.

"Room service," Sgt. Jeffreys announced as he walked in with a tray of food. "The Captain was concerned that our civilian passenger would give us a bad travel guide rating, so he sends this with his compliments. You did say you wanted breakfast, didn't you?"

"Sure did! I'm starving."

"Good, because I brought you breakfast, bagels, eggs, bacon, hash browns," Sgt. Jeffreys identified the entrees as he unloaded the tray onto the small table.

"Since when do waiters wear BDU's?" Mark asked with mock horror after Sgt. Jeffreys had finished laying out the platters.

"The Navy folks were all busy, they're the ones who wear the whites."

"Good gracious!" Mark said.

Sgt. Jeffreys looked up quickly, brow furrowed.

"Where are the grits?" Mark continued. "You're serving a southerner breakfast without grits! This is cruel and unusual punishment. You'll lose your travel rating for certain now."

"Don't tell the Captain. He tried so hard," Sgt. Jeffreys responded, unsuccessfully trying to keep the smile off his face.

"Captain? He'll be busted down to swabbie after this debacle," Mark deadpanned, before they both started laughing. After catching his breath and piling food on his plate Mark asked, "So what's the schedule today?"

"Today? You slept through most of it!"

"It's five o'clock in the morning," Mark replied defensively, glancing at the clock on the wall.

"That's the problem with you Army types," Sgt. Jeffreys tried to deadpan. "You think five o'clock is early. Half the day is gone already."

"I'm a civilian," Mark responded. "And we civilians need our beauty rest after all."

"Sure, sleeping beauty, anything you say."

"That's it, next time I book with the Carnival cruise line; I bet their waiters are a lot nicer to their customers."

Sgt. Jeffreys laughed. "I can't believe you're dissing Navy cruise lines. The Captain will be so disappointed. But to answer your original question, Captain says that once you eat, if you're ready, you can make another contact. Timeframe is yours."

"Don't tell me that the Captain is already up," Mark said.

"Oh, I bet he has been up for a while," Sgt. Jeffreys replied.

"Okay, tell him I can be in Sick Bay in about," Mark paused, "Say, forty-five minutes. That should give us plenty of time. I'd like a leisurely meal for a change."

Sgt. Jeffreys pulled out his radio and made the report, before helping himself to some more food.

Forty minutes later Sgt. Jeffreys and Mark walked into Sick Bay and were immediately ushered into Mark's normal room. "Doctor Martins will be with you shortly," a corpsman reported. "She is finishing up with a patient."

"Oh damn!" Mark said.

"What?" Sgt. Jeffreys asked.

"I forgot to call my wife again. She is going to kill me. I wonder if we can set up a quick call…" The rest of the sentence was interrupted by Dr. Martins walking in.

"You ready for another adventure?" Dr. Martins asked.

"As ready as I'll ever be," Mark replied. Turning to Sgt. Jeffreys, he added, "Remind me to call Beth when we are done here."

"You mean when you wake up afterwards," Sgt. Jeffreys corrected.

"Yes, then," Mark said. "She is going to kill me."

"Do you want to do it the same way as before, with the monitors?" Dr. Martins asked, ignoring the side conversation with Sgt. Jeffreys. "Or do you want to skip it?"

"I don't care," Mark truthfully responded. "As long as it doesn't involve needles, I'm fine. Or drugs," Mark hastily added.

"Might as well do the monitors," the doctor decided. "It's easy to set up and doesn't hurt anything." Mark stripped off his shirt and lay on the bed, allowing technicians to attach leads to the various monitors. As they were finishing, the Captain arrived with another officer carrying a lock box containing the cube. The room still felt crowded when the unauthorized personnel departed, leaving the Captain, the doctor and Sgt. Jeffreys crowded around Mark's bed.

"That thing doesn't bite," Mark joked as he watched the Captain unlock the box and without touching it himself, use tongs to carefully place the cube next to Mark.

"It seems to bite you pretty good sometimes," the Captain replied. "Sucks out all your energy."

"Yea, I guess it does," Mark agreed.

"Have a good trip," the Captain instructed. "See if you can figure out what our friends are trying to tell us."

"I will. I just wish they'd stop being so obscure, I'm dying to figure out their message." With that Mark reached over and touched the cube.

Mark was back at the helm of his ship. That is, his host was. Once again he was sunk into the command chair as three separate scenes floated above him, two showing views of space, while the third contained unrecognizable alien symbols. Mark studied the displays, trying to locate the Earth or any recognizable reference point. In the distance a reddish hued planet slowly filled up one of the views. Another object entered his view, this one much closer. It was a silvery, oblong, like a flattened egg. On the wider ends there were two bright, pulsing orbs, one on each side of the ship, held away from the ship by slender supports that reminded Mark of flying buttresses on the Notre Dame in Paris. The engines? He couldn't tell its size without a frame of reference. As he approached and the ship filled his vision, he realized it was much larger than the ship he was in. His ship slowly approached and then rested against the larger ship before it slowly sank through the bigger ship's hull, just like the cubes had sunk through the top of the table. A few minutes later his ship was docked. The displays winked out of existence as his host disengaged from the chair, which seemed to re-inflate, pushing him out. Weightless, his host pushed off and floated down a shaft before exiting through an airlock into a corridor. Mark floated down several circular corridors before arriving in a small circular room with three chairs facing each other in a triangular formation. Two chairs were occupied, multiple views hovering above them. Mark's host floated through a star field as he headed for the empty chair. As he sank into it, additional scenes materialized above him.

Symbols swam above him as lines, curves, and other geometric shapes superimposed themselves upon the stars. Mark tried to make sense of what he was watching, but the scenes were too alien to decipher. A flash of light in one of the scenes caught his attention. Studying it carefully, he made out two, no, three ships in the star field. Two of the ships had graceful, curving designs, similar to the ship Mark had entered. The third ship was much smaller, but faster. It had a jagged design, like two parallel circular saw blades with eight giant flattened teeth, connected in the center by an angular black structure. The teeth pulsed with bright, purplish light.

A bolt of light flashed out from the jagged ship and skated across the blue-gray ship. The blue-gray ship glowed and the light disappeared, only to be replaced by another bolt. Mark stared, fascinated at the ongoing space battle. He watched as another jagged type ship shot past, firing several blasts of iridescent light. The view changed, showing another jagged ship near an asteroid. The asteroid had a ring of small glowing dots above it. The dots spread out until they formed a glowing halo above the asteroid. A moment later the asteroid disappeared into the halo, reappearing a moment later in another view above a white planet resembling Earth's moon. The asteroid sped towards the moon's surface and then impacted, sending up a huge cloud of debris.

The view shifted again, now showing a head on view of one of the jagged ships. Bolts of light shot out from it directly at the view screen. A number of the views flicked out of existence and an alarm sounded in the distance. The blue-grays appeared agitated as they worked on their controls. More views flicked out of existence. Alien symbols danced over Mark's head. The tension among the blue-grays was palpable, even without the missing 'emotion' channel. Suddenly, an explosion behind Mark's host sent debris shooting past his head, only to hit the wall and float back. Mark's seat spun so he faced the blasted airlock. A cat creature wearing a form-fitting suit, complete with a clear helmet and faceplate, leaped into the room. The cat pointed an object at the blue-gray next to Mark. A blinding white beam shot out and the blue-gray's head disappeared in a cloud of black particles as a snapping sound filled the air. Mark's host was still sitting as he brought up the metal rod Mark had seen used on the cats before, but not fast enough. The cat twisted in the air and brought its weapon to bear on Mark's host. A dazzling white light filled Mark's vision as a beam of light flicked towards him, hitting him in the chest. Time stopped, then searing pain flooded Mark's senses...

Sgt. Jeffreys had taken up his customary position in a chair in the corner of the room while Mark lay on the hospital bed with his hand resting on the cube. There was no telling how long these sessions would last so Sgt. Jeffreys had pulled a small paperback novel from his BDU cargo pocket and was reading. The key to life in the military, he reflected, was to know how to take advantage of down time. The Captain had left after Mark made contact and the doctor was tending to some other duties in Sick Bay, coming back occasionally to check on Mark. The only noise came from conversations in the other rooms, the hum of florescent ceiling lights, and the steady beep, beep, beep, of the cardiac monitor. Sgt. Jeffreys' book was not stimulating enough to overcome the hypnotic effect of the cardiac monitor and his eyes kept drooping. Suddenly, an alarm broke the hypnotic effect. Sgt. Jeffreys jumped up and stared at the monitor, its green screen showing a jagged saw tooth pattern, where before it had shown the classic sign of cardiac activity seen on billboards and sides of ambulances. The doctor ran in as Sgt. Jeffreys was processing what he was seeing.

"What did you do?" the doctor asked urgently, while checking the leads and the monitors.

"I didn't do anything. I was sitting in the corner when the alarm suddenly went off."

The doctor checked another lead and then felt for a pulse. "Code blue!" she shouted. "Get the crash cart." Sgt. Jeffreys was pushed out of the way as a group of corpsmen rushed in pushing a cart. The room filled with people and shouted commands as they worked on Mark. Sgt. Jeffreys moved around the people and secured the cube, placing it in the lock box before backing into the corner of the room where he could watch, but was out of the way. He pulled out his radio and called the command center, informing the watch officer to notify the Captain that Mr. Williams was in cardiac arrest. After that all he could do was watch and pray. He felt useless just standing there, but there was nothing he could do. He watched as one corpsman performed CPR, while another started an I.V. as the doctor readied the defibulator.

"Clear," the doctor shouted, as she positioned the paddles on Mark's chest. Mark's body jerked. All eyes watched the monitor. Nothing changed. "Clear," she shouted again after the paddles recharged. Mark jerked again, and once again all eyes went to the monitor as the paddles recharged. "Get me 10cc's of epinephrine," the doctor said. "Clear." She shocked him again. The green line on the monitor jumped. Everyone seemed to hold their breath as they waited. It jumped again, then again. Sgt. Jeffreys saw the doctor visibly relax as she handed the paddles to a nearby corpsman. Mark moaned. "Mr. Williams, Mr. Williams, can you hear me?" She asked. Mark moaned again and tried to move. "Mr. Williams lie still. It's okay. You've had an incident, but you're okay, you need to rest. Do you understand?"

Sgt. Jeffreys moved over so he could see Mark's face. Mark's eyes fluttered open and he seemed to take a moment to try to focus. "Chest hurts," he whispered as his free hand tried to rub his chest.

"I know, I know," the doctor responded. "It will be all right." She turned and started giving some instructions to a nearby corpsman.

"At war. Shot." Mark whispered, before losing consciousness.

The doctor looked back and then quickly checked the monitors. She noticed Sgt. Jeffreys standing nearby, looking concerned. "He's asleep. His vitals are strong now," she added, studying the monitor. "He needs to rest, regain his strength. We'll keep a good eye on him." She turned to the corpsmen and gave them some further instructions. After watching the monitors some more, she made a final check on her patient before stepping out of the room.

Sgt. Jeffreys heard the Captain's voice in the other room. He sounded out of breath. 'He must have sprinted down here,' Sgt. Jeffreys thought as he listened to the doctor explaining the situation. "I don't know what happened," the doctor was saying. "He was touching the cube when suddenly he went into v-fib. No warning at all. I reviewed the tape. There was a brief moment of increased heart activity, like he was excited or exercising and then he v-fibed. No idea why. We brought him back with the defibrillator and now he has strong cardiac rhythm. He's asleep, like he usually is after touching the cube. He should be fine after that. Except I don't know why he went into arrest. There is no obvious reason for it."

"Could the cube have caused it?" the Captain asked.

The doctor hesitated before answering. "I would think the cube had to have caused it. I can't say for sure, but someone his age and physical make up should not just v-fib while sleeping." Sgt. Jeffreys listed to them talk for a few minutes more, but the doctor could not provide any further information.

"Okay," Sgt. Jeffreys heard the Captain say. "Let me know the minute he wakes up."

"Yes, Sir."

The Captain stepped in to check on Mark and Sgt. Jeffreys snapped to attention. "Captain."

"Yes, Sergeant?"

"I have the cube. It's secured in its container," Sgt. Jeffreys held out the lock box for the Captain.

"Good thinking. I'll send someone down for it shortly."

"Yes, Sir. And Captain?"

"Yes?"

Sgt. Jeffreys lowered his voice so the corpsman attending to Mark would not overhear. "He did say something before he fell asleep."

"What?"

"He said his chest hurt."

"Yes, the doctor told me that."

"Yes, but after that, while the doctor was talking to a corpsman, Mr. Williams whispered: 'At war, shot.'"

"At war, shot?" the Captain repeated. "Are you sure?"

"Yes, Sir. I was standing this close," he motioned.

"Do you know what he meant?"

"No, Sir. That's all he said."

"I guess we'll have to wait for him to wake up. Stay with him. Notify me the second he wakes up."

"Yes, Sir."

"This certainly complicates things," the Captain added, more to himself as he turned to leave. Sgt. Jeffreys couldn't agree more.

CHAPTER 16

Once again Mark woke up feeling like a truck had run over him, or in this case, had parked on his chest. He moaned and absently rubbed at his chest. When he opened his eyes, Sgt. Jeffreys and the doctor were standing over him. He was about to say something when he remembered the vision. He gasped and grabbed his chest.

"Easy, easy," the doctor was saying as she and Sgt. Jeffreys held Mark down, both looking very concerned. Mark rubbed his chest, feeling skin rather than the gaping, charred hole he remembered. He relaxed as he distinguished reality from his vision and realized the doctor was waiting for a response.

"What?" he mumbled.

"How are you feeling?" the doctor repeated.

"You keep running me over with a truck," Mark complained, but managed a weak smile. While the doctor questioned him, Mark noticed that Sgt. Jeffreys was talking in hushed tones on the radio. He also noticed the I.V. in his arm.

"Before you pull that out," the doctor said quickly, noting Mark's irritated look at the IV. "Can I explain?"

Mark nodded. "You went into full cardiac arrest. We had to defibrillate you. You've been asleep since and your vitals are all now strong. You can take it out if you want, but I would recommend leaving it in a while longer. Until we are sure that you are back one hundred per cent."

Mark closed his eyes as he processed this new information. 'So the cube could be fatal,' he thought. 'Great, just another minor little complication.' Opening his eyes, he said, "Ok. How long have I been out this time?"

"About six hours," the Doctor replied, glancing at her watch.

"Can I at least sit up?" Mark asked. Maybe get something to eat?" They raised the bed up and started him off with Jell-O, promising something more substantial when he proved his system was working. He had taken several bites and was already feeling much better when the Captain came in and, after getting a nod from the doctor, stepped over to Mark.

"I see you're back. Gave us a bit of a fright," the Captain said. "Do you know what happened?"

"I was shot." When no one responded, Mark continued. "Shot in the chest by the cat alien. Hurt like hell, too. Blew my chest apart... and evidently stopped my heart from what the doctor is telling me," Mark added.

"Could that have caused it?" the Captain turned and asked the doctor.

"No idea," the doctor responded. "I don't know how that cube works. But there is no other medical reason for it. He's fit. It's possible it was shock. Or… I don't know," the doctor trailed off.

"How are you feeling now?" the Captain asked, noting that Mark was rubbing his chest.

"Oh, fine. I'm just relieved that I can feel my chest and not… a big hole." Mark went on to explain what he had seen in the vision. "This one was pretty easy to figure out," he continued. "There is a war going on between the blue-grays and the cats, who are clearly an intelligent race, by the way. There appeared to be a stellar battle around Mars. I'm guessing Mars based upon the reddish hue of the planet. And also near some asteroids. Someone, I'm assuming it was the cats, was sending asteroids to bombard the planet. I saw one fired at the moon. There were a number of space ships engaged in a battle, although it was pretty slow, not like *Star Wars*. Then the cats attacked the ship I was on. The cats boarded us, blew the door and stormed into the control room, shooting the blue-gray next to me and then shooting me in the chest. That's when the vision ended, when my host died."

"And so did you," Sgt. Jeffreys added in a whisper.

"And so did I," Mark repeated quietly. After a moment's reflection he added lightly, "I think the blue-grays will have to fix that little glitch if they want to replace our DVD's with their cube technology. Wouldn't do killing all your viewers every time they watch an action movie."

"No," the Captain agreed. "That would be a serious drawback. And speaking of viewers, are you up for a conference? A lot of folks are waiting to hear from you."

Mark stretched experimentally. "I'm tired. But I otherwise feel pretty good."

The Captain glanced at the doctor for confirmation. "I don't know," the doctor hesitated. "I would really like to keep him here a little longer, just to make sure. It was pretty close, and he arrested here where I could start working on him immediately."

"Okay," the Captain decided. "Why don't you stay here? We'll have you describe the whole thing again on video, which I will send to Washington so they can start chewing on it. Then, when you're ready, we can bring you in live to the conference. Doctor, does that sound satisfactory?"

"That'll work for me," she answered.

"Mark?"

"Sure."

"Sgt. Jeffreys," the Captain continued. "You stay here with our guest. I'll send someone down with the video equipment."

"And can I get some real food?" Mark asked, motioning with disgust at the Jell-O container.

"Now I know you're okay," the Captain answered, shaking Mark's shoulder. Mark thought of several retorts, but finally just smiled. He was still having trouble accepting the fact that the cube had killed him.

About thirty minutes later, Mark provided a very detailed account of the vision for the video from his hospital bed, with Sgt. Jeffreys off camera asking questions when needed to provide additional details. The video lasted almost an hour and Mark sank back in the bed exhausted, when the camera was finally turned off. He opted out of attending the conference and the doctor agreed with his decision. So instead, he and Sgt. Jeffreys ordered "room service," as Mark liked to call it, and enjoyed a meal of surf and turf brought to them from the Officer's Mess.

"Man, I am going to get spoiled," Sgt. Jeffreys remarked as he served himself some more shrimp.

"Why? You eat pretty well in your mess hall," Mark commented.

"True. But the service here, delivered to your room, that's just too much."

"Nice not having to do the dishes afterwards," Mark agreed. "But it would be a lot neater if I didn't have this," Mark added, raising his arm with the IV.

"Yea, that probably sucks. Boy, you scared us to death."

Mark started laughing, almost choking on his drink. It took a couple of minutes for him to calm down, finally wiping tears from his eyes as he caught his breath, while Sgt. Jeffreys looked on quizzically. "Sorry," Mark finally managed to say. "You weren't scared to death. I was scared to death, literally." He started chuckling again. "Gallows humor, I guess. It's all kind of catching up with me."

"The game certainly got a lot more serious this last go around," Sgt. Jeffreys observed. "So do you think that is what happened, that you were literally scared to death? Or do you think the cube actually... killed you?"

Mark paused to consider.   "I really don't know. When I'm in contact with the cube, I still know who I am. I don't believe I'm a blue-gray, even though I can feel what they feel and see what they see.   But this time the shock was so great. I really had very little warning when the cats broke in.   It was just a matter of seconds from the time they blew the door and blasted the blue-gray next to me and then shot my host.   The shock of being shot.   And then the pain, unbearable, searing pain.   I guess it was just too much."

"But what if it happens again?   Can you break contact?"

"No.   I tried that when they drugged me.   I tried everything I could to let go of the cube, but I could not control my human body any more than I could control the host body.   But perhaps if it happens again it will not be such a shock and I can be an observer, rather than a participant."

"So you're going to touch the cube again?   After what just happened?"

"I don't think I have much choice," Mark answered after a momentary hesitation. "We need to be able to communicate with the blue-grays and right now I seem to be the only one who can do it.   And now that we know there's a war going on, it seems much more important to know what they're trying to send.   The only thing that really bugs me..."

"Other than the fact that touching the cube can be hazardous to your health?" Sgt. Jeffreys interjected.

"Right, other than that minor inconvenience. But why are they doing it this way? You would think they would know our language by now, that they could communicate with us directly. Why hide in the Mariana Trench and send the cube? Particularly as it is missing a channel; thoughts or emotions."

"Maybe they're hiding," Sgt. Jeffreys said after a long pause. "Maybe they're hiding from the cat aliens."

Mark frowned. "But if what Dr. Benson said is correct, then that war occurred sixty-five million years ago. Why are they hiding now? I can't imagine a war lasting sixty-five million years."

"Maybe they're hiding from us," Sgt. Jeffreys suggested.

"As advanced as they have to be, why would they hide from us?"

"Maybe they're afraid we'll nuke them before they get a chance to communicate with us and that's why they're hiding where we can't reach them. We do have some pretty awesome firepower at our fingertips here."

"If they're afraid of that, why did they almost land on top of a carrier task force? Why not land in the middle of the desert, or Kansas? Why here?" Mark objected.

"I don't know," Sgt. Jeffreys conceded. "Of course, landing on top of the carrier group guarantees an audience with the most powerful people on the Earth."

"That does make some sense. It just provides more incentive to getting to the end of their message."

"Just make sure the end of their message is not the end of you."

"Amen to that," Mark agreed. "In the meantime, let's see if the doctor will let me lose this IV. I need to move around if I'm going to be ready to touch the cube again. And I need to call Beth and somehow not tell her that this last trip was fatal."

"That should be an interesting call," Sgt. Jeffreys deadpanned.

"No kidding," Mark agreed.

"I can't believe how tired I am from that short walk," Mark complained as he sat at a communications console, waiting for the technician to patch his call through to the States.

"You are back from the dead," Sgt. Jeffreys deadpanned.

"Great, zombie jokes already," Mark laughed. "You better stay in the Marines, because your bedside manner is deteriorating."

Sgt. Jeffreys retort was cut off when the technician motioned to the phone, "Your call is going through."

"What time is it there?" Mark asked as he picked up the receiver.

"Twelve fifty-six in the morning, Saturday morning," the technician replied.

The phone was picked up on the fifth ring and a sleepy, female voice said, "Hello?"

"Hey honey, it's me," Mark said. "Sorry it's so late…"

"Are you all right? What's going on? You haven't called in days!"

Mark was always amazed how quickly Beth could go from fast asleep to wide-awake. It was certainly not a trait he shared. "I'm fine," Mark replied. "Things have been a bit hectic. And to answer your next question: No, I haven't figured out the native's language yet, but I am certainly getting closer."

"What are they saying?" Beth asked.

"I can't really say," Mark answered as the censor looked up at him. "More of a history lesson right now, I think. I'll give you all the details when I get home."

"When will that be? You've been gone a week."

"I know. Hopefully, it will not be much longer. Is everything okay back home?" Mark got worried when there was a pause. "What's wrong?" he asked. "Are you okay?"

"I'm fine," Beth responded slowly.

"Then what's going on?" Mark repeated, concern creeping into his voice.

"Oh, everything's alright," Beth replied. "I wasn't going to tell you, because I didn't want you to worry."

"Tell me what?"

"You remember those government men who came by the other day?"

"Yes."

"Well, I had another run in with them. But don't worry," Beth continued before Mark could interrupt. "I don't think they will be bothering me again."

"So what happened?" Mark asked impatiently.

"Calm down and I'll tell you," she replied. "Let's see, it was two nights ago. I had gone to bed, but was awakened by the dogs barking. When I looked out, the dogs were standing at the fence, looking toward the barn. I started to go back to bed, but then worried that something might be going on back there with the horses, so I decided to check it out."

"You went out to the barn alone in the dark?" Mark interrupted.

"You weren't here," Beth answered defensively. "But I did take my .357 and your mag light." Mark could picture Beth walking down to the barn with a .357 on her hip and his mag light, the same light that police officers carried that doubled as a billy-club and was bright enough to light up the trees from a hundred yards. "When I got to the barn…" Beth's words shook Mark from his mental image. "I heard a noise and flashed the light into the barn. I surprised this guy in a suit setting up some piece of equipment that looked like a small satellite dish. The light blinded him and he started to jump up, until he heard me pull the hammer back on my .357. It's amazing how loud that is in the middle of the night." Mark laughed as Beth continued the story, telling how she had the stranger lie in the dirt as she called 911 on her cell phone and kept him there until the deputies arrived.

"They ended up letting him go," Beth finished the story. "Evidently, he was a federal agent of some type and they had to release him.

"Are you sure," Mark asked.

"Sure I am," Beth responded. "I talked with John personally."

"John, the Sheriff?" Mark asked.

"Yes, that John. And he told me that Washington called and he had to let the guy go. Some people with NSA credentials came and picked him up from the jail. Oh, and the equipment that he had. John said it was a hi-tech microphone."

Mark thought about this, while a hundred questions swirled in his mind. "Why set it up in the barn?" was the first question he asked.

"They were aiming it at the house. You know how rural it is here," Beth answered. "John figures they couldn't do it from a car or van because they would have been seen. They found his car in the woods up near the highway."

"But why are they spying on you?" Mark asked. "It's not like I'm keeping any secrets over here. They know everything I'm doing."

"Wasn't it NSA people that you had thrown off your tour?" she asked thoughtfully.

"Yes, it was," Mark said. "But government is government, isn't it. We are all on the same side."

"You have a rather naïve view of Washington," Beth responded.

"Maybe I do," Mark conceded. "But why not just bug the phone?"

"I figure they probably are," Beth said, which made Mark pause. They talked some more, most of it spent by Beth trying to assure Mark that she was perfectly safe.

Finally, Mark reluctantly hung up, promising to call again as soon as he could.

When Mark hung up, he was furious. "How dare they harass her," he complained to Sgt. Jeffreys as they left the communications area. "Who do they think they are?" Sgt. Jeffreys listened patiently while Mark vented. By the time Mark finally wound down, they were at Mark's berth. "I need to talk to the Captain about this," Mark said.

"You need to get some sleep," Sgt. Jeffreys said. "I will talk to the Captain for you," Sgt. Jeffreys said when Mark tried to object. "You get some sleep, you need it. I will call for another escort to stand by here and I will go talk to the Captain. There is nothing that you can add and you need the rest before you contact the cube again."

Mark started to object, but then gave up as he realized the Sgt. Jeffreys was right. He was exhausted. The short walk back to his berth had taken it out of him. So with Sgt. Jeffrey's promise that he would go to the Captain immediately, Mark lay down and surprisingly, fell right to sleep.

CHAPTER 17

Mark woke up the next morning to find Sgt. Jeffreys standing outside his door. "Don't you ever sleep?" Mark asked.

"Not as much as you do," Sgt. Jeffreys' replied. "That's all you do."

"What time is it?"

"Zero-seven-hundred," Sgt. Jeffreys replied. That's seven a.m., Sunday morning, for you civilians."

"I know what time zero-seven-hundred hours is," Mark said.

"You've been asleep for almost twelve hours," Sgt. Jeffrey's continued.

That gave Mark pause. He never slept twelve hours! He never contacted aliens either. And his internal clock had still not adjusted to ship time, even though he had been here a week. It was all just too strange. Mark and Sgt. Jeffreys made a quick stop at the Officer's mess before heading to sickbay. After the doctor readied Mark for contact, the Captain arrived and asked the others to step outside for a second so he could talk to Mark privately.

"Sgt. Jeffreys told me about your phone call with your wife last night," the Captain began. "So I called a friend of mine last night who works in G-2, military intelligence, and asked him to look into it for me. He called me back this morning. He wasn't able to find out anything, but he did get some high level heat telling him to back off. So whoever is backing this operation, has some high level contacts."

"So what do I do?" Mark asked.

"I don't know," the Captain said. "However, I think it is safe to say that whoever it is…"

"NSA," Mark interrupted.

"We don't know that," the Captain said. "However, you are probably right. Anyway, they are probably pissed that they got kicked off this ship and are trying to get information from any source possible."

"So why eavesdrop at my house?" Mark asked. "I'm here. The only information she can get is what I tell her and I have to call her to do so. All they have to do is tap my phone. Which I'm sure they probably already have done. Why set up a microphone in the barn?"

"I have no idea," the Captain said.

"How can I concentrate when Beth is being harassed?" Mark complained.

"It sounds like she took care of herself," the Captain replied with a laugh. "I think they got the worse of it."

Mark laughed as he pictured Beth holding the agent at bay with her .357. "Yes, they will think twice before they step on the farm again." Mark paused before adding, "I guess we should get this show on the road."

"You sure you are ready to do this?" the Captain asked.

"As ready as I'll ever be. I think I've taken off as much time as I can. Besides, I let the doctor hook me up, just in case," Mark answered.

"Be careful," the Captain said as he motioned to the door for the others to join them.

"I will." Mark felt that he should say more, but couldn't think of anything else to say. In the movies they always said something profound in a moment like this, but he was at a loss. So instead, he just reached over to touch the cube. His body betrayed him, stopping his finger just short of touching the cube. It was like intentionally trying to touch an electric wire. He could get close, but couldn't quite touch it. He glanced at the Captain, embarrassed, and then gritted his teeth and forced himself to grab the cube, almost knocking it over in the process.

Once again he was sitting in the control room of an alien ship. But this was a different ship than the one he had been killed in. His host, a different host than before, was studying the scene above him: stars, distant ships and an occasional flash. The battle was evidently still raging. He saw two spaceships locked in a web of lightning, bolts flashing in intricate designs. Suddenly the web expanded as the blue-gray ship exploded, vaporized by the flashing bolts.

Another scene appeared, showing an approaching cat ship. His host began tapping frantically with his hands and feet and the view quickly rearranged. Part of the scene continued to show the approaching ship, while another part showed an asteroid field. Alien symbols flashed in the air, which Mark still did not understand. But he did understand that the trajectory lines superimposed on the two ships intersected before the asteroid field. What if the cats killed his host again? Would he be able to survive it? He watched as the ship approached, his host clearly becoming more agitated as his fingers flashed across the controls. Lightning-like energy beams shot from the cat ship. A web of energy began to grow, much like the web that had destroyed the other ship.

He tried to let go of the cube, but as before he had no control over his human body and could only sit and watch. His breathing came fast and he could feel his hearts pounding in his chest: bip, bip, bip, bip. Hearts? He realized the breathing and heartbeats were his hosts, not his own. He had no contact with his human body. It was the host body he was feeling. Only his thoughts were his own. He would have to control them to keep from being scared to death again.

He studied the scene above him. Part of it appeared to be malfunctioning. He could see the stars sharp and clear, but the asteroid in the center had disappeared, replaced by a black circular void surrounded by a thin sparkling ring. The ring expanded as they headed towards its center. As they got closer he realized it was similar to what he had seen above the asteroid before it disappeared, presumably being teleported or shot through hyperspace towards the moon. Mark glanced back at the other views. The energy web between the ships had grown exponentially. New symbols flashed. Judging by his host's actions, the indecipherable symbols were not providing good news. The black void was rushing towards them while the enemy ship continued to fire. Views started winking out of existence while an acrid smell filled the room. Would they be able to make the jump in time? Or would the ship be destroyed before it made the jump? If the ship was destroyed, could Mark survive? The black hole filled the forward-looking view, while the rear view danced with energy. The two ships were locked together by the pulsing energy, which peeled off to the sides of the black hole. The view danced with colors, pulsing like a living creature, brighter and brighter. Then a flash knocked out the views and he was in the bare control room. The ship lurched and the room stretched and bent. 'No,' Mark thought 'they've given me drugs again. Not now!'

Time stood still. Finally, the room took on normal proportions and a view appeared above his chair showing stars sliding crazily as if the ship were spinning. His host frantically entered commands and the stars slowed and stabilized. Mark got a glimpse of the cat ship tumbling through space behind them and then disappearing in the distance.

The vision abruptly shifted. He was still in a command chair, but the only thing in front of him now was a view screen with a white, cratered asteroid filling the view. Mark watched, fascinated, as they flew low over the asteroid and another planet came up on the horizon. The planet was approaching incredibly fast before the ship started decelerating. Mark watched as a web of energy materialized in front of the ship. He saw numerous objects circling the planet. Other spaceships? Were they going to get into another battle? He recognized one of the ships. 'No, it couldn't be!' They entered the atmosphere, the ship blazing as it shot towards the surface. Just before impact it slowed almost to a stop, before plunging into the ocean, making several course changes before finally settling into the depths of the ocean floor.

Mark awoke. He opened his eyes and was back in sickbay, his hand resting next to the cube. "That can't be it," he whispered. "There must be more." And before anyone could answer, he reached over and grabbed the cube again.

Mark was back in the alien ship, his host now standing with two other blue-grays. One blue-gray pointed towards his host and then pointed to an isolated scene floating in the air. The scene was animated, Mark realized, as it did not have any of the details of the prior views. It showed the blue-gray ship at the bottom of the ocean and a depiction of the submarine and the carrier task force above him. The scene shifted up into space and he saw a cat spaceship approaching the Earth. It showed the ship entering the atmosphere and attacking the surface ships with bolts of lightning. The animation shifted and showed the blue-gray ship rising from the depths and attacking the cat ship. The animation shifted again, showing Navy fighter jets attacking the cat ship. It ended with the cat ship blowing up and the blue-grays standing next to the humans on the flight deck of the aircraft carrier.

Mark opened his eyes and once again he was in sickbay. Sgt. Jeffreys was standing nearby and saw the movement. Mark felt the crushing fatigue overwhelming him. But first, he had to warn them. "War, the cats. They're coming to Earth. They're coming…" he managed to whisper before he passed out.

CHAPTER 18

Consciousness slowly returned. But instead of opening his eyes, Mark lay quietly in bed contemplating the vision he had just seen. He knew he would be besieged with questions when they realized he was awake, but he needed a moment to make sense of it for himself. Finally, his parched throat would not allow him to delay any longer so he opened his eyes. Sgt. Jeffreys was in his customary spot in the corner and a cup with a straw was already placed next to his bed. Mark tried to reach for the cup, but his body was too slow to respond, so he only managed to knock it over. Sgt. Jeffreys jumped up immediately, checked on Mark and then ran for a refill. He was back in a moment, followed by the doctor. Mark enjoyed the cool water flowing down his throat, while the doctor checked the monitors and Mark's pulse. 'Odd,' Mark thought, 'water never tasted so good.'

By the time the Captain arrived, Mark had been cleared medically and was eating a bowl of Jell-O. After a cursory exchange, the Captain came right to the point. "Your last words have caused quite a stir. Would you care to elaborate upon them?"

"What did I say?"

"War, the cats. They're coming to earth. They're coming... You don't remember?"

"I remember. I just didn't know if you heard me."

"Sgt. Jeffreys heard. He seems quite good at picking up your whispers. So what did you mean?"

Mark frowned. "The blue-grays finally sent a message I could understand. If I understood it correctly, and I think I did, they are telling us that these cat creatures that they are fighting are coming to Earth. The war is coming here and they want us to take sides, to help them fight the cats." He then went on to provide the Captain with a brief synopsis of what he had seen the in vision.

When he finished the Captain asked, "Are you up for the conference? I don't think you can sit this one out."

"I need to eat. Something real, not this," Mark said while motioning to the Jell-O. "But then I should be ready. Can you give me an hour?"

"I can give you an hour," the Captain responded. "Normally I could give you longer to set up these conferences, but after your last comment I suspect they will be very quick about turning this one around. Sgt. Jeffreys, you still have that radio?"

"Yes, Sir."

"Keep an ear to it. I'll call you when I have it set up."

"Yes, Sir."

With that the Captain left to make the arrangements, while Sgt. Jeffreys placed an order with the Officer's Mess. Mark sat back and replayed the vision in his mind, concentrating on the details he knew would be asked when the conference started.

It actually took an hour and a half before Mark was sitting in the conference room and the video link was being established. After the testing was done and all parties had a clear signal the person Mark considered the moderator placed his hand to his ear, obviously listening to an earpiece. Mark couldn't overhear his reply, although he did hear someone say impatiently, "Let's get this thing going. I don't have all night."

"Night?" Mark wondered as the moderator held up his hand for silence, saying, "Just a minute, we have one more link to establish."

"What time is it in Washington?" Mark whispered to the Captain.

"A little past midnight, Saturday night," the Captain whispered back.

A minute later a new voice tested the link, after which the moderator said, "We are ready to begin." But instead of asking Mark or the Captain to proceed, as he normally did, he announced, "Ladies and Gentlemen, the President of the United States." A screen appeared with the President sitting at a desk wearing a polo shirt. Mark glanced at the Captain, who looked back equally surprised.

"Mr. Williams," the President said. "I heard what happened when you touched the cube earlier and I would like to thank you personally, and on behalf of all of us, for your willingness to contact it again." Mark nodded, a bit embarrassed. "I also understand you have a message for us."

"Yes, Sir. But you're not going to like it. To save time, I'll provide you with an overview of what I saw. The blue-gray aliens are at war with the cat aliens. It is a war that was raging, according to Dr. Benson's calculations, sixty-five million years ago and which resulted in half of the Earth's population, including the dinosaurs, being wiped out after the cats launched two asteroids against the Earth. Two ships, one blue-gray and one cat, were locked in a battle with some type of energy weapons. The blue-gray ship tried to escape by creating what I can only describe as a wormhole or black hole. Both ships went through it and both ships emerged spinning out of control. The blue-grays regained control of their ship first and ultimately flew to Earth, present-day Earth.

"I was in the cockpit of their ship as they entered the Earth's atmosphere. I saw the carrier task force and the two fighter jets flying towards the alien ship. I saw the blue-grays maneuver around one of our submarines and finally settle in the bottom of the Mariana Trench. All of this I saw from the blue-gray ship. I saw the blue-gray ship approach our submarine underwater, which must have been their first attempt to contact me. And I saw them prepare to launch the cube from their ship to the surface. All of this was contained in the memory of my blue-gray hosts.

"And then the oddest thing occurred. I saw two blue-grays standing next to a view screen and then one pointed to me and then to the screen. An animation appeared. It was clearly an animation. It appeared to be a patched together presentation of various images. The animation showed a view of the sky, a starry night sky, and then it zoomed out and showed the cat ship approaching the Earth, and then attacking this carrier group with energy weapons. The animation continued, showing the blue-gray ship rising up and attacking the cats, along with our fighter jets and surface ships. The footage was, as I said, cobbled together. It was like YouTube video clips from World War II, Vietnam, Iraq: showing ships firing and fighters flying. The scene shifted to the cat ship, which exploded.

"The graphics were pretty basic 'B' rated movie stuff. The last scene showed a blue-gray standing on the deck of this aircraft carrier with a number of humans. The vision ended there." Mark paused for a moment before continuing. "Mr. President, I think we finally have their message. The cats are coming to Earth and we are being drawn into a war between these two alien species. The blue-grays are clearly asking for our assistance in this war."

There followed several seconds of silence before multiple voices tried to address the President. The President held up his hand. "Mr. Williams, since you are in contact with the aliens, I would like your opinion first. Should we accept their request and fight with them?"

"Mr. President, I am afraid that I am a biased observer. I watched the cat creatures almost destroy the Earth. I watched, and felt them kill my host, which also killed me, quite literally. I am terrified of the cats. They have already demonstrated their ability to destroy life on Earth. And they hate the blue-grays. I don't think they will let the mere fact that we are here stop them from doing whatever they can to kill the blue-grays, even if that means wiping us out. And I would hate to go down without a fight, even if our technology may be the equivalent of bows and arrows against cruise missiles."

"However," Mark continued as others attempted to join the conversation. "I have had a little longer to think about this and I am a trial lawyer, which means I am used to analyzing both sides of every issue. So let me give you the other side. All of the information that we have is from the blue-grays. Although what they are sending me feels real, there is no guarantee that it is. We do not know the other side of the story. We could be watching the equivalent of a Nazi propaganda reel and be thinking 'those poor Nazis, we need to help them.'"

"So to answer your question, Mr. President, I do not know what we should do. When you were elected, I told my wife I would not want to be sitting in your seat with the impossible decisions you would have to make. Well, those issues are nothing compared to the decision you have to make now. My only concern is that we may not be allowed to choose. We may be innocent civilians caught between two armies besieging a town. But this time, the town is our planet, and we can't leave. So, if we choose wrong…" Mark let the last statement hang in the air.

"Do you have a timeframe for their arrival?" the President broke the silence.

"No, Sir. I would search space carefully. Look for an approaching ship. The visions are not always good with timeframes. Sometimes they skip. But I did see the cat ship emerge from the black hole. That may be why the blue-grays have been at the bottom of the Mariana Trench. I think they are hiding from the cats. Their ship may be damaged or unable to beat the cats alone. They were trying to run in that last vision and the cat ship was chasing them. My guess, and this is really only a guess, is that it will not be very long, hours or days, perhaps. But not much longer."

Once again the President stopped the roar of voices that followed the last comment. "Mr. Williams, is there any other information that you can provide me at this time?"

"No, Mr. President. Only more details as to what I saw in the vision, but nothing that would really change anything."

"Okay, thank you Mr. Williams. I appreciate all you have done for us. If anything else comes up, let me know."

"Yes, Sir."

"Gentlemen," the President continued. "I will leave you to continue this meeting. I will call a meeting with my advisors shortly. Please be ready to discuss, as best you can, our options at that time." With that the President's screen went blank. Mark endured another two hours of questioning, although it was obvious he had no further information to provide. Ultimately he excused himself, telling the Captain that he had to take a break and move around and then he wanted to contact the cube again.

CHAPTER 19

"How about this explanation?" Sgt. Jeffreys said. He and Mark were sitting in a corner table in the Officer's Mess, where they had ended up after leaving the last debriefing. Mark was picking at a fruit salad, worrying about his wife's last encounter with the NSA.

"What explanation?" Mark asked.

"The NSA theory," Sgt. Jeffreys continued. "Let's assume there is a power struggle in Washington. You read about it in every book or magazine. The NSA wants to control the contact with the aliens. But their two agents, our friendly doctors," Sgt. Jeffreys added with a chuckle, "get kicked off the ship. So they can't control it first hand. We can assume that they get your reports, either by being briefed or monitoring the communications. We know there isn't anything transmitted which the NSA can't pick up, that's there job after all. Anyway, they want more info."

"But why eavesdrop on my house?" Mark objected. "I'm not there. Any information Beth has is from me over the phone. And you already said that they can monitor anything."

"Right," Sgt. Jeffreys continued, undeterred. "They are not looking for what you have to say, they want to hear what she has to say. They want the rest of the story."

"What rest of the story?"

"Why you are here. Why you were chosen by the blue-grays."

"I already told you, and them," Mark said. "I have no idea why they chose me. I haven't figured that out either."

"Sure. And I believe you," Sgt. Jeffreys said. "But the NSA does not. They think you are holding out on them. Particularly since you treated their representatives so well." Sgt. Jeffreys held up his hand when Mark started to protest. "I'm not saying you did anything wrong," Sgt. Jeffreys continued. "I'm just laying it out from their perspective. Anyway, since they can't do anything else here, they are investigating your home, trying to figure out what you are hiding and why you were chosen to make contact."

"So they figure my wife knows," Mark continued Sgt. Jeffreys' line of reasoning. "And are just waiting for her to tell the neighbors."

"Something like that," Sgt. Jeffreys said. "Like I said, it's just a theory."

"Well then, I guess I should just tell them the truth," Mark said. Sgt. Jeffreys raised a questioning eyebrow. "That we are keeping a blue-gray in our guest bedroom while Beth is negotiating Earth's surrender. Meanwhile, I am distracting everyone half-way around the world by playing this cat and mouse game with the memory cube."

Sgt. Jeffreys chuckled. They fell into silence while Mark pushed the food around his plate. Bits and pieces of conversations washed over them as officers moved to nearby tables. Finally, Mark broke the silence at their table. "I'm going back to contact the cube again."

"Don't you need to rest some more," Sgt. Jeffreys asked.

"No. I'm fine. And I've got too much in my head right now to sleep. Might as well find out what else is on that cube." Sgt. Jeffreys picked up his radio to notify command of Mark's intention.

An hour later Mark was in his customary room in sick bay with the corpsman finishing up placing the leads for the monitors and inserting an IV. Once the nonessential personnel had left the room, Mark nodded to the remaining observers and reached over and touched the cube. Nothing happened. Mark looked up puzzled. He let go of the cube and touched it again. Nothing. He rubbed it, squeezed it, and still nothing. "I don't understand, it's not working." One by one the others touched the cube as well, although not expecting any results since it never worked for them anyway. Mark tried one more time, but to no avail.

"Maybe the message is over," Sgt. Jeffreys suggested. "The last vision brought us up to the launching of the cube, so now there's nothing more on it."

"He may be right," Mark admitted to the Captain. "I'm certainly not getting anything else here." Mark reached over and rubbed the cube one more time for emphasis. Nothing happened. "I guess you can take all this stuff off, doc. Looks like I won't be needing it." The leads and I.V. were removed and Mark got out of the bed. Putting on his shirt, he turned to the Captain. "So what do you think is next?"

"I was going to ask you that," the Captain responded. "After all, you are the alien interpreter."

"Evidently not anymore," Mark complained. "I feel like a medium who has suddenly been abandoned by the spirit world."

"What about the other visions that you've received, the ones from the submarine? Are you still getting those?" the Captain asked.

Mark was still a little bit uncomfortable talking about those visions. But as they had not shown up in the last couple days he answered truthfully, "Not for a while. I actually was a bit relieved." When the Captain looked at him quizzically, he explained. "I can psychologically prepare myself before I touch the cube. The other visions come without warning and although I was getting better at dealing with them, they were still a bit... unnerving."

"I'll contact Washington and let them know that you're not able to make contact anymore. We'll see what they suggest. In the meantime it looks like you have some free time. You may have a while too. After that last bombshell you dropped, I'm sure Washington will take all day to discuss it. After all, it is about six a.m. Sunday morning in Washington."

"Six a.m.? That would be five a.m. in Pensacola. I need to call Beth. I don't remember the last time I called."

"That's fine," the Captain said. "Just remember the ground rules."

"Don't want the NSA to know what is going on?" Mark joked. The Captain ignored the jibe. "After I call home," Mark continued. "Do you mind if I take a real tour of your ship, now that I can pay attention? It's really the first time since I got here that I don't feel like a truck ran over me."

"Sure. Just stay with Sgt. Jeffreys. He can give you the tour and he's my way to contact you if I need you," the Captain added, pointedly looking at Sgt. Jeffreys' radio.

"I'll take care of him, Sir," Sgt. Jeffreys responded, snapping to attention.

"Just make sure he doesn't spend the entire time touring the mess hall. I don't want to have to replenish our food supply while underway."

"Actually," Mark interjected. "I need to see that exercise room again. Since all I have been doing is sleeping and eating, I need to work off some of this extra weight." Mark concluded while patting his stomach.

The Captain laughed. "Well I can't think of a better tour guide than a Marine Sergeant to take off a few extra pounds for you." With that the Captain turned and left sick bay.

The first thing Mark did was to have Sgt. Jeffreys take him to communications so he could call home.

"Good morning, honey," Mark said when his call home was patched through.

"Where are you? Are you all right? When are you coming home?" Beth asked without taking a breath.

"Hey, one question at a time," Mark laughed. "I'm still on my trip and I'm fine. Actually, more rested than I have been the whole trip. I may even take a tour now that I have some free time."

"So what is going on," Beth asked, prompting a look from the communications officer who was monitoring the call.

Mark had already prepared a response. "I have finished my Rosetta Stone course and will probably be coming home soon as it appears that my work here is done."

"Really?" Beth asked. "Did you learn the new language? Did you get a chance to try it out on any foreigners?" Beth said.

"I will give you all the details when I get home," Mark said. "But no. I got to listen to some recordings and finally figured them out, but I was not able to try my skills live with anyone."

"How disappointing," Beth said. "Can you tell me what the recordings were?"

"Not over the phone, I'm afraid. It's a bit complicated," Mark replied. "But, I did finally get to the end of the recordings and figured out the meaning. Now that is over, I should be able to come home soon. I am just waiting for the president of this tour group to decide when that will be. But you will probably have to call my office and extend my absence a little longer. Perhaps kill off another of my relatives."

"You sure you are coming home soon," Beth asked.

Mark hesitated. "Probably pretty soon. It looks like my portion of the tour is over, so it will just depend on what they decide. I'll let you know as soon as I do. How are things going there? Any problems with those trespassers?" Mark added, trying to change the topic of the conversation.

"No," Beth said. "I haven't seen them since we last talked.

They talked a little more before saying goodbye, Mark promising to call again as soon as he had more information about his return.

The next several hours were spent touring the ship, which Mark felt certainly qualified as a workout. The tour finally paused at the Enlisted Mess, where Mark gratefully sat down to rest his aching legs and replenish some of his lost calories. "How much more ship is there?"

"You're not tired are you?" Sgt. Jeffreys asked, sounding like a Drill Sergeant about to inform a new recruit that they were about to climb yet another mountain.

"You're enjoying this!" Mark accused Sgt. Jeffreys.

"Who, me?" Sgt. Jeffreys asked, feigning a look of pure innocence. "Now why would a Marine Sergeant want to show up an Army Captain?"

"I'm not an Army Captain anymore," Mark protested. "And that was twenty years ago! So you can go knock out the next twenty miles by yourself, I'm going to eat. And then I'm going to go to my room and sleep. It's almost eleven o'clock at night. It's about time this cruise lived up to its reputation, fine dining and relaxation."

Sgt. Jeffreys just shook his head. After they ate, he led Mark back to his cabin. "Will that be all," Sgt. Jeffreys asked.

"Yes, that will be all Jeeves," Mark said with a laugh. "You can take the rest of the night off. But bring the car around in the morning and we will take a morning tour. After all, I appear to be currently unemployed."

Sgt. Jeffreys rolled his eyes as Mark broke into laughter. "Ah, the idle rich," Sgt. Jeffreys muttered as he closed the door.

Mark didn't sleep well that night. His dreams were disjointed, full of aliens and exploding planets. He dreamed he was being chased by aliens, but couldn't run or was helplessly floating in space. When he finally dragged himself out of bed in the morning, he staggered to the shower, hoping the cold water would wake him up. Sgt. Jeffreys was his usual chipper self, which only made Mark feel more exhausted.

Mark followed Sgt. Jeffreys to the Officer's Mess, convinced that Sgt. Jeffreys was setting an intentionally fast pace. They had to wait in line, while the smell of bacon, eggs and sausage wafted around them. Although he didn't feel hungry, Mark filled his plate with eggs, grits, and bacon, hoping that a good meal would wake him up after the shower had failed. They found a corner table and Mark slid into his chair, still feeling like he had stayed up all night. "This is not fair," he complained. "I'm as tired now as I was after touching the cube." Mark dug his fork into his food, lifted it to his mouth and slumped to the table. He awoke a few moments later to find Sgt. Jeffreys and two other crewmen standing over him. Sgt. Jeffreys was wiping some food off of Mark's face. He had evidently collapsed in his meal. 'How embarrassing,' Mark thought.

"You okay?" Sgt. Jeffreys asked. Mark nodded. "Seizure," Sgt. Jeffreys said to the other sailors. "Thanks, I can handle it now." Turning back to Mark he asked, "Do you want me to call sick bay?"

"No, I'm okay. It just takes..." The room faded but did not completely disappear. A star field emerged and was replaced by the room again. Mark blinked and the room became more substantial. Aware of Sgt. Jeffreys staring at him intently, Mark opened his mouth to speak and the star field started to appear again, only to abruptly disappear, the room taking it's place once again, sharp, clear and solid. "This is really weird," Mark managed to say before the Star field replaced the room once again. Unlike prior visions, this vision did not completely replace his consciousness. It was more like watching a traditional movie, rather than the blue-grays' usual total immersion experience. Consequently, Mark was aware of his surroundings, even while watching the alien sent vision. Realizing it was not ending, Mark succumbed to the inevitable and whispered to Sgt. Jeffreys. "This is something new. Better get me back to sick bay."

Mark was aware of Sgt. Jeffreys talking on the radio and then having two nearby sailors assist in carrying Mark out of the mess hall and down the corridor. At some point they met two corpsmen carrying a stretcher. Mark was transferred to the stretcher and then carried down seemingly endless corridors. Mark watched as the gray pipe filled corridor ceiling gave way to stars, space, and a ship. And then the half vision ended. By the time Mark was transported to sickbay, he was once again fully alert. He was still tired, but not exhausted like after touching the cube. The doctor checked his vitals, but other than a slightly elevated heartbeat, everything was normal. The doctor was completing an EKG when the Captain arrived.

"I guess I don't get a day off," Mark joked, as the doctor pronounced the EKG normal.

After ensuring that the room was clear of all unauthorized personnel, the Captain asked, "So what's going on now?"

"This one is really weird," Mark started to explain, realizing that this whole experience had been weird. "I'm getting a new vision, but unlike any I've received before. The cube was total immersion. The visions I received from the submarine were total immersion, but lasted only seconds. This one is overlapping. It's like two films are being played at one time, one on top of the other. And this was not total immersion. It was visual only."

"What did you see?" The Captain asked a bit impatiently.

"Oh, sorry. It was space, out in space, stars, and then a ship. I think it's the cat ship."

"Are you sure?" the Captain asked.

"I think so," Mark replied. "It was a view from a distance so I can't say for sure, but it looked like a cat ship, a double flat sphere with jagged edges. That's what the ship looked like that attacked the blue-gray before the wormhole collapsed.

Is it coming now?" the Captain asked.

"I don't know. It might be, based upon the last vision we got from the cube. But I couldn't tell you from this one. I saw stars and the ship. But nothing I recognized. I don't know where it is."

The Captain's phone beeped and he listened to the message, ending it with, "I'll be right there." Turning to Mark, he said, "We're getting a new signal from our friends downstairs. It was transmitted to the submarine, which forwarded it to us. Can you make it to the bridge?"

"I think so. I might need a little help." The Captain and Sgt. Jeffreys escorted Mark up to the CIC. There they were shown to a screen that showed what the submarine had received. It was a static picture of a group of stars.

The Captain confirmed from the operator that it was the entire message. Turning to Mark, he asked, "Does this make any sense to you?"

Mark studied the screen carefully. "Yes. These are the stars. The ship should be right about here," he pointed to the screen. Can you identify these stars?" Mark asked.

"We'll see," the Captain said as he turned to a operator to relay the order, noting that this should be sent to Washington immediately. About 10 minutes later the Captain informed Mark that they had identified the constellation shown in the photograph and NORAD and a number of other observatories were now searching that area of space for the cat's ship. "If it's anything like the ship our friends downstairs have, it will be a tricky business," the Captain explained. "The only thing we could get on it was visual. We never could pick up a radar signature on it."

Mark stared again at the constellations on the screen and then slumped and would have fallen had Sgt. Jeffreys not caught him and assisted him to a nearby chair. "It's coming again, Mark managed to whisper as his view of the room with the Captain and Sgt. Jeffreys staring down at him overlapped with a view of the command room on the blue-gray ship. He blinked his eyes and tried to adjust to this double vision, fighting a wave of nausea as he did. "I'm on the alien ship, the blue-gray ship. I'm in their command room," Mark whispered. The vision changed. "They're watching us. It's a view of the *Ronald Reagan* from sea level, like from a periscope." Mark blinked to clear the vision. Then he closed his eyes, finding it was easier to concentrate on one vision rather than two. He continued to describe what he was seeing. "The view has zoomed in. They're looking at us now, at the tower."

"Is this a real-time vision?" the Captain asked.

"I don't know," Mark admitted. "Let me tell you what they see and you tell me if it's real-time. There's a sailor outside on, what do you call it? A balcony? He has binoculars and is scanning the ocean."

"Go check," the Captain said to Sgt. Jeffreys, who immediately went outside to check.

Still sitting in the chair, eyes closed, Mark continued his narrative. "Sergeant Jeffreys just came out onto the balcony, a floor above. He's looking around. He's looking down at the sailor with the binoculars. He's going back inside, now."

Sgt. Jeffreys came back in the room and started to report what he had seen, but was interrupted by the Captain. "I know, he told me. Go back out there and make a couple of signals, completely random. I want to make sure this wasn't just a lucky guess."

"Sergeant Jeffreys has come back outside," Mark continued. "He's raising his right hand. Now he's waving. Now he's saluting. He's turning around in circles, now jumping up and down. He went back inside."

Sgt. Jeffreys came back in and told the Captain what he had done. It matched. "Okay, we have a real-time vision. So what does this mean?" the Captain asked Mark.

Mark opened his eyes to respond and started feeling dizzy and sick as the overlapping visions confused his senses. "I don't know, I…" Mark closed his eyes as the vision changed again and another wave of nausea struck him. "I'm back in the blue-gray ship. Looking at their monitor. It's the view of space, the cat ship is coming."

"Coming when?   Now?" the Captain asked. "Are they coming here?"

"I don't know, the vision is..." Mark reeled back and gasped, as he was suddenly flooded with the full vision. When the intensity let up, he caught his breath and blurted out, "Now! They're coming now! The blue-grays are alarmed.   They're maneuvering. Captain, they're arming their weapon systems!" Mark opened his eyes, even though the double vision sent another wave of nausea through him.   But he had to make sure the Captain had heard. The Captain was giving commands to contact CINCPAC immediately.

"Captain," Mark said and waited for the Captain to turn towards him.   "I think you should notify the President it's going down now. You don't have time for channels and the President asked me to contact him directly if something like this happened. And Captain, if the blue-grays are correct in what they showed me earlier, we are about to be attacked."

The Captain stared at Mark as he processed this information.   He turned and barked some commands, most of which Mark missed due to the changing vision. However, he did not miss the sound of a klaxon and a voice stating "battle stations." Mark closed his eyes and tried to block out the frantic activity on the bridge so that he could concentrate on the vision. The blue-grays were doing something on their bridge, but Mark could not figure out what they were doing. The ship was clearly maneuvering, but where? Mark felt movement and it took him a few moments to realize he was feeling the aircraft carrier picking up speed and changing course. A few minutes later he heard the unmistakable sound of jet engines spooling up as strike aircraft prepared to launch.

A new vision rocked him and it took a moment for him to interpret it. He opened his eyes, and saw Sgt. Jeffreys kneeling down in front of him, watching him intently. "They're coming here," Mark said to Sgt. Jeffreys, his voice coming out in a whisper. "The blue-grays are coming to this ship." Sgt. Jeffreys stood up and turned, but did not leave Mark's side. "Captain," Sgt. Jeffreys yelled across the bridge. Mark saw the Captain turn. "Mr. Williams says the blue-grays are coming here, to our ship, right now."

"Sonar, report," the Captain commanded.

"Nothing, Sir."

"Go active," the captain ordered.

"Yes, Sir, going active." There was a long pause and then, "Nothing, Sir. No, wait." Another pause, "I've got something rising fast, Sir. Directly beneath us and rising fast."

"Two miles? How could they be watching us from periscope level?" the Captain questioned.

"Maybe a remote pickup," the XO offered.

Mark had to close his eyes as the scenes from his senses and the vision started to overwhelm him again. He was back on the blue-gray bridge, watching the view screens as the ship rose. Mark opened his eyes again and saw Sgt. Jeffreys watching him intently. "Tell the Captain,

I think the blue-grays intend to land on our ship." Mark closed his eyes again to concentrate, while trying to shut out the bridge noises.

The Captain's voice broke into his consciousness. "Mr. Williams." Mark opened his eyes to see the Captain looking down at him. "The blue-grays are coming here? To our ship?" Mark nodded. "Where is the cat ship?"

"It's still in space. I can't tell you how far out or how long, I don't understand their displays. But I don't think it will be long. The blue-gray ship is getting close to us," Mark added.

The Captain turned away and Mark heard a flurry of orders. "No one is to fire unless I give the direct order. Make sure everyone holds their fire. Where is Washington?" Several other voices reported. Moments later someone shouted, "There it is." Mark didn't have to look out the window to know what was going on. From his vision, he knew the blue-gray ship had risen out of the water and was now hovering about 100 yards off the stern of the *Ronald Reagan*. On the blue-gray view screens Mark saw sailors staring at the ship, while others were training weapons, although to their credit no one fired. The blue-gray ship maneuvered until it hovered 20 feet above the aircraft carrier's flight deck, about 100' to the stern of the tower. Mark's vision changed as a new vision was introduced. "Captain, they want me to go to their ship." Mark announced.

The Captain looked at Mark with concern. "They want me now. They are in a hurry." When the Captain did not respond immediately, Mark added, "I don't think I can chicken out now. I've got to do this."

"Okay," the Captain decided. "Sergeant Jeffreys, take Mr. Williams down there. Follow his instructions. And Mr. Williams," the Captain added. "Be Careful."

Sgt. Jeffreys helped Mark out of the command center. Mark found that if he concentrated on his surroundings, it was easier to block out the alien vision. When they stepped out of the tower onto the flight deck they stopped and stared up at the alien ship hovering about one hundred feet away.

"It looks like a giant egg standing on end," Sgt. Jeffreys remarked as he stared at the hovering ship. It did look like a giant egg: completely smooth, aluminum gray, standing about 90' tall and 20' wide, with a horizontal, pulsing, purplish ring running around the center of the ship. "Is this the ship from your visions?"

"I don't know," Mark responded. "I've always been inside the ships. And the time I was on the planet running to the ship, I was drugged, so I couldn't see clearly. It is not the ship I landed on in space though, wrong shape. But see that pulsing purple band across its middle," Mark added, pointing.

"Yes, it's hard to look at."

"I've seen that before, I think that's its engine," Mark said.

"So what now?" Sgt. Jeffreys asked.

"I guess I go over and talk to them," Mark answered, not really sure himself.

"Then at least take this," Sgt. Jeffries said as he ordered a nearby Marine to take off his Kevlar vest.

Mark hesitated at first, and then allowed Sgt. Jeffries to help him put it on. The weight of the vest made him feel a bit more protected as he started walking down the flight deck towards the blue-gray ship. "I probably should do this alone," Mark whispered to Sgt. Jeffreys, who was walking next to him.

Although clearly not pleased with Mark's suggestion, Sgt. Jeffreys hesitated only a moment before complying. "Okay. I'll follow in the catwalk over there. You be careful." With that he sprinted to the side of the ship and jumped out of sight. As Mark continued to slowly walk towards the blue-gray ship, he spotted Sgt. Jeffreys walking along the edge of the ship, only his head visible. When Mark was 50 feet away from the alien ship he stopped, wondering what he should do next. He did not have to wonder long. An opening spiraled out of the lower part of the ship and a blue-gray effortlessly leapt out, landing easily on the deck 20' below. It looked at Mark, and came walking towards him. Mark thought it looked like the same blue-gray he had seen on the alien bridge in the last vision. Mark watched him approach, realizing only then that he was no longer receiving the alien visions.

The blue-gray was about his height and moved in a fluid motion, although not as fast as Mark had seen before. Mark wondered if this was to keep him from becoming alarmed. Out of the corner of his eye he saw Sgt. Jeffreys to his right, with an M-16 trained on the blue-gray. The blue-gray stopped about 5 feet away from Mark and held out his hand, palm up. In his palm was a cube.

But this cube was different. The memory cube was perfectly square. This one looked about the same diameter, two inches, but was multi-colored and had twice as many facets to it. 'Like a double cube,' Mark thought. Hesitantly, Mark stepped forward and reached for the cube. His fingers brushed it. The resulting vision was overwhelming. Mark staggered back, wobbled, and fell to his hands and knees. His heart pounding as he took several deep breathes to try to clear his senses. Using all his willpower he managed to get shakily back to his feet. The blue-gray still stood there, palm extended. Bracing himself, Mark reached for the cube again. The force of the vision overwhelmed him.

As his senses cleared for a second time, he realized he was sprawled on his back on the flight deck. His vision blurred by a bright streak that seemed to be racing towards him. In the distance he heard Sgt. Jeffreys yell out a warning, but could not comprehend what was said. Mark rubbed his eyes and looked up just in time to see a huge fireball shooting towards him from the sky. Involuntarily, he rolled onto his stomach, covering his head with his hands. When nothing happened, he uncovered his head and looked up. A second ship hovered 100 feet over him. Mark instantly recognized the jagged saw blade shape of a cat ship. Several bolts of lightning streaked out from the cat ship as sounds like arcing electricity filling his ears. Lightening bolts struck the blue-gray ship and danced across the aircraft carrier's bridge, sending out sparks and starting fires.

A cat alien leaped down from the second ship, landing on all fours on the deck and raced towards the blue-gray ship. Switching to a two-legged run, the cat pulled out a weapon and shot the blue-gray, the bolt catching the blue-gray in the chest. Mark watched in horror as the blue-gray's chest disintegrated and its body was thrown to the ground. Mark was still sitting when the cat fired a shot absently at him as it bounded past towards the blue-gray ship. The shot struck Mark square in the chest, knocking him across the flight deck in a cloud of burning particles and static charges.

From his vantage point 75 feet away in the cat walk, Sgt. Jeffreys trained the sites of the M-16 he had commandeered from another Marine on the blue-gray's forehead. He barely resisted squeezing off a few rounds when Mark staggered back and fell to the ground after touching the cube the first time. Only by watching the prior contacts with the cube did Sgt. Jeffreys realize this was probably a normal reaction and not an attack. He watched Mark sit up and try a second time, only to be thrown back again.

Mark appeared to be recovering when a glare covered the flight deck. Sgt. Jeffreys looked up in time to see what appeared to be a meteor streaking towards him. He shouted a warning to Mark as he ducked for cover. Instead of the expected explosion, Sgt. Jeffreys heard a loud buzzing sound, like hi-voltage electricity arcing. He looked up in time to see a large cat-like creature leap from it's glowing, hovering ship and bound across the flight deck, shooting and killing the blue-gray in the process. Sgt. Jeffreys didn't have time to bring up his M-16 before Mark was shot in the chest, the bolt throwing him 10 feet across the flight deck, leaving a trail of burning parts behind. Sgt. Jeffreys sighted his M-16 on the bounding cat, the shot easy at this distance. But his Marine training kept him from firing. Mark was dead. He had failed to protect him. But he was under orders not to fire and shooting now wouldn't help Mark.

Sgt. Jeffreys pushed his emotions aside. He would deal with them later, after this was over. When the cat leaped inside the hovering blue-gray ship, Sgt. Jeffreys sprinted across the flight deck to Mark's body. He was not going to leave him there. And if the cat came out while he was exposed, well that was what his M-16 was for. When he got there, he was amazed to see that Mark was still breathing. The Kevlar vest was destroyed, having been blown apart by the alien's weapon, but Mark appeared to be conscious and intact. "Hang on there, Sir," Sgt. Jeffreys said as he knelt down to pick up Mark. "I'll get you out of here."

"Wait," Mark whispered urgently. "Get the cube."

"I can't, it was blasted," Sgt. Jeffreys responded.

"No," Mark insisted. "The other one. It's attached to his hip, his right hip."

M-16 at the ready, Sgt. Jeffreys ran over to the dead blue-gray. Trying to recognize the charred mess, he finally identified a small satchel attached to the hip, which he grabbed. It came easily off the dead body. Running back, he shoved the satchel into his cargo pocket and then bent down and swung Mark over his shoulder and headed for the relative safety of the catwalk as fast as he could run with Mark's additional weight. When he got to the edge of the flight deck, he lay Mark down and jumped to the catwalk, quickly turning and pulling Mark unceremoniously off the flight deck. As he pulled Mark to safety, the cat leapt out of the blue-gray ship and headed for it's own, stopping briefly to search the dead blue-gray before taking another unnecessary shot at the corpse, further disintegrating the body. The cat effortlessly leapt 100' feet into the air, landing on the edge of its ship and disappeared inside.

Although obviously in pain, Mark insisted on inspecting the satchel Sgt. Jeffreys had retrieved from the dead blue-gray. Sgt. Jeffrey's pulled the satchel out of his cargo pocket and handed it to Mark who was propped up in a sitting position on the catwalk. Mark turned the satchel over and a multi-faceted cube dropped into his hand. A blank look came across Mark's face, which Sgt. Jeffreys recognized from Mark's sessions with the memory cube. Several minutes passed in eerie silence, the only sound on the normally noisy flight deck coming from the wind and the waves, broken by the occasional roar of a passing fighter jet. The alien ships hovered silently above them. Crouched down behind a stanchion, Sgt. Jeffreys noted that Mark was still immersed in his vision. He was debating about breaking the contact when he heard a rushing noise above him. Looking up, he saw a dark circle slowly expanding above the cat's ship, which was now hovering over the blue-gray's ship. Hoping that Mark would recognize this anomaly from his visions, Sgt. Jeffreys pulled Mark's hand off the cube.

"Wake up!" Sgt. Jeffreys demanded, shaking Mark roughly. "Wake up, I need your help." Mark's eyelids fluttered as his normal expression returned. "Stay awake," Sgt. Jeffreys commanded, fearing that Mark would fall asleep, like he did after the long visions. "I need your help. What's that?" Sgt. Jeffreys asked, pointing to the expanding black circle that now had a noticeable white sparkling border.

Mark stared sleepily where Sgt. Jeffreys was pointing and then came fully alert. "We've got to stop them," Mark whispered, and then repeated louder.

"What?" Sgt. Jeffreys asked.

"We've got to stop them. Shoot them."

"We can't shoot without the Captain's orders."

"Then call him. Fast."

"I can't get through, comm's knocked out."

"Shoot, then. Shoot," Mark ordered frantically as he started to get up, adrenaline counteracting the effects of the cube.

"Why?"

"That's a black hole they're creating. They're going to destroy our ship."

"I can't, not without orders."

"But I can," Mark said and with surprising strength, sucker punched Sgt. Jeffreys in the solar plexus, dropping him. "Sorry," Mark apologized as he picked up Sgt.

Jeffreys' M-16 and climbed up onto the flight deck to get away before Sgt. Jeffreys could recover and try to stop him. He ran about 50', stopped, took careful aim at the cat's ship and started shooting. Round after round he fired at the cat ship until his magazine was empty.

The other sailors saw him shooting and when they couldn't raise command, the entire comm having been knocked out by the cat's attack, they started shooting as well, including the side gunners with their .50 caliber machine guns. Mark watched as tracers rose up at the cat ship and then harmlessly veered towards the sides of the expanding black hole, which looked like a giant, jet-black window, with a sparkling edge spiraling open above the cat's ship.

Lieutenant Commander John Sterling was banking his Hornet for another pass by the carrier. He had launched just before the first alien ship had arrived with orders to get on station, but to take no hostile action unless specifically ordered to by the Captain. Circling the carrier, he watched in amazement, as the blue-gray's ship hovered over the deck and had to abort a run past the ship when the second alien ship streaked down. He watched the second alien ship attack the carrier and targeted it several times, but never fired, as he could not raise the carrier on the radio. Oddly, all his communications were out. He couldn't raise the other ships or aircraft. Frustration mounting, he continued to circle the carrier, straining to figure out what was happening. As he approached the carrier on another low pass he spotted the unmistakable flashes of small arms and tracers arcing towards the second alien ship.

'Ok,' he thought. 'That looks like a go to me.' He quickly swung his hornet away and looped around so he could approach from the side of the carrier as he lined up his shot. He couldn't get radar-lock on either alien ship, but he acquired a thermal-lock on the second ship as it was still radiating some heat from its fiery entry into the Earth's atmosphere. Approaching about 200' above the water, he noticed an odd, black line above the alien ship. He dropped a little lower, closer to the deck so he could shoot up, minimizing any interference from the carrier, and noted that the line now appeared as a huge black hole. Hitting his afterburners, he fired two heat-seeking missiles and pulled away.

Mark was running back to Sgt. Jeffreys to get more ammunition when LTC Sterling started making his run. He did not notice the hornet coming straight at him as he was focused on getting to the catwalk. However, the fighter caught his eye when it suddenly veered off, leaving two missiles streaking in straight at him. Mark registered this in just enough time to dive to the deck, still 50' from the relative safety of the catwalk. The missiles streaked in and exploded over his head. There was a double bright flash, but no sound, no shockwave, no shrapnel tearing through his body. Mark rolled over and looked up. Above him the black hole continued to expand, the alien ships apparently intact. Mark's heart sank. If those missiles didn't touch it, then there was nothing they could do in the time they had left.

Mark grabbed the empty M-16 and rolled back onto his feet. He had to do something. He made it two steps. Time slowed. Mark stared at Sgt. Jeffreys, who was frozen, climbing up out of the catwalk. Another fighter was sitting in the sky, frozen as it banked. The ships in the distance all stood still, their bow waves curled up and stopped like a photograph. Mark took in all this detail as he studied the tableau in from of him, having all the time in the world, as he too stood frozen in time. Then all turned liquid and flowed up into the sky like an upside down waterfall. Sgt. Jeffreys became a long streak as he streamed into the sky. The ships in the distance became blurs. Mark could almost touch the blue-gray's ship, although his feet were still on the carrier. Mark had a momentary sensation of weightlessness before gravity reasserted itself. There was a crushing pressure and all went black.

CHAPTER 20

Mark awoke slowly, completely disorientated and hurting everywhere. He wondered if his alarm had gone off. Maybe he had overslept. He would have to see what time his first appointment was scheduled. Slowly he opened his eyes and then had to blink to clear his vision. He heard a moan and realized that it was him. Someone came over and wiped his face with a cool cloth. He heard a voice, a male voice. What was a male doing in his bedroom? He blinked his eyes and as his vision cleared he saw a Marine Sergeant standing next to him. What was a Marine doing in his bedroom? Groggily he looked around at the fluorescent lights and took note of his surroundings. He was in a hospital, not his bedroom. How did he get here? And why was there a Marine here, rather than a nurse? Where was Beth? What had happened? He tried to think back, but could not come up with any details.

"Where am I?" he managed to whisper.

"You're in sick bay," the Marine answered.

Sickbay? The words did not register. Sickbay, what was that? A Navy term, he told himself. Why was he in a Navy sick bay? Why would they take him to the Navy

Hospital?   There   were   three   civilian   hospitals   in
Pensacola, and they were closer to him than the Navy
Hospital.

"Why not Sacred Heart?" he asked, referring to the
hospital near his office. A confused look came across the
sergeant's face, but before he could respond a female
came over dressed in a military uniform and started
checking on him. Mark recognized the silver oak leaf and
medical caduceus on her shirt.

"How are we doing?" the doctor asked.

Irritation and a sense of déjà vu came over him.
'Obviously, we are not doing well if we are in the
hospital,' Mark thought. Particularly when he had no idea
why he was here. 'Must have been a car accident, and
they took me to the nearest hospital.'   He tried to
remember, but still couldn't come up with what
happened. This was seriously irritating. He tried to move
and waves of pain shot through him, causing him to
moan involuntarily. "I hurt everywhere," he whispered,
as the pain receded.

"I'm not surprised," the doctor responded.   "You
had a pretty good fall from what they tell me.   But
nothing's broken and the scans are all negative."

'Fall, what fall?' Mark thought. "What happened?"
he finally managed to ask.

"What do you last remember?" the doctor asked.

Mark thought back, but could not answer.   He
remembered driving, his office, appointments, but none
in any particular order. What had he done last? "I don't

know," he finally admitted. "It's all a jumble." He moved and winced as pain hit him again.

"You have burns across your upper torso," the doctor explained. "Fortunately, only first and second degree. Where else do you hurt?"

Mark gingerly started to move his arms and flex his legs. He felt pain whenever his burned skin moved, but also felt pain deeper. "Everywhere," he responded. 'What happened?' Mark wondered, imagining a car accident and resulting fire. But they had said something about a fall. None of this made any sense.

"Captain wants to talk to you," the doctor said. "He'll be here shortly." With that the doctor left, leaving him alone with the sergeant.

"I'm glad you're back with us," the sergeant said with emotion. "I really thought they had killed you."

'Killed me? What was he talking about? That didn't sound much like a car accident.' Mark thought. "What happened?" Mark asked again for what seemed like the hundredth time.

"I'm not allowed to discuss it," the sergeant said apologetically. "Captain said he is to be the first to talk to you. He should be here any minute now. I did tell them what you told me on the flight deck," he added conspiratorially.

As if on cue, another Navy officer walked into the room, followed by the doctor, who was summarizing Mark's condition. Mark assumed it was the Captain, based upon the eagles on his collar. The Captain was all business. Without even a cursory, how are you doing, he asked, "What happened down there? Why did you fire? Washington is climbing down my throat and I need answers."

Flight deck? Washington? Why did you fire? This did not seem like car accident questions. It should be the Highway Patrol asking who had the green light and whether he was wearing a seatbelt. Mark strained to remember what had happened, but could not recall anything else. "I'm sorry," Mark finally said, the words coming out more as a hoarse whisper. "I really don't know what you are talking about. Why am I here, rather than Baptist or Sacred Heart."

Mark's comments clearly shocked his listeners. "Where do you think you are?" the doctor asked.

"Navy Hospital, Pensacola. Right?"

"No," the Captain said. "You are on board the *USS Ronald Reagan*, an aircraft carrier sailing in the Pacific Ocean. You don't remember coming out here?"

Now it was Mark's turn to be shocked. "I'm where? What am I doing here?"

"You wouldn't believe me if I told you," the Captain said as the doctor motioned him aside. Mark overheard the doctor say "concussion", "PTSD" and "cube," while the Sergeant looked on mutely. Mark couldn't make out the rest of the conversation until the Captain said loudly, "I can't fly a blessed thing off this ship unless it has rotors and I can't spare any right now, so as long as he is stable you're stuck with him. The Captain turned back to Mark. "I'm sorry. I didn't realize you had a memory problem. I guess I shouldn't be surprised. You've been out over thirty-six hours. The doc will see if she can help you remember. In the meantime, I have to get my ship fixed. It took one heck of a beating. Right now it's a great big floating parking lot. So I have to go. But," he added. "The minute you remember anything, call me. I have a lot of questions." With that he turned and left, leaving Mark more bewildered than ever.

Mark looked at the Sergeant and the doctor. "Okay, is someone going to tell me what is going on?"

The doctor answered, "Post traumatic stress disorder is not my specialty. And of course in your case the cube could have caused it, which takes it out of everyone's specialty. I really don't know."

"What is the cube?" Mark asked, his frustration increasing.

The doctor looked flustered. "I'm going to have to check on this," she said and left the room.

"That's helpful," Mark complained to no one in particular.

The sergeant stepped over to Mark's bed. "Do you remember me?" he asked, concern in his voice.

"I'm afraid I don't," Mark answered, although he immediately liked him.

The sergeant looked at the open door and continued in a hushed voice. "I'm a friend. I was assigned to protect you. I'm sorry. I didn't do a very good job. We were in a battle. You were... shot. And then there was an explosion and you were tossed around by it. That's probably why you hurt so much. Just relax. You're safe now. It's over. Just relax. I'm sure you will remember. I had buddies in Iraq and Afghanistan who had PTSD, and they all recovered. It just takes a little time."

Mark could feel the emotion in the sergeant's words, the first person that he could relate to. As if reading his mind the sergeant continued. "You got along with the Captain real well. He's just real stressed right now. We took a hell of a hit. Knocked out comm, controls, computers, fried a bunch of electronics and took out part of the flight deck. Big depression scooped out of it. For a while we were actually adrift. Planes had to fly to Guam or ditch. Nothing could land. Rumor has it we almost lost the reactor. A lot of it has been jury rigged now. We are underway, heading to port for repairs. Still nothing can land except the copters."

A million questions rose up as Mark tried to process what he was hearing. "But I'm a civilian," Mark finally said. "How come I'm in a Navy battle in the Pacific?"

The sergeant hesitated before answering. "You were specifically requested to come out and help. And then things kind of got out of hand."

"But why?"

"I don't think I should tell you. Its very complicated and I think it would be better if you remembered it on your own. That's what they tell us, anyway. Just rest. Try to remember it first; if not…"

The doctor entering the room interrupted the sergeant. "I've got something for the pain," the doctor said as she injected a needle into Mark's IV. "Relax, and we will talk when you feel better."

Mark was about to object, but the drug took effect and he fell asleep.

CHAPTER 21

Once again Mark woke up slowly. Eyes still closed, he started to roll over when a wave of pain brought him fully awake. As usual, Sgt. Jeffreys was at his side in an instant, offering him some water. "Don't you ever get any time off," Mark asked between sips.

"You remember me?" Sgt. Jeffreys asked.

"Why wouldn't I remember...?" Mark paused. "Is this the second time I woke up?"

"Yes."

"You know, I have a vague, dream-like memory of waking up at the Navy Hospital in Pensacola."

"That's where you thought you were," Sgt. Jeffreys replied. "Scared me to death."

"Did I talk to anyone?"

"Just me, the doctor and the Captain. But you didn't remember anything."

"Well, I remember now," Mark assured Sgt. Jeffreys. "What happened in the... explosion? Was anyone hurt?"

"Only you."

"Lucky me."

"Hold on a second, I've got to tell the doctor you're awake," Sgt. Jeffreys said before stepping out of the room. He was back in a second, followed shortly by the doctor.

"Sgt. Jeffreys tells me that you are back to your old self."

"My memory is back, if that's what you mean. Physically, I feel a little bit worse for the wear."

"That's to be expected," the doctor stated as she checked his vitals and monitors.

"Any way you can unhook any of this stuff," Mark asked, motioning to all the leads running off his body.

"You plan on going anywhere?" The doctor asked.

"I need to get out of this bed, move around or I'm going to turn into a potted plant," Mark complained.

"You are by far my worst patient," the doctor said with a laugh. "I can unhook you, but you won't like it. Why don't you just leave it for a little while?"

Mark reluctantly acquiesced. He was sitting up in bed, a corpsman checking the monitors, when the Captain arrived. The corpsman quickly finished and departed the room, leaving the Captain and Sgt. Jeffreys alone with Mark. "They tell me you're back with us," the Captain stated.

"Yes. I don't know what that was all about before, but I'm back now."

"Tell me, what happened? Why were you shooting at the alien ship?"

"They were going to kill us."

"That's what Sgt. Jeffreys said you told him. How do you know?"

"I recognized the wormhole. I knew how it worked from my visions. It was going to suck up the ship, this ship. I had to stop it. We tried to contact you, but the comm was out. And we didn't have much time. Not enough to get to the bridge and back."

"You sure about all this? Washington is in an absolute uproar. Thinks you may have brought Earth into a galactic war," the Captain stated, and then looked surprised when Mark laughed.

"Sorry," Mark said. "Its just ironic. There was a war all right. But we didn't start it, we were just pawns. They are gone now."

"Are they coming back?" the Captain interrupted. "We're not in the best of fighting strength right now."

"I don't know." Mark answered. "Can you tell me what happened when the missiles hit? I'm not real clear after that."

"The missiles didn't do anything. They just disappeared. But moments afterward there was a flash, a black flash, and both alien ships were gone," the Captain replied.

"That's it?" Mark asked. "No streaking of light?"

"Not that I saw," the Captain replied. "Sergeant Jeffreys?"

"No, Sir. Just that weird black flash. And Mr. Williams landing in that depression dug into the flight deck."

"What did you see?" the Captain asked.

"My perspective was very different," Mark began slowly. I was starting to run back to the catwalk for more

ammunition when the missiles hit. I saw them streak in.
I hit the deck by reflex and they exploded, both of them,
right over my head." Mark paused as he remembered the
event. "It was odd, two flashes of light. No sound. No
blast."

"There wasn't any shrapnel," Sgt. Jeffreys objected.
"I've seen lots of explosions. There should have been
shrapnel everywhere. And loud. That close the sound
alone would have knocked you off your feet."

"Nothing was found," the Captain confirmed. "The
only damage to the flight deck was that smooth concave
depression carved out right below the alien ships."

"No one else saw the missiles explode?" Mark asked.

"No," the Captain answered while Sgt. Jeffreys shook
his head.

"That's strange," Mark agreed. "But it gets weirder.
After the missile flash lit up above me, I expected to be
blown away, literally. When I realized I was still alive,
that nothing had happened. I glanced up. The ships
were still there with the wormhole gaping huge above
them. Nothing had changed. I got up and started
running towards Sgt. Jeffreys, who was climbing up onto
the flight deck. I made it about two steps before the
world turned bizarre. Everything stopped. And then
kind of stretched out. Like a Salvador Dali painting. It
was like everything turned into liquid and was stretching
up towards the wormhole. I couldn't feel my body, the
wind, anything. It was like I didn't exist. I was
insubstantial. And then just as suddenly, I was so heavy.
I was tumbling though the air, the wind roaring in my

ears. And then I hit something real hard. That's all I remember."

"So the aliens went through the wormhole," the Captain stated, rather than asked.

"They must have," Mark agreed. "That's how they travel."

"Are they coming back?" the Captain asked again.

"I don't know," Mark answered slowly. "There is no reason for them to come back. We are absolutely insignificant to them. The blue-grays were only here because they were trying to hide from the cats. With the blue-grays gone, there's no reason for the cats to return."

"Looks like the blue-grays are out of the picture now," Sgt. Jeffreys interjected. "That cat creature didn't look like it was taking any prisoners."

"You're probably right," Mark agreed. "And I really know nothing about the cats, other than they hate the blue-grays."

"Let's hope they don't take it out on us for being with the blue-grays," Sgt. Jeffreys said.

"Or shooting at them," the Captain added. "That's what has Washington in an uproar. It would be hard to defend yourself from someone who can throw asteroids at you from space." This observation was met by silence as each of them tried to consider the consequences of such a confrontation. "Well," the Captain finally broke the silence. "Are you up for a conference? I need to set one up now that you are awake."

"Yea," Mark responded unenthusiastically. "I guess I am."

"Good. I'll set it up." As the Captain prepared to leave, he leaned over and whispered to Mark. "Be forewarned. There are a number of folks in Washington who want your head. So be careful. Pulling back, he added conversationally, "We have a video you might like to see. It was taken from the base of the bridge with a hand held video camera. It's the only video on board that survived the cat's attack. It's a bit jerky in places, but you can see what's happening. Sergeant Jeffreys."

"Yes, Sir?"

"As soon as he is ready, take Mr. Williams to the briefing room next to the CIC conference room. I'll make sure the video is ready for him there. He needs to review it before we get Washington on line.

"Yes, Sir."

The doctor was not too keen on allowing Mark to leave sickbay after having been unconscious for over 36 hours. But she knew that in this matter she would be overruled. As a compromise she insisted that two medics carry Mark up to the conference room in a stair chair and that she personally attend to him during the conference. "At a minimum, you've received burns over twenty percent of your body, had a concussion and been in contact with that alien cube. Only God knows what it does to you."

Mark started to object, but when pain and overwhelming fatigue simultaneously washed over him as he tried to get up to walk across the room to go to the head, he merely replied, "You're probably right." The doctor nodded in reply and started making the necessary preparations.

Twenty minutes later Mark was in the conference room with the doctor and Sgt. Jeffreys. He was glad that he had acquiesced to the doctor's recommendation as the mere act of getting dressed and being carried up to the conference room had been exhausting, not to mention painful.

"Do you want some pain medication for that?" the doctor asked, noticing Mark wince as he adjusted his shirt over his burned shoulder.

"No, thanks," Mark replied. "I think I need to keep my head clear for this conference."

"Okay, just let me know," the doctor added, motioning to the corner of the room where a large medical kit was sitting.

Mark nodded as he tried to find a comfortable position in the hard chair. A technician programmed the display and Mark and Sgt. Jeffreys watched the video. It was odd watching himself, Mark thought as the video showed him approaching the blue-gray. "That was like sticking your finger in an electric outlet," Mark said when the screen showed him being tossed back after touching the cube.

"You are a glutton for punishment," Sgt. Jeffreys added when Mark touched the cube a second time. They continued watching in silence. Mark grimaced and the doctor gasped when the cat shot Mark. "I really owe you for the Kevlar vest," Mark said to Sgt. Jeffreys. They continued to watch as Sgt. Jeffreys ran out and carried

Mark to safety. "And for getting me out of there, also," Mark added after the cat blasted the blue-gray a second time. Several minutes passed while nothing happened and then the wormhole began to form above the cat's ship. From the perspective of the camera it appeared as an empty black sphere slowly growing immediately above the alien ship.

"Look at the tracers," Sgt. Jeffreys commented when the 50's opened up. They're not touching that ship. They're swerving over to the sides of the wormhole. I could have sworn they were hitting the ship dead on when I was watching. But from this angle... " He let his sentence hang. A minute later the missiles streaked in and disappeared. No bright light, no explosion, no fireball. Just disappeared.

"I know I saw them explode," Mark objected. "I know it." Then the camera focused on the alien ship. A moment later the screen went completely black. When the picture returned the wormhole and both ships were gone, replaced by an empty blue sky.

"Wait. Can you back it up," Mark asked the technician. "Play the last minute over." The technician complied and they watched again in silence. "Again," Mark asked, and watched it again. "Can you slow it down?" Again the technician complied.

"What are you looking for?" Sgt. Jeffreys asked Mark after watching the same sequence five times.

"The edge of the wormhole. I think it wavered. Can you enhance it or enlarge it?

"I can a little," the technician responded. "The equipment I have here is not very good. Most of it got fried in the attack. Give me a minute."

As the technician was working on enhancing the video, the XO walked in. "Captain sent me down with these," he said, placing some flash drives on the table. These contain video from the fighters and some of the other ships. He wanted you to see it all before the conference begins. Thought it was good that you saw everyone's perspective before... "

"Before I commit to a story?" Mark finished for the XO.

"Let's say he wants you to be fully informed so that you can provide the best explanation for the events that transpired," the XO continued.

"Now that is spoken like a true defense lawyer," Mark said with a laugh.

"It is in everyone's best interest that we get a well reasoned account and not some emotional or political twist to the events," the XO responded somewhat defensively.

"I couldn't agree with you more," Mark stated. 'Particularly since it is apparently my neck on the chopping block,' Mark thought, but did not state aloud.

"So, what are you doing," the XO asked Mark, while glancing at the technician who was still working on the display.

"I'm trying to see if he can enhance the image. I think I saw the wormhole wobble right before the ships disappeared."

"Wormhole?"

"Wormhole, black hole. I'm not a physicist, but I think wormhole is probably the better description," Mark clarified.

"Ok. So is this wobbling significant?" the XO asked.

"It could be critical."

"Sir," the technician turned to the XO. "I really can't do much with this equipment. Most of our equipment got fried. This junk is hopeless."

"What do you need?" the XO asked. The technician rattled off a number of components, none of which made any sense to Mark. When he had finished the XO replied, "Okay. Contact your Chief. Tell him what you need and to get it here ASAP. If any ship in this battle group has it, it's yours. But I want it here and ready to use now! Not ten minutes from now. Understand?"

"Yes, Sir!" the technician said as he jumped to comply.

"In the meantime," the XO continued to Mark. "You probably should review these other tapes. See if they help."

"I will, thanks," Mark answered. "Oh, do you know when that conference will be scheduled?"

"No. We don't know yet. But if you need it, it might take a little longer on our side to work out the technical glitches to set it up."

"That would be good. I would like to try to figure this out before the grilling starts."

"We'll see what we can do. But we can't buy too much time. Maybe an hour or two."

"Then that will have to do," Mark replied. While the technician worked on getting better equipment, Sgt. Jeffreys and Mark watched the other tapes. There were two gun camera tapes from the fighter aircraft, one from the jet firing the missiles and a second from his wingman. The third tape was from an escorting ship. "That's odd," Mark said as they watched the other tapes.

"What?" Sgt. Jeffreys asked.

"You see that bottom ring on the cat ship?"

"That part that looks kind of like a glowing circular saw blade?" Sgt. Jeffreys asked.

"Yea, that," Mark said. "In my visions there were two rings, one on top and one on bottom. In this video there is only one, with that structure sitting in the center of it."

"Maybe they turn the top one off when they land," Sgt. Jeffreys suggested.

"Maybe," Mark said. "Or maybe it's a different ship."

"Look at this," Sgt. Jeffreys exclaimed as they watched the feed from the first fighter jet. "When the fighter drops down you can see the black hole, but when it rises up level with it all you can see is a black line, which disappears completely when it rises above it. This is awesome."

"Yep, some scientist will have a field day with this. Probably have to rewrite Einstein's theory of relativity or something," Mark agreed. "But none of it shows what I saw. The missiles still just disappear and from this distance I can't get any good detail on the edge of the hole."

"Let's play them again slowly while the technician works on enhancing the other tape," Sgt. Jeffreys suggested.

"Might as well," Mark agreed. They watched and re-watched the tapes, looking for something that would explain what occurred. During that time, more equipment arrived and the technician worked on the original tape. About an hour later the XO came in and announced that the conference would start in thirty minutes. By this time just sitting and watching exhausted Mark. He relented to "doctor's orders" and took a break for some food that was brought up before watching the original tape one more time.

"I hate to say it," the doctor commented between bites of food. "But for someone who is looking at this video footage fresh, without the background that we have, you running out there and firing that M-16 at the alien ship does not look good." She waived aside Mark's objection with her fork. "I'm not saying what you did was wrong," she continued. "I am just warning you that it could easily be taken the wrong way if one were so inclined. Not a real friendly way to greet an alien race."

Mark nodded his head, but Sgt. Jeffreys objected. "They shot him. Nearly killed him, and would have without that vest."

"And he was consorting with their enemy," the doctor replied. "If they were really our enemy, they would have destroyed the entire ship."

"They were going to," Sgt. Jeffreys replied hotly.

"Says who?" the doctor rejoined.

"Mr. Williams..." Sgt. Jeffreys started to answer, but stopped when Mark held up his hand.

"I see where you're going with this doc," Mark interjected. "Thanks for the warning." The doctor nodded her head. "Let's look at the original video one more time. They watched it again, slowed, enlarged and enhanced. "Again," Mark instructed. "Just the last five seconds." He watched it again. "Stop! Back it up a couple frames. Okay. Can you loop that portion? There it is!" Mark said excitedly. "I knew I saw it wobble."

"What's that mean?" Sgt. Jeffreys asked.

Mark's answer was interrupted by the XO, who walked in at that moment. "We're almost ready. Can I get you to come in and take your seat?"

"Sure," Mark replied. "Are you going to have these tapes available during the conference?"

"If you need them. Just tell Adams here what you need."

Mark gave some instructions to Adams while the doctor spoke to the XO. "I'll bring him in. Let me have just a minute to check my patient's vitals."

"Don't take too long doc, there will be a bunch of brass waiting on him."

As the XO left the room, the doctor said, "Bear with me. We're going to take you in that wheelchair. With the pillows it will be a lot more comfortable than the conference room chairs. And I want you to have this..."

She pulled an I.V. out of her medical kit and hung it on the pole attached to the chair.

"Wait a minute," Mark objected. "You know I don't..."

"Listen," the doctor interrupted and then waited for the technician to leave the room with his equipment before continuing. When it was just Mark, Sgt. Jeffreys and the doctor, she explained. "This isn't a courtroom that you are going into and I've spent some time in Washington. It can be brutal."

"But I don't need those drugs," Mark continued to object.

"You don't," the doctor explained with a smile. "You need an edge, so you have time to get your message across. Trust me on this one." With that, she quickly set up the I.V. on a stand attached to the wheelchair and wrapped the I.V. tube in tape around his arm, but never inserting a needle into his arm. Mark smiled when he understood what she was doing and then sat back as she rolled him out of the room.

The doctor personally wheeled Mark into the conference room, I.V. rocking on the chair's stand. There was a moment of confusion as people had to rearrange when they realized that Mark would not be sitting in the empty chair next to the Captain. The doctor whispered something to the Captain and they got everyone repositioned with Mark's wheelchair now situated in front of his customary chair. Most of the conference attendees, including those on video were already on and Mark wondered if the doctor planned his entrance so that all could see the medical attention being paid to him. 'That is probably the last special treatment I can expect during this conference,' Mark thought wryly. Although Mark felt he had made the right choices, he nevertheless felt nervous when someone announced: "Ladies and Gentlemen, the President of the United States."

Like before, as the senior member present, the Captain started the briefing. "Mr. President, I'm Captain Joseph Peters of the *USS Ronald Reagan*. I've been informed that you have been fully briefed, so I will skip the background briefing. Mr. Williams awoke a couple of hours ago and our flight surgeon has medically cleared him to attend this briefing, despite his wounds. Doctor Martins, our flight surgeon, is in attendance should Mr. Williams need her assistance during the course of this briefing.

'Nice touch,' Mark thought as the Captain mentioned his medical condition. 'They must think this is going to be bad since they are going out of their way to try to load up the sympathy factor.'

"So without any further delay," the Captain was saying. "I will turn this over to Mr. Williams."

Mark noticed the cameraman shift his focus to him. 'Show time,' Mark thought as he tried to control his nerves. 'I'm as nervous as opening statement at trial.'

"Good Morning, Mr. President," Mark began before realizing that he did not know what time of day it was either here or in Washington. 'How to start?' Mark wondered. He had spent so much time reviewing the tapes and trying to figure out what had happened, that he had not had time to prepare a presentation. 'Great.' he thought. 'Perhaps the most important presentation of my life, and I have to wing it.'

"Mr. President," Mark extemporized while he organized his thoughts. "Is it safe to assume that you have seen the videos taken of the recent events?"

"It is," the President simply responded.

'That's not a good sign,' Mark thought. 'Not a very warm and fuzzy greeting. Okay Mark, time to use those advocacy skills of yours.' he coached himself.

"In that case, let me provide you with the events from my perspective. Then if you have any questions, I will gladly answer them." Mark paused. When there was no response, he continued. "As you have probably been informed, shortly before the blue-gray's ship rose to the surface, I started to receive visions from them alerting me to the imminent arrival of the cat's ship. The blue-gray ship came to the carrier and requested, through the vision, that I meet them. They communicate through those cubes and they tried to do that with me on the flight deck. Unfortunately, the cube was too strong for me, much like their earlier attempts to communicate with me on the submarine.

"You probably saw that both times I tried to touch the cube, the contact threw me to the ground. Before I was able to touch the cube a third time, the cat ship arrived. What happened there is clear on the video, the cats attacked both the *Ronald Reagan* and the blue-grays with some type of energy weapon. I've been told that the attack wreaked havoc on the *Ronald Reagan* and you saw what it did to the blue-gray and me." Mark watched his audience, they were as unreadable as a jury. So far he had told them what they already knew. It was time to tell them something new and convince them that he had not dragged Earth into a galactic war.

"But you knew all that," Mark stated the obvious. "Let me tell you what you don't know." Mark noted that his audience seemed to lean forward with that remark. Now he had to deliver on his promise. "You probably saw on the video that when Sergeant Jeffreys came out on the flight deck to save me, he went back to the dead blue-gray for a moment. He was retrieving the blue-grays' personal cube. That cube is like a personal computer, a smart phone and much, much more, all rolled into one. When Sgt. Jeffreys got me to the catwalk, I touched the dead blue-gray's cube. Suddenly I was the blue-gray. The experience was much more intense than my sessions with the memory cube. You will recall that I had always thought I was missing a channel during those visions. I could see, hear, taste, and feel during the visions, but I could not access their thoughts, emotions or speech. As it turns out, they did block those channels. When I touched the blue-gray's personal cube, I received all the channels, including his thoughts. So now I have the uncensored version, rather than the censored version they sent us." Mark paused for dramatic effect before continuing.

"There was a war, a galactic war between the blue-grays and the cat people. That war was fought sixty-five million years ago when the blue-grays first visited Earth.

Their purpose in coming here was to conduct genetic engineering. They were looking for a species to use as a weapon against the cats. And they found one, the dinosaurs, specifically the velociraptors. My first vision showed the blue-grays observing the velociraptors hunt. They hunted in packs as Dr. Benson confirmed for us from the fossil record. You will recall that the velociraptors failed in their first hunt, the prey got away. The blue-grays then started their genetic engineering. I saw it in the second vision. It was a velociraptor egg they were manipulating. The third vision showed the genetically enhanced velociraptors conducting a hunt. The blue-grays sent them out and they were very successful. They killed all the prey and did so before eating. This is what the blue-grays wanted. Their intent was to take the velociraptors and plant them on the cat worlds, like commandos, to go and kill the cats. Blue-grays had done this before with other species from other planets and that's what the blue-grays were doing on Earth sixty-five million years ago. But they were discovered and the cats attacked.

"The blue-grays had some warning, which I saw in the vision when they were evacuating the planet. The cats attacked by crashing two asteroids into the earth. One struck in the Gulf of Mexico and the other in the Indian Ocean. This was the KT event that Doctor Benson told us about, the event that wiped out fifty percent of life on Earth and wiped out the dinosaurs. I saw how the cats did this in the next vision. They created a black hole, or perhaps wormhole would be the better term, above the asteroid and the asteroid was sucked into it and then emerged above the Earth. The blue-grays had some warning of this attack, but not much. They were evacuating the planet when the asteroids struck. Meanwhile, a space battle raged in our solar system between the cats and the blue-grays, a battle that the cats appeared to be winning.

"During this battle a cat ship started chasing a blue-gray ship, which happened to be a research vessel my host was on. It had some weaponry, but was no match for the cat ship, which was a fighter. The blue-grays tried to escape to the asteroid belt, but were not fast enough. The cat ship started firing and the two ships became locked in a web of energy. The same type of energy bolts we saw when they attacked the *Ronald Reagan*, but on a much larger scale.

"The blue-grays were desperate to get away so they attempted a jump. They had the same or similar technology as the cats, so they opened up a wormhole and attempted to jump through it to safety. But the two ships were locked together by those energy fields and the cat's ship was sucked into the warp along with the blue-grays' ship. The energy fields reacted with the wormhole and something went wrong. Instead of being transported through space, the two ships were transported through time. Sixty-five million years. They emerged in our time in our solar system. Emerged out of control and on different tangents. The blue-grays regained control of their ship first and fled, ultimately coming here to hide in the deepest part of the ocean, the Mariana Trench.

"The blue-grays' cube answered some questions that have puzzled me from the very beginning of this trip. I could never reconcile the dinosaur visions with the blue-grays being present here in our time. Think about it. If the visions shown to me of dinosaurs were from our past, which it turned out they were, then the blue-grays were over sixty-five million years old. So why hadn't they evolved way beyond us? If the blue-grays were time travelers, then why would they bother with our technologically inferior culture? Either way it didn't make any sense. The answer is that they were neither. They existed sixty-five million years ago. But they were not time travelers, not intentionally anyway. These two ships accidentally, not intentionally, traveled through time. But I digress. Let me bring us back to the present.

"The blue-grays' ship was damaged and outgunned. They fled to the Earth to get away from the cats, recognizing it as the planet they had been on, to them, only hours before. They also realized there was a different dominant life form here, a more advanced one compared to the dinosaurs they had just left. Despite our technological inferiority, in desperation they decided to enlist our aid in their fight against the cats. They hoped that if the cats found them, which they knew they would, we might get lucky and either kill the cats, or more likely distract them long enough for the blue-grays to successfully attack. All this I learned from contacting the blue-grays' personal cube."

Mark paused again, this time to gather his thoughts for what he knew would be the most important and most difficult part of his presentation. "As we know, the blue-grays' plan didn't work. The cats attacked before they had successfully communicated with us and the blue-grays were killed. So what happened next?" This was the key, the part the Captain and the doctor had warned him about. Mark took a deep breath and continued. "While I was lying on the side of the deck, still in contact with the blue-grays' cube, Sergeant Jeffreys saw the wormhole opening and he broke my contact with the cube to see if I knew what was going on. I recognized it from my contact with both cubes, as this was a standard form of travel for both of the alien races. I also realized that something was wrong. A wormhole only has to be as big as the object entering it. When Sergeant Jeffreys woke me up, the wormhole was already expanding larger than the alien's ships. The only explanation was that cats intended to pull their ship and the blue-gray's ship through the wormhole, along with the *USS Ronald Reagan.*" Mark paused to allow the implication of that statement to sink in.

"Yes, they intended to transport the *Ronald Reagan* with them into space. Of course, everyone on the *Ronald Reagan* would be dead the minute we entered the vacuum of space. That's when I told Sergeant Jeffreys that we had to stop them. He tried to communicate with the Captain, but comm was down after the attack on the bridge. I knew from watching the expanding wormhole that we did not have much time, certainly not enough time to get to the bridge and back. So I sucker-punched Sergeant Jeffreys, took his M-16 and ran out onto the flight deck before he had a chance to recover. I was desperate to do something. I really didn't think an M-16 would do any good, and it didn't. Evidently, the other sailors saw me shooting and must have assumed that the command had been given, so they opened up as well. Again it did no good. If you watch the videos carefully, you will see the tracers veer off to the edge of the wormhole. They never touched the cat's ship.

"I started to run back to Sergeant Jeffreys to see what else we might have when the missiles came in. From the videos it appears that the missiles simply disappeared. They didn't. From my vantage point directly below the expanding wormhole I saw them explode, both of them. Or I should say I saw the light from both of the explosions. The explosions should have killed me. But I never felt the blast. There was no sound, no shrapnel. I can only assume, and here I am making an assumption, that the wormhole sucked up the entire explosion, the fire, shrapnel, even the sound. Only the light from the explosion escaped. I can't explain it any other way. When I realized that I wasn't dead, I looked back up and the alien ships and the expanding wormhole were still there. I jumped up to run back to Sergeant Jeffreys when the wormhole collapsed. I have tried to describe this to the Captain. What everyone else observed and you can see in the videos is a black flash. The alien ships and the wormhole are simply gone, along with part of the flight deck. What I observed was very different. It was like I was frozen in a moment of time. I couldn't feel anything, not even my own body. I was insubstantial. Everything around me was frozen in place. Sergeant Jeffreys looked like a statue of someone running with one foot held up. Then everything blurred, no, streaked would be a better description. It was like you had painted a watercolor picture and then held it vertical while it was still wet and watched all the colors run down the canvas. But in this case, everything ran up, streaking up towards the wormhole. And then the black flash, followed by gravity. Overwhelming gravity. And then blackness." Mark paused and reached for some water, wincing as he did when his burned skin moved.

"So what happened? Where did the alien ships go?" the President asked in the intervening silence.

Mark put down his glass of water. "I think I know the answer to the first question, but not the second. You will recall that I said the wormhole 'collapsed.' The aliens opened and closed wormholes. How they did that I have no idea. But they did. But I think this one collapsed. I have studied the videos very carefully and you can see the edge of the wormhole wobbles right before it disappeared. That's not normal. In fact it's very dangerous. A wormhole has to be balanced. The blue-grays' memories are absolutely clear on that. This wormhole wobbled and then blinked out of existence, taking the cat's ship, the blue-gray's ship, and part of our flight deck with it. I don't think it closed, I think it collapsed. The blast from the missiles must have hit the cat ship and damaged their equipment or somehow interacted with the wormhole, because a second later it starts to wobble and then collapses. I believe the two alien ships were most likely destroyed in that collapse. If not, there is no telling where or when they were transported, or whether they even survived the transit."

Mark paused. There was a lot more to tell, and a lot more that he was not willing to tell. But he figured it would be best to let them ask their questions now. He had laid the foundation for his story. He would now have to convince them individually that his actions were justified. He paused and took another sip of water, waiting for the inevitable questions. There was a moment of silence as the attendees waited to see if the President was going to ask any questions. When it became obvious that he was not, there was a clamor of voices asking questions. The moderator finally regained control and the questioning began.

"How do you know they were going to take the aircraft carrier with them?" the first questioner asked.

Mark sighed before answering. He wasn't sure that he appreciated the easy question or was irritated by its stupidity. "I already explained," Mark began. "The wormhole was expanding larger than the cat's ship. The only reason for that was to bring in a larger ship, which in this case could only be the *Ronald Reagan*."

"And you know that because?"

"Because of my visions and contact with the blue-grays' personal cube, I have seen this before."

"Even if they were going to take the *Ronald Reagan*," someone else asked, "How does that justify you attacking the cat ship?"

This was the question Mark had been expecting and dreading. "Other than the fact that the cats were trying to kill all aboard this ship?"

"The *Ronald Reagan* is a small price to pay to avoid a war with a species that can destroy the Earth," the speaker continued.

'Spoken from someone who was not aboard the *Ronald Reagan*,' Mark was tempted to respond. Instead, he answered, "We are insignificant to the cats. Their war is with the blue-grays and that's why they attacked the Earth sixty-five million years ago, to fight the blue-grays. You saw the video. The cat shot me as he was passing, more of an afterthought than anything else. The cat's decision to take out the *Ronald Reagan* was probably just anger at us for dealing with the blue-grays, just the same as they took out the dinosaurs, which the blue-grays were trying to use against them."

"But that's just your belief, you don't know that. You have no proof."

"That's true, I don't." Mark agreed, bringing a mutter from the crowd. "But you have no proof that I am wrong either. The cats may have intended to travel out to the asteroid belt and send a couple of asteroids back to finish what they started sixty-five million years ago." That comment brought a contemplative silence to the audience.

"But you didn't know," another speaker objected. "You took it upon yourself to make a unilateral decision of immense importance and fire upon the cats against orders. You did not have the authority to do that."

"Please," Mark said, exasperation clear in his voice. "Does anyone have authority to declare war on an alien race?" He continued before anyone could respond to his rhetorical question. "What would you have me do? We literally had just a couple of minutes to act. I did not have time to make it to the bridge to tell the Captain, let alone try to set up some bureaucratic conference to debate the pros and cons for a decision for which no one had enough facts to decide with any degree of confidence. No. The cats were trying to kill us, so I tried.... and did... stop them."

"But you were under orders not to fire."

"Not to split hairs, but I am a civilian. I was under no orders from anyone." Mark held up his hand stopping the next objection. "But even assuming that I was, I would have done the same thing again."

"What's to say that the cats aren't in the asteroid belt right now, about to destroy us," an irate voice asked.

"Like I said before, we know they were going to destroy the *Ronald Reagan*..."

"According to you," the speaker interrupted.

"Yes, according to me. And there is no evidence to refute it," Mark added. "And we don't know if they intended to attack the Earth afterwards, whether I shot at them or not. We will never know that. But right now we are alive and I believe that they were probably killed, or if not, transported to God only knows where when the wormhole collapsed. Either way, we are the least of the cat's worries. We pose absolutely no threat to them. We can barely get to our own moon, let alone attack them.

So, right or wrong, I made a split second decision to protect the *Ronald Reagan* from the cat's attack. I still think it was the right decision. But right or wrong, I had to make it and I did and only time will tell if I was right."

"You may have doomed the human race!" someone accused.

Mark reached for his water as a flurry of redundant questions and accusations were raised. Mark did not bother answering. He had stated his case the best he could and thought that it would be best just to rest his case at this point. He didn't have the energy or patience to sit in a prolonged meeting debating his actions endlessly.

"Mr. President," Mark said. He had to repeat himself to be heard.

"Yes, Mr. Williams," the President answered, bringing silence to the meeting.

"Mr. President, I had refrained from allowing the doctor to administer any drugs for my injuries before this conference so I could be as lucid as possible. I have explained to the best of my ability what transpired and why I took the course of action that I did. If you have any questions, I would be glad to try to answer them. Otherwise, I would ask that you excuse me so I can go back down to Sick Bay and rest." As if on cue, the doctor got up and moved next to Mark.

The President paused to consider Mark's request before replying. "That would be fine, Mr. Williams. We will consider what you have told us and when you are better, we will talk with you some more. I'm sure we will have some further questions."

"Thank you, Sir," Mark replied. "And if I may leave you with this thought," Mark added, the lawyer in him wanting to have the last word. "Both the blue-grays and the cats considered us inconsequential. They looked at us only as a potential weapon, and not a particularly dangerous one at that. Neither race paid any more attention to us than we would a colony of ants, fire ants perhaps, but ants nonetheless. And neither race cared about our existence any more than we would that colony of ants. We have met two alien species and to them we were insignificant. Fortunately, their war was sixty-five million years ago. Both races are probably extinct today and the last representatives of these species, the ones who traveled to our time, are now most likely dead and gone. They are, like both their species, ancient history."

CHAPTER 22

Sitting at his office desk waiting for his next appointment to arrive, Mark thought back to the events 10 months before. It had taken several days for the *Ronald Reagan* to travel to Guam. During that time the Captain was too busy trying to get his ship operational to see Mark. Sgt. Jeffreys continued as Mark's escort, although Mark did not travel very much because of his injuries - confining himself to his room, sick bay and an occasional trip to the Officer's mess. Once they arrived at Guam, Mark was taken off ship and subjected to multiple debriefings. But in the end they had accepted his account, or at least had let him go home. Of course they really had no choice, Mark realized, since there was no other version to conflict with his. And as time passed and no asteroid suddenly appeared above the Earth, Mark's prediction that the cats were either dead or indifferent seemed more plausible, although Mark had a lingering doubt as to whether his interpretation was correct. There were just too many unknowns.

Mark had not told the debriefers everything. He couldn't. And he didn't trust them, especially after the NSA interference. He never confessed the influence the cat visions had on him. Nor did he enlighten them about the cube that the dead blue-gray was trying to hand him. Everyone had assumed it was another memory cube. It was not. It was a control cube. The same type of cube the blue-grays used to control the dinosaurs. Fortunately it had been too strong for Mark. If he had made good contact, he would have been under the blue-grays' control. As it was, his brief contact with it had flushed him with an almost overwhelming hatred of the cats. That information alone would probably have jeopardized Mark's ability to sell his version of events, giving the evidence needed by those who wanted to lock him up for threatening the human race, or crimes against the universe, or some such charge. They would not have believed that the control cube's influence ended when the cat blasted it.

Some of the debriefers had suggested detaining Mark until he provided them with the secrets of the alien technology. Fortunately, Mark had convinced them that he had no such information and what he had 'seen' in the visions was useless, that he could not explain any of the alien achievements. He smiled as he thought back to that conversation. "Imagine," he had argued, "that you were magically transported back say a mere three hundred years, to the early 1700's, the time of sailing ships, horse and buggies, a time before electricity or combustion engines. How would you describe our world? We have computers, cell phones, a space station orbiting the Earth. You could tell them how you used a computer, cell phone or GPS, but you probably couldn't tell them how they worked or how to build them. I know I couldn't. I couldn't even describe what parts they contain, let alone how to build them or what they do. What is a memory chip, a hard drive, or even a diode? I don't have a clue. And this is our technology, which just 300 years ago would be nothing short of magic. The blue-grays had space ships, conducted gene splicing and traveled by wormhole, or something. And I saw or felt them do it by moving their fingers and toes. And that's all I can tell you about it. The fact that they could do it is nothing more than what science fiction writers have been describing for decades. But as to how they did it, their technology, I don't have a clue."

It was a shame, Mark thought as he sat in his office, that he couldn't tell anyone, except his wife, about the best closing argument he had ever made, and to the President of the United States no less. But the government was intent on keeping the whole thing secret and amazingly had managed to hush up the whole incident, covering it with rumors about an explosion of an experimental space re-entry vehicle. After an initial flurry of news only the *National Enquirer* paid any more attention and no one believed their space alien stories. Mark had even been threatened with the National Secrets Act if he divulged any information about the encounter. Although he pointed out that he had never signed the document, he assured them nonetheless that they had nothing to worry about as it would not be good for his business to advertise that he was a lawyer who communicated with aliens. After all, the only hard evidence of the whole encounter were the two remaining cubes and the Navy videos, all of which Mark was certain were locked up tight somewhere. The deck of the *Ronald Reagan* had been repaired and neither cube, which appeared to be some type of solid crystal, worked after the blue-gray's ship disappeared. Mark figured he would probably never know whether the government ever managed to unlock their secrets.

But Mark had kept his own secrets as well. He never told anyone about all of the information he had received from the blue-gray's personal cube, the one Sgt. Jeffreys had retrieved for him from the dead blue-gray. That cube was completely different. Where the memory cube acted as a video that you were immersed in, the personal cube was like being inside the operating system of a computer. You could immerse yourself into the various files, like the memory cube, or you could skim over them, viewing them like a video table of contents.

When Sgt. Jeffreys had broken Mark's contact with the cube to show him the wormhole, the lingering effects of the cube continued and all the data on wormholes had flashed through Mark's mind, which is why he instantly "knew" what the cat was trying to do. It was also how he "knew" the wobble or waver he had seen at the edge of the wormhole was evidence of a collapse and not it simply closing. Mark could have spent a lifetime exploring the personal cube, living and learning the blue-gray's history. Unfortunately, the destruction of the blue-grays' ship shut down the cube, leaving Mark with memory fragments, many of which made no sense without the larger context.

Mark did learn that the blue-grays had sent the cat visions so he would believe the cats were single-minded killers. That, coupled with the cat's attack on Earth, would convince him to side with the blue-grays. Mark wondered if the blue-grays appreciated the impact the depth of the cat's emotions would have on Mark or if the blue-grays could even understand that emotion. Even the blue-gray's "missing channel" did not have such a depth of emotion.

There were still a number of questions Mark couldn't figure out and more than once he wished he could have spent more time exploring the blue-gray's personal cube, filling in the gaps in the visions and answering nagging questions, like why him? Of all the millions of people on Earth, why had the blue-grays chosen him? During his brief contact with the blue-grays' personal cube he had learned that he had a particular genetic code that they needed, but did not learn how they had found him among the millions that inhabited the Earth. He hadn't seen anything in his visions to suggest that the blue-grays could detect him from space. So how did they find him? Did they send out other probes before their ship landed? This would probably be one of his many unanswered questions. Another nagging question was why were the alien ships so small? They seemed so much larger in the visions. He could not reconcile the ships he had seen in the visions with the much smaller ships he had seen over the *Ronald Reagan.*

The intercom announcing the arrival of his next client interrupted Mark's thoughts. He sighed. It had been an exciting, exhausting, and at times terrifying experience, which had put mankind's existence in perspective and not a very flattering one at that. Now that it was over, he was back at work as if nothing had happened. The whole event had been hushed up so he certainly couldn't talk about it. He felt a little like a super-hero who was back in his secret identity, but with no ability to become the super-hero again. Mark pondered that for a moment. Maybe that wasn't such a bad thing after all. Although he was pleased that his split-second decision ten months ago saved everyone aboard the *Ronald Reagan*, he had nagging doubts as to whether some of the debriefers may have been correct and that it could have caused the destruction of the planet. That was not something he had contemplated when he saw the expanding wormhole. He had only acted on instinct, trying to stay alive. He had not even contemplated whether his actions were jeopardizing the Earth.

With a sigh, Mark put his thoughts aside. He got up from his familiar desk, walked through his perfectly ordinary office, to meet with a client about a routine will.

EPILOGUE

The third planet from the sun had almost completely circled its star, but still the watcher remained. She was hidden in a crater on a small asteroid between the fourth and fifth planets in this system. The inhabitants of the third planet called this asteroid 4 Vesta, one of the larger asteroids in their so-called asteroid belt, but the watcher neither knew nor cared about this designation. The watcher's sole concern was to fulfill her mission: to find and destroy her sworn enemies. She stretched her lithe body, fur bristling and claws snapping out. This long period of inaction was maddening, cooped up alone in her small ship. But she would continue to wait for her enemy to reveal themselves. Then she would avenge her mate. She would destroy her enemies' mothership and then the planet below.

Read on for an excerpt from
DAVID HIERS'

FIRST
CONTACT
RETURN

Available on Amazon and Kindle

or

www.dhiers.com.

PROLOGUE

The third planet from the sun had almost completely circled its star, but still the watcher remained, hidden in a crater on a small asteroid between the fourth and fifth planets of this system. The inhabitants of the third planet called this asteroid 4 Vesta, one of the larger asteroids in their so-called asteroid belt, but the watcher neither knew, nor cared about this designation. The watcher's sole concern was to find and destroy her sworn enemies.

She stretched her lithe body, fur bristling and claws snapping out. This long period of inaction was maddening, cooped up alone in her small ship. But she would continue to wait for her enemy to reveal themselves. Then she would avenge her mate. She would destroy the enemy mothership and then the third planet where her mate had died.

CHAPTER 1

Fireball detection

IR sensors aboard US DOT satellites detected the impact of a bolide over central China on 15 August 2012 at 08:41:15 UTC. The object was traveling roughly east to west. The object was first detected at an altitude of approximately 110km at 31.13 North latitude, 121.28 East longitude and tracked down to an altitude of approximately 11 km at 24.53 N., 103.24 E. The impact was simultaneously detected by space-based visible wavelength sensors operated by the US Department of Energy. The total radiated energy was approximately $1.29 \times 10^{\wedge} 12$ joules.

Mark awoke with a start, the dream fresh in his mind. He had been hurtling through the blackness of space towards a small planet shining blue and white in the distance. Green and brown continents had taken shape as he drew closer until he recognized India on the horizon, with a quickly expanding China in the foreground. His vision blurred red upon entering the upper atmosphere, was replaced by landscape zooming towards him, a quick glimpse of jagged stone structures, then impact. Upon awaking, Mark could recall every feature of the stone structures: row upon row of tall, jagged, oddly serrated, stone pillars that looked like they had weathered millions of years. A beautiful, eerie, almost alien landscape.

Reluctantly, Mark peeked open an eye, focusing on the glowing numbers on his alarm clock: 3:46. Relief. He still had over two hours before his alarm would go off. He settled back into his pillow, wondering if he could replay his dream. Maybe this time he could control the flight and soar across the Earth. That would be fun. He lay in bed, willing himself to fall back to sleep, the dream fresh in his mind. But he couldn't recreate it. Instead he had a feeling that he was lying on the ground, waiting to be found. Maybe if he called out someone would find him...

The 6:00 a.m. alarm jarred Mark awake. He dragged himself out of bed, amazed at how just waking up once during the night had broken his sleeping rhythm. He felt like he had not slept at all. An hour and two cups of coffee later, he was still exhausted as he pulled into the back of a 1928 house that he and his law partner had renovated to make into an office. That was pretty typical in downtown Pensacola, where professionals who preferred working out of the old buildings were renovating the historic city center. Although there were some glass or brick hi-rises, there were only a few and the tallest was only nine stories, as Pensacola seemed determined to buck the overdevelopment trend of the rest of Florida. Mark was relieved that his partner's car wasn't in the parking lot. He really didn't feel like talking to anyone yet and his partner was a morning person, way too chipper for Mark's current mood. Mark's secretary knew to keep conversation to a minimum in the morning and would have a pot of coffee ready.

Mark walked in the back door, hung his keys on a hook in the kitchen, poured himself a cup of coffee, and grunted at his secretary as he walked into his office. His secretary had already started his computer and the screen showed his day planner. He glanced at it as he opened the Wall Street Journal, which was in its customary spot in the center of his desk. Beneath it were several files. He would look at them later. He glanced at his day planner and confirmed that he didn't have any appointments today, rather he would be drafting documents. That was a mixed blessing. Although he would not have to be civil, drafting legal documents was mind numbing on the best of days. He hoped that four cups of coffee would do the trick. It didn't. By noon he was still trying to draft a relatively simple trust provision for a will. He just couldn't concentrate and knew that he would have to recheck the conveyance language carefully.

He broke for lunch, placing a sticky note to himself on the file to recheck the trust provisions. Foregoing the local restaurants, he went to the downtown YMCA, hoping that a three mile run would energize him for the afternoon. His route was an easy one. He merely ran under the I-110 overpass up to Maxwell Street and back. The mostly flat, grassy, park area under the overpass allowed him to stay out of the Florida sun for most of the run, which was crucial if you intended to survive running at noon in August. Although most people opted for running along the edge of Escambia Bay in hopes of getting a breeze off the bay, there were too many busy streets to cross. Getting run over during lunch hour was not Mark's idea of good exercise. Besides, his solitary run allowed him to concentrate on office projects; the ultimate in multitasking, he always told himself.

But this run was different. No matter how hard he tried, Mark could not shake the dream. It consumed him. He turned around at Maxwell Street and started heading back. 'Half way,' he encouraged himself as he stared fixedly at the dirt path. It felt like he was running in an oven. Wiping sweat from his eyes, he glanced up to judge his distance and saw a towering stone pillar. He stumbled, but somehow managed to catch himself. He staggered to a halt and bent over, hands on his knees, as he gasped for breath, beads of sweat falling from his head like rain to the dry dirt at his feet.

Stone pillar? He was under the interstate. There were no stone pillars. After several deep breaths, he looked up again and saw a double row of uniform cement columns holding up the interstate. That was more like it. After a few more deep breaths, he stood up and began walking back towards the YMCA. Overheated, Mark told himself. Hallucinating. But what an hallucination! He had seen the stone pillar in every detail, down to every crack on its surface. It was the same stone pillar from his dream.

Mark walked the rest of the way back to the YMCA, warily glancing at the cement columns as he passed them. The stone pillar did not reappear. Matt took a cold shower, followed by a Gatorade. He was still sweating when he put on his suit and headed back to his office. At least I am sweating, Mark reasoned. That rules out heat stroke. But heat exhaustion did not explain the hallucination.

"I had the worst day at work," Mark complained to his wife, Beth, over dinner that night. Beth Williams was Mark's wife of twenty-seven years. She was an accountant in a local firm. They had met when she was an expert witness in a case he had tried. They had hit it off and started dating shortly thereafter. Twenty-seven years and three children later, they were facing "empty-nest syndrome" as their youngest headed off to college. "I just couldn't concentrate all day and then I had the oddest hallucination while running at lunch time."

"I told you not to run at noon," Beth interrupted. "It's way too hot. You'll get heat stroke for sure."

This was Beth's favorite mantra. A morning person, she worked out early, before it got too hot. But Mark was not a morning person and the thought of getting up, let alone doing so to exercise, was repugnant. No, he would take his chances with heat stroke. "I had a dream last night," Mark continued. "Woke me up around three and then I couldn't get back to sleep. All day today I have been dragging. And then during my run today, when I made the turn at Maxwell, I had this vivid hallucination that I was running towards a stone pillar. I saw it plain as day. It was really weird."

"Would you like some more pasta?" Beth asked as she helped herself to some more.

"No, thanks," Mark replied. "It was the same stone pillar from my dream," Mark continued. "It was so real."

"This morning you said the dream was in space," Beth said.

"Yes, approaching Earth and then impacting somewhere in China," Mark said, a bit surprised as he had not thought his wife had been paying attention that morning.

"Maybe it's left over from one of those visions last year," she replied.

Mark thought about that for a moment before replying. "No, I don't think so," Mark replied hesitantly. "Those visions occurred when I touched that alien artifact."

"The cube," Beth said.

"Right. The memory cube. Then I became the alien who sent it, seeing, touching, feeling, what he felt. In this dream I was not an alien. I just saw the Earth approaching. It was as if from a meteor's perspective."

"But you also had visions last year when you weren't touching the cube."

"That's true. But those were very different. Fast, fleeting. And even in those I was an alien, had an alien body. And when the vision was in space, I was still in an alien's body in a space ship. This is different."

"Maybe it's PTSD," she said. "You were almost killed and came home all burned and bruised."

"I don't think so," Mark said. "Granted, I did have some nightmares, but they were more general and stopped over six months ago. No, this is totally different. It's probably just a dream. It's just odd that it's hanging on so long."

The dream haunted him the rest of the evening. When he finally fell asleep, he dreamed of an alien landscape, with valleys filled with stone structures, rising up, jagged and sharp, climbing up in nonsensical piles above the valley floor. And through it all was a call: "*Come find me.*"

"How was your day?" Beth asked when Mark got home late the next night.

"Exhausting," Mark said. "It was just like yesterday. I just couldn't…"

"You didn't have another hallucination, did you?"

"No. I didn't…"

"You didn't run did you?"

"No, I didn't run today," Mark finished saying. "I was just tired all day. Couldn't concentrate with that dream lingering in the back of my head all day. Took me forever to finish a simple trust. That's why I'm so late getting home."

"Why don't you have a glass of wine and go to bed early tonight?"

"That sounds like a great idea," Mark said. "Maybe I'll have two glasses."

But later that night, Mark still lay wide awake in bed while the call, "*Come find me,*" kept swirling through his consciousness. Finally, he climbed out of bed and took his laptop into the den. "Just out of curiosity," he muttered to himself as he searched the web, typing in a Google search for recent meteor sightings. He perused a number of hits, none of which satisfied his curiosity. He was about to exit when an entry caught his attention. Clicking on it, he saw a brief reference to a reported meteor in China Wednesday afternoon. He almost skipped past it as his dream had been early Wednesday morning, but then he remembered that China time would be hours ahead of him. He checked the world time on his cell phone. China was thirteen hours ahead of him. He re-read the entry. It merely mentioned that a number of people reported seeing a meteor streak through the late afternoon sky near Shanghai, heading west, and there was speculation as to whether the meteor had actually impacted or burned up in flight. Could that be it? Mark wondered. If only he knew the exact time, then he could be certain. 'The North American Aerospace Defense Command would have it,' he thought. 'Like he could call NORAD and ask them for information on a meteor,' he chided himself.

"This is stupid," he said aloud as he closed his computer and headed back to bed. But sleep would not come. The continuing command to "*Come find me*" kept him awake. 'What if I did dream about that meteor over China? So what?' Mark thought. But he knew there was only one answer to that question: a vision. Succumbing to the inevitable, he started to get back up.

"You getting up again?" Beth asked.

"Can't sleep," Mark said. "I keep hearing that call. I'm starting to wonder if you were right. Maybe it is some type of vision."

Beth rolled over to face him. "How could it be?" she asked. "You said the cube stopped working when the alien ships were destroyed."

"It did. But maybe this is a new one," Mark said without any real conviction. "A different type."

"Think about it," Beth said. "Last year NORAD tracked that alien ship when it landed in the Mariana Trench. Don't you think they would contact you if they thought this meteor was another alien ship."

"But what if they didn't see it?" Mark said.

"NORAD tracks everything. You told me that yourself after one of your debriefings."

"True."

"And besides, even with that genetic coding of yours, you still had to touch the cube, or be close by in order for the aliens to send the visions to you. You knew nothing about them until the Navy flew you to the *USS Ronald Reagan*. So just how can you be receiving a vision from a meteor half-way around the world from us?"

"Your talents are wasted as an accountant," Mark said as he lay back down. "You would make a great lawyer."

"I would settle for some sleep," Beth replied.

They lay in silence for a while. "How can you explain my dream about a meteor at the same time and place that an actual meteor landed?" Mark broke the silence.

"What?" his wife asked sleepily.

"Landed. That's the key," Mark said. "I need to determine whether it actually landed and confirm the time. If they match my dream, then that is just too coincidental. It would have to be related to the blue-grays."

"Why the blue-grays?" Beth asked.

"Because they were the ones who sent the last visions. It's their technology. It would mean that they survived the wormhole's collapse and are back. I need to learn more about that meteor."

"Well, do it quietly. I need to sleep," Beth replied as she rolled over.

Mark got out of bed and went back to the den to turn on his laptop. Now, how to confirm the time? He couldn't call NORAD. They didn't even know who he was and he doubted they would take calls from civilians asking about meteors in China. How about Space Watch, the folks who mapped approaching asteroids? He remembered a reference during a briefing last year that Space Watch had actually spotted the meteor before NORAD. He started with Space Watch's web site. When that didn't yield any further information, he checked the Department of Energy website, where he found a number of meteor entries, but none recent enough. He always wondered why the Department of Energy monitored meteors.

He found the U.S. Meteor Society and then jumped to its international counterpart. Finally he found a time entry hidden within the text of a blog on the Chinese meteor. A quick calculation confirmed it was within minutes of when he had awakened. But what about the coordinates? It took him another fifteen minutes on the computer before he found a site that would translate the latitude/longitude findings into something he understood. It was in the southern portion of China, heading east to west.

A cold chill went down Mark's spine. He had dreamed of approaching Earth and crossing China from east to west about the exact time this meteor had been sited. It had to be a blue-gray artifact. There was no other explanation for the dream. But had it landed? Try as he might, he could not find any confirmation that it had landed.

What should he do? The last time he had not known about the blue-grays until the Navy transported him to the South Pacific and he touched the artifact. But this time he felt like he was being called personally. So what should he do? Whom should he call? Who would believe him? Could he call the President? And what would he tell him? I dreamed of a meteor? Could he even get through to the President? And what if he was wrong? He would look like the ultimate fool. But what if he was right and did nothing? What if a blue-gray artifact had landed in China? What would happen?

The questions would not stop. And no answers were forthcoming. He finally decided that he would have to alert someone. He could not live with himself if something happened and he had done nothing. But whom? Last year the President had called him personally after Mark refused to believe the local navy officer's story of a strange meteor that appeared to be of alien origin. Should he call the President? Who else could he call? The whole event last year had been hushed up, not many people even knew about it.

But how does one contact the President of the United States? He finally decided he would have to do it the same way he did last year, when he needed to confirm that he was in fact talking to the President of the United States and not some friend of his trying to fool him with a very good impersonation. So, feeling rather like Chicken Little, he called the contact number for the White House listed on the government website.

"This is the White House, how may I help you," a chipper female voice answered. How could someone sound so chipper at one in the morning, Mark wondered?

"Yes," Mark replied. "Ah, yes, this is Mark Williams…" The last time he had said that, he had been patched right through to the President. But that time the President had called him first and was expecting his return call. That was a year ago. This time they weren't expecting him.

"Yes, Mr. Williams, what can I do for you?" the operator repeated, still chipper.

"Please give the President the following message," Mark continued. "Tell him that Mark Williams called and he thinks the blue-grays have returned. Ask him to call me." After having her repeat the message, Mark finished by leaving his cell phone number and then hung up, feeling very foolish and wondering if the message would be delivered or merely placed in the crank call log. If the message was delivered, he would receive a return call immediately. But would they wake up the President for a message they did not understand? Probably not. Not unless his name was on some important person list. Mark chuckled, unlikely. Five minutes passed, then ten. Nothing. Okay, let's assume that didn't work, Mark thought. What should be the fall back plan?

Now that he had decided to take some action, he could not wait for morning. Who were those two Navy officers that had come to his office last year? He remembered they came from Corry Station, but could not remember their names. He wondered if Captain Peters was still commanding the *USS Ronald Reagan*. They had become friends during Mark's short stay and Captain Peters knew all about the blue-grays. A quick Google search confirmed that Captain Peters was still in command and the carrier group was still stationed in the Pacific. He could help, Mark decided. The trick was getting a message through. Now how to do that?

Mark decided the best way would be to go to the Navy base and send a secure message to the carrier. He decided to go to Corry Field since it was a Naval Intelligence and Cryptology station, while Pensacola NAS was only a training command. Also, the two officers who had contacted him before were from Corry. So with some misgivings, he went back into his bedroom to get dressed, while trying not to wake up his wife.

"Where are you going?" a sleepy voice asked after he dropped his shoe the second time.

"Can't sleep," he replied. "I'm still thinking about that meteor. I'm going to run down to the Navy base and send a message to Captain Peters, have him check it out."

"Ok, don't let the cat in," Beth replied as she rolled over and fell back to sleep. Mark was always amazed at how fast she could fall asleep. In all likelihood she had never awakened and would not remember this conversation in the morning. He chuckled as he thought he should have answered: "A UFO landed in the back yard so I thought I would hitch a ride to Pluto for a pizza." Better leave a note on the kitchen counter, he decided as he headed for the door.

He drove down to Corry Station, arriving at the gate close to 2:00 in the morning. Not having a military I.D., Mark knew he would have trouble getting on base and probably even more trouble getting his message sent. But his time in the Army and experience in life had taught him that if you acted like you were in charge and knew what you were doing, people usually assumed that you did, particularly military personnel. Mark pulled up to the front gate. "I need an escort to the Communications Duty Officer," Mark said officially as he handed his driver's license to the armed gate guard.

"What's the nature of your business?" the guard asked unimpressed.

Mark was ready for that response. "Classified." He merely responded. The guard hesitated. "Do you have any military identification?"

"I am not in the habit of carrying military identification for everyone to look at," Mark answered, hoping that the guard would assume that more was implied in that sentence.

The guard was still not impressed. "Are you expected?"

"No," Mark responded, now ad-libbing. "An unexpected event has occurred and I need to send a secure, classified message out ASAP. That's all I can tell you. So if you will hurry and have someone escort me." The guard still hesitated. "Listen," Mark added forcefully. "You do not want to be the one responsible for holding up this communiqué. So I suggest that you get on the horn before you end up guarding a sand dune in the Mojave desert."

The last threat did the trick and the guard stepped into the guardhouse and made a call, while another armed guard watched him suspiciously. A minute later the first guard came back. "They want to know what this is all about."

"Well, you tell them that I am not going to explain it to a gate guard. Either they will have to come here or you can take me to them. I'm not trying to blow up your base. I can leave my car here and you can have ten guards take me to them. I don't care. But we have to do something now. We are running out of time." Mark glanced at his watch for emphasis.

Clearly undecided, the guard went back into the guardhouse and got back on the phone. When he returned he said, "Okay, park your car over there and we will escort you."

"Thank you," Mark replied and pulled his car into the indicated parking spot. A military van pulled up and

Mark got in the passenger side while the second guard drove him onto the base. Mark glanced into the back of the van. They were alone. Mark chuckled to himself. If he were really a terrorist he could disable the lone driver with a quick blow to the head and then he would be on base, unsupervised, with the guard's weapon. Now how secure was that? The driver stopped in front of a nondescript, three story, 1940's era building and escorted Mark inside. After traveling down several corridors they arrived at a room marked "Duty Officer." One more hurdle to go, Mark thought to himself as a young Ensign looked up from his desk.

"What's this all about?" the officer asked.

"I have a coded message that needs to be sent by secure transmission to Captain Joseph Peters on the *USS Ronald Reagan.*"

"What is the message?"

Mark looked at the guard and then back at the officer. "Let me have a piece of paper." The officer complied and Mark wrote:

Mark Williams is at our location. He says the blue-grays have returned. Wants you to contact him immediately.

"You will have to add your contact information to the end of that," Mark instructed. I will wait for his reply."

"What does this mean?" the duty officer asked.

"That's classified," Mark responded.

"I have a top secret clearance."

"That's not high enough for this," Mark replied calmly.

"How do I know you're not some nutcase off the street?" the officer asked.

"You don't," Mark answered. "And like I told your guard at the gate, you don't want to be the one who holds up this message. You can couch it with anything you want to cover your butt, but just get that portion of the message I wrote down through, now. It's about 1500 hrs. ship's time, I'll wait for the response. If he doesn't know who I am, then you can have me prosecuted for interfering with the military or any other charge you want. But if I am right..." Mark let the last part hang in the air.

The officer hesitated, trying to figure out what to do. He tried to size Mark up, fifty something, fit and trim, graying hair, civilian clothing, casual, yet expensive looking. He had an air of confidence and a sense of authority about him. Not someone who looked like a lunatic. If he were in uniform, he could easily pass as a Captain. The last observation did it. "Wait here," the officer commanded. "I'll get your message sent. But I'm warning you, if this is some type of joke, you'll be in big trouble."

"Make sure it is sent secure," Mark instructed, ignoring the threat. Mark glanced at his watch and sat down and waited while the guard stood by the door. 'I give it fifteen minutes,' Mark thought. 'I should have a reply by then.' The reply actually came back in twelve.

The young Ensign rushed into the room. "Captain Peters is on the comm," he stated breathlessly. "He wants to talk to you. Come with me." With that he escorted Mark down another hall to a communications center and motioned to a telephone. He's on that line."

"Is this line secure?" Mark asked.

"Yes, it is."

As Mark reached for the phone he pointed to the guard and said, "He needs to step out of the room."

"Of course," the Ensign answered and motioned the disappointed guard out of the room.

"You, too," Mark said. The Ensign paused for just a moment before complying, stationing himself outside the glass door where he could watch.

Mark picked up the phone. "This is Mark Williams," he said.

"Mark, Joseph Peters. I didn't expect to hear from you again." Came the friendly reply. Mark had wondered what type of reception he would get from Captain Peters. He had spent the majority of his time as Captain Peters' "guest" onboard the *Ronald Reagan* and had hit it off quite well. But when he left he had not been able to say goodbye, as Captain Peters was too busy trying to get his ship seaworthy after the alien attack. It had actually been adrift for a while, its nuclear reactors in jeopardy while they desperately tried to get the electronics back on line.

"I didn't expect to be calling either," Mark answered. "But I think I've had a new vision and I can't contact anyone over here. Probably because it's past midnight. So I need your help to confirm it."

"Your message says the blue-grays are back," the Captain remarked.

"I think they might be," Mark clarified and then told the Captain the details of his dream and his continuing feeling that he was being contacted again. "I tried to confirm it on the Internet," Mark concluded. "But I could only get bits and pieces, but what I did find was a reference to a meteor in China within minutes of when I was awakened by this dream. That and the continuing sense of contact made me feel that I just couldn't ignore this any longer, the potential ramifications are too great if the blue-grays have come back.

"So, can you contact NORAD and see what they have on it, particularly whether it landed? I think they track this sort of thing. If I'm wrong and it was only a dream, then I owe you dinner the next time you're in Pensacola. But if their satellites confirm what I saw at the same time and place and particularly if it landed, then my only conclusion is that the blue-grays are back and I don't know why. Or for that matter, how. I thought they were gone for good after the wormhole collapsed."

"Okay," the Captain responded. "I'll check with NORAD. Where can I get back to you?"

"Hold one moment." Mark said as he waived at the Ensign who was watching through the glass door. "Captain Peters has to check on something and will call me back. Can I wait here?" Mark asked.

"I suppose you can," the Ensign replied.

"I'll wait here for your answer," Mark told the Captain. "I assume you know how to contact me here, or do I need to put this officer on?"

"You said you were having a little difficulty on that end?" the Captain asked.

"Yes. You know how it is with us civilians. No respect."

The Captain chuckled, "Let me speak to the duty officer."

"He wants to speak to you," Mark said to the officer as he handed him the phone.

"This is Ensign Johnson," the duty officer said and then straightened up as he listened to the Captain.

Mark did not know what Captain Peters said to the young officer, but the change was dramatic. After the call it was all "Sir, this and Sir, that. Do you need anything, Sir?" This was more like it Mark thought.

"Do you have a cot or a sofa?" Mark asked. "It's rather late and I haven't had any sleep. I don't know how long this will take and I wouldn't mind getting a short nap." Mark was shown to a sofa in the XO's office with assurances from the Ensign that he would be contacted the moment Captain Peters called back. Mark looked at his watch. It was past three in the morning. Now that he had taken some action, he was exhausted. He lay down on the sofa and quickly fell asleep.

Mark was awakened several hours later by a commotion outside the door. "What do you mean there's a civilian sleeping in my office?" a very irate voice was shouting. The answer was lost as the door burst open and a senior officer stormed in. "Just what do you think you're doing?" he bellowed.

Mark sat up slowly and rubbed his eyes. "I was sleeping," he replied.

This was not the answer the Commander expected and after a moment of shocked silence, he went off. Mark just sat back and smiled. It was nice being a civilian, no fear of rank. Mark ignored the tirade and when the Commander took a breath, Mark turned to the Ensign cowering in the corner and asked, "Has Captain Peters called back yet?"

"No, Sir," the Ensign replied timidly.

"Just what is going on? Who do you think you are…" the Commander went off again while Mark continued to sit on the sofa.

"Are you the commander here?" Mark asked during a lull in the tirade.

"I'm the XO," came the reply. "And you have a lot of explaining to do."

"I'm afraid I can't do that," Mark replied calmly. "My mission is classified."

"Classified? Let me assure you, I have clearance. This is the Center for Information Dominance. So what is going on?"

"It's classified," Mark repeated.

"And I told you, I have clearance."

"Not this high." Mark said. The XO started to sputter, threatening to put Mark in jail and "other" threats.

"Look. I'm not trying to give you a hard time," Mark continued. "Why don't you contact Captain Peters on the *Ronald Reagan*? He can decide what information to share with you. I can't."

This answer was not satisfactory to the XO. He shouted some more and then called for security. "You're going to the brig!" he declared.

"Might I suggest that you contact Captain Peters, first?" Mark calmly asked again. "He can probably clear this up real fast."

"I am not going to be intimidated by your fast talking," the XO raved. A minute later a military policeman arrived and was instructed by the XO to handcuff Mark and take him to the brig.

Mark stood up and calmly presented his wrists. As he did, he turned to the Ensign, "Please make sure that Captain Peters knows where to locate me." He then turned to the XO. "I'll say it one more time, if you will contact Captain Peters you can avoid making a very poor career choice here." The minute Mark said that, he knew he had phrased it wrong. It was like pouring gasoline on a fire. The military policeman had to stand aside while the XO screamed in Mark's face, while Mark calmly stood there handcuffed.

As he was winding down, a sailor burst into the room. "Sir, Sir, Sir!"

After three attempts, the XO turned on the unfortunate sailor. "Don't interrupt me…"

To his amazement, the sailor did, "Sir, the President is on the line!"

"The President? The President of what?" the XO sputtered.

"The President of the United States," the sailor responded.

"The President is calling for me?" the XO asked in disbelief.

"No, Sir. For him," he said, pointing to Mark.

Mark tried to suppress his smile. He held up his handcuffed hands to the military policeman as he quietly said, "I probably should take that call."

AUTHOR

David Hiers has had many adventures as a lifeguard, firefighter, Army Captain and as a lawyer. He currently lives on a horse farm outside Pensacola, FL with his beautiful wife and daughter, an overactive imagination, and too many critters.

www.dhiers.com

Made in the USA
Columbia, SC
23 May 2018